NO WHERE TO RUN

The sound became loud and clear as Timmy moved cautiously through the woods. When he saw the man suddenly and unexpectedly, he dropped to his belly behind the twisted roots of a large tree. It wasn't a stake being driven into the ground that he heard—it was a hole being dug by a pickax.

And then Timmy saw the other thing.

It lay upon the ground just beyond the hole and looked like a bundle of blankets wrapped in a short, round oblong shape like the cocoon of an unborn butterfly. Parts of the blanket were stained almost black, and Timmy recognized the pink and blue plaid with a stinging coldness growing and spreading over his skin. It was a blanket from one of the bunk beds. But there was a difference in this blanket. There was a large red flower among the pinks and blues—not a red flower but red, fresh blood!

Time hung suspended in Timmy's moment of mesmerized horror. He began pulling away, searching blindly for safety. What he saw was death—and what he knew was that he was going to be the next innocent victim. . . .

HOME SWEET HOME

BY RUBY JEAN JENSEN

ZEBRA BOOKS
KENSINGTON PUBLISHING CORP.

ZEBRA BOOKS

are published by

Kensington Publishing Corp.
475 Park Avenue South
New York, NY 10016

Fourth printing: October 1986

Printed in the United States of America

Prologue

The child looked up through the meager protection of her fingers, crisscrossed over her eyes and her mouth. Although there was a quiet and desperate fear in her china-blue eyes, there was also defiance.

"I don't want it," she said. "I don't want it."

The large man said in a tone wheedling and singsong, "Now, now, little Susie. Don't be that way. Little Mother made you a nice supper. Why don't you be a good girl and eat it?"

Her eyes flickered. She said, "No."

The man pushed the laden spoon against her fingers. The edge cut into her flesh, and the stacked contents of the spoon dripped onto the front of her blouse.

"Eat, goddamn you, eat!"

She turned her face away, dropping her wounded hand. She began to cry. "No, please, Uncle Dan, I don't want it."

The spoon trembled in his fingers. Her jerking head tipped it, and more of the cooked grits spilled.

In a sudden grip, his free hand tangled in the uncombed mass of pale, fine blond hair.

"Eat!"

He forced the spoon into her wailing mouth. The tears mixed with the grits and spilled down her chin. He dropped the spoon and dug his hand into the man-sized bowl in front of her and began pushing the food into her open mouth. She gagged. He bent her head backwards, his fingers locked into her hair, straining the scalp.

On the other side of the long, plank table a dark-haired, brown-eyed little boy stared in silence. He was eating. Like an automatic toy even while he stared in dread fascination, his right arm, bent at the elbow, lifted spoonfuls of mush to his mouth, slid it in, and went back for more. As the girl was afraid to eat, the boy was afraid not to.

Over her nearly empty bowl the girl began to vomit.

"Goddamn! Damn you, you little bitch!"

Dan slung the vomit off his arm. In uncontrolled frustration and fury he dragged her frail body out of her chair and carried her with one hand across the room, as if she were a rag doll, holding her by her clothes. He stopped at the door, pulled down the old razor strop that hung on a nail there, and began beating her. The slap, slap, slap of the strop against her body fell like hailstones among her tears.

"When Little Mother cooks, you eat what she cooks, do you hear me? Don't you dare disobey Little Mother, ever! In no way !"

In disgust at last he threw the strop to the floor and hauled her along by the arm down a narrow hall and into a bedroom where there were four sets of narrow bunk beds.

He threw her onto one of them.

"When you're ready to eat," he said, "let me know. You can apologize to Little Mother later."

The door slammed shut, and he was gone.

Susie huddled under her blanket in the twilight corner of her bunk, curled in a knot as small as her body could make. She looked at the spider who lived in a web where the logs of one wall met the logs of another, in the corner of her bed. It was within her reach, and sometimes she touched the firm web with one finger, and the spider came running as if to see who was at her door.

Susie wasn't afraid of the spider anymore.

It was almost a friend now. Someone who had come into the mountain cabin to escape the winter outside and had stayed into the summer. Someone who came eagerly to the door when Susie knocked.

The room darkened, and the spider faded into the darkness, along with the curves of the logs and the patterns of her blanket.

Susie stared into the dark and waited for the little boy, Terry, to come in to bed. As she waited, as time passed, she grew tense again, her legs, arms, her spine straining against this new dread.

Had Uncle Dan taken Terry to see Little Mother tonight?

At last she heard it, that ultimate horror.

The scream. The cry, at first, the begging, the pleading.

And then the inhuman scream that no longer belonged to a little boy, not this one nor the others before him. When at last they screamed, they all sounded alike. And yet, they didn't sound like themselves anymore.

Susie huddled under her blanket, afraid to move, even to breathe.

Even after the screaming had stopped.

One

Steve was not accustomed to drinking alone, to stopping on his way home for any purpose unless it involved a grocery store, or some other family-oriented mission. And this evening of all times he was torn between hurrying on and delaying as long as he dared without heaping more worries on Connie, his wife.

He sat at the end of the bar in Rialto's and looked into the half empty glass of pale amber. It was draft beer. It wasn't so much the alcohol he had needed as time alone, just a few minutes, before he faced Connie with her problems, his problems, those medical facts that scared him more than he wanted to know.

On Sunday she was scheduled to check into a large hospital fifty miles from home, and on Monday morning a gynecologist, to whom the family doctor had referred her, and his team of surgeons, would remove her uterus and the tumor it held, uncovering their fears, and at best forever removing her hopes in having a second child.

It was the tumor that scared him.

He was aware of a fathomless fear, an unspoken fear. Of losing her forever to that hospital and those surgeons.

Occasionally the muted noises in the bar diverted him, drew his mind away from problems he couldn't separate and identify. The family doctor had been so calm. *It probably is a benign tumor, but just to be on the safe side she should have the best care, the best surgeons.* Too calm. The clink of glasses now, the voices of the bartender and the two men he was mixing drinks for, the television on the wall with some unwatched game show, the low murmurs from other scattered voices in the dark recesses of the room—they all entered upon his thoughts so there continually failed to be a solution to problems confused in his mind. What about Timmy? No grandparents anymore. No aunts or uncles living near. No trusted babysitter in these past two years since most of their activities had been such that Timmy was included, or safely asleep in his own bedroom. The light here in the bar was dim and soft too, like the voices, so different from the late afternoon sunlight outdoors now that summer had come and the sun hung around longer and longer into the evening. There was, in the bar, a feeling of change in reality, which was what he needed most for this few minutes' delay in getting home.

The door opened, bringing another customer. A familiar voice spoke to others nearer the door. Steve Malcolm looked up. The man he saw was square and heavy, and because of his breadth, appeared

10

shorter than he actually was. He was dressed in a light blue summer suit with dark shirt open at the neck. His hair was sunbleached, or, as Connie had once laughingly said, professionally streaked. Who could tell? His opinion and Connie's were often at variance where Dan Walker was concerned.

For some unaccountable reason Dan turned Connie off. She had definite likes and dislikes while he was more accepting. He liked Dan Walker fine, okay, so-so. They had played many a poker game together, shot a lot of pool, talked about nothing over too many drinks to remember. Dan had the friendliness, the outspokenness and outward confidence of a successful salesman, which he obviously was. Steve considered Dan a friend, but today he wasn't looking for comradeship.

He wanted to be alone, to think, to feel, to remember . . . Connie when she was twenty-two years old and standing beside him in her long, white wedding gown. How beautiful she had been. But no more beautiful than two years later when she had been brought from the delivery room of the local hospital, her hair damp against her forehead, brushed back by a hand he hadn't seen, sleeping, pale, exhausted from long hours of labor, the new mother of a healthy son. But the ultimate in her beauty, in his heart, came yesterday when she stood before him and looked up into his eyes with her own so sad and so silently frightened, and briefly gave him the message. "I have to have the operation now, Steve. I can't put it off any longer, the doctors agreed." He enveloped her in his arms, as though he could hold her forever safe. Even now he could feel the combined beating of their hearts.

"Hey, Steve!" the familiar voice of Dan Walker spoke in a lift of surprise. "That can't be you, can it? Stopping off for a beer on your way home? If I didn't know better I'd say there's trouble brewing on the home front. This is a record, for you, isn't it?"

Dan was coming closer, taking the stool just around the forty degree-angled turn of the bar. Steve's moments of solitude were gone. He tried to match the cheerfulness in Dan's voice.

"I thought you were out of town, peddling cameras."

"That was last week. I made my sales, and here I am, back again. Always good to be back." He raised his voice. "Bring me the usual, Pete."

"Business going good, umm?" Steve said, to keep the conversation away from himself, to fill the moment of silence as Dan received his drink and paid for it.

"Yeah. Camera equipment is always in greater demand in early summer. Everybody is out to capture the beauties of nature. They forget about the bugs."

Steve smiled and looked into his beer. He felt Dan's eyes reading him more closely than usual.

"There is trouble, eh, old Steve? Something's bothering you. If you want to talk about it, I'm here."

He hadn't intended saying anything at all about Connie, but suddenly he was talking, his fears and thoughts spilling, as confused as he felt. "It's Connie, Dan. She's had trouble ever since Tim was born, and our family doctor wanted her to have a hysterectomy a couple of years ago, but she refused because she wanted to have more children. She especially wanted a little girl now, to make the family complete, you know? That's her way of looking at it. I would rather she had followed the doctor's suggestions, but she didn't. Now she has to. There's a tumor fast growing, and a chance that it could be malignant. She has to have surgery, and it's scheduled for Monday morning, in Shreveport."

Dan was looking at him steadily, as though he absorbed every word in depths unknown to Steve.

"Hey, that's tough," he said softly, and Steve was briefly under the impression that Dan had not spoken his real thoughts, but it was a fleeting impression and unimportant to Steve. Dan's hand reached over and clasped itself for a moment to Steve's shoulder. "But they've got the best surgeons there, and you'll be back to normal in no time, eh? She'll be feeling better, and the worry will be gone."

"Yeah. That's what I try to tell myself. But you can't keep from worrying."

"Of course not. Are you going down with her?"

"Yeah. Sure. They can't keep me away. I've taken a couple of days off from work, and if I need more I'll take it. No problem there. My boss is pushed right now, so I told him I'd work Saturday to help out. Then I can stay with Connie Monday, Tuesday, and Wednesday."

"What about Tim?"

"I don't know." Steve raised a hand to his chin and rubbed, feeling a short, prickly stubble of beard. Had he forgotten to shave this morning? "I don't know. I hate to take him along, he'd have to stay in the waiting room. Kids aren't allowed in hospitals, especially that one. I thought about sending him to some kind of camp for the summer, but this came up so fast—"

"Why not let an old buddy help?"

"Huh?"

Dan shrugged, smiled faintly, motioned fleetingly with his hands. "Well why not? I always wanted a boy of my own, and since none of my marriages produced one for me I have to borrow my nephews now and then. It'd be a pleasure for me, Steve. I've been planning a trip up to the mountains anyway. I want to do some wildlife shooting, my old hobby you know, kind of neglected lately. No, not guns, cameras. I'd be glad to take care of Timmy for a couple of weeks. By that time Connie should be home again, right?"

"Two weeks?" It seemed a lifetime. It was, it could be, a lifetime.

"Sure, why not? For Timmy it'll pass in a hurry once we get going, and he won't have to know his mother is sick at all. Have you told him?"

"No, not yet. But I'm sure that he should know."

"Why should he? It would only be a worry for him. You could tell him she's going to the hospital without letting him know the extent of your concern, right? And I'll keep him entertained, and you won't have to worry about him. I've got enough extra cameras and equipment, he can shoot his own pictures. He'll have a great time, Steve. No problem."

"I hate to saddle you with a ten-year-old boy for two weeks, Dan."

"Hey! What do you mean saddle me? I wanted to take him along camping last year, remember? Just for his company. It'll be a pleasure for me. I love kids, you know that. Timmy's a great little guy."

"Well, thanks, Dan. I'll talk to Connie."

"Tell her it's settled. I'll be over Sunday morning to get him, and I won't take no for an answer." He slid off the bar stool and clasped a hand once more to Steve's shoulder. "Gotta be going now. See you early Sunday morning."

Steve watched him cross the room, pause at a table to talk for a moment with a man and his girlfriend, and go on toward the door. A part of his unidentified worries had gone with Dan, leaving him feeling tired and relieved, and ready to go home. At least Timmy would have a great two weeks ahead of him.

Two

"I don't want to go with him, Mom."

He stood by the kitchen cabinet, on one foot, the other foot propped against his ankle. He rubbed his leg with the lifted foot, dirty sneakers against clean jeans. He wasn't sure she had heard him. Much of the time lately when she was busy she didn't hear him. But she was only making a salad, she should have heard, she should be listening, for his statement was quietly urgent.

The peanut butter sandwich in his hand had one bite taken out of it. He started to take another, then held it away and looked at it. His stomach had closed and felt as though it came all the way up into his throat. Why did they want to send him away?

"Why don't you want to go with Dan, Timmy?" she asked, her voice gentle as it almost always was, but oddly distant too, as if she only half listened. Her real thoughts were on other things. The salad, maybe.

"I just don't. Why can't I go with you and Dad?"

17

She stood looking down into the salad bowl, her hands still now, her hair touching her cheek in soft curls. The half-broken head of lettuce fell from her hand into the big green plastic mixing bowl. To Timmy's surprise she turned and dropped to her knees in front of him, pulled him into her arms and held him, her face pressed against his chest. Her hug was solid and almost fierce for a moment, then she sat back on her heels and smiled at him. Her face was below his. He looked down into her eyes. They were dark, like his own, and misty and bright as though she were going to cry. But if the mistiness was caused by tears they were far back, unreleased, unshed.

"Timmy," she said softly. "Daddy didn't tell you that we're going to a big hospital in Shreveport, did he?"

He shook his head, frowning faintly. "Why are you going to a hospital?"

She glanced away. "I'm going to have some things done, some tests, and that sort of thing. It's nothing much. It won't take very long. You know, the way you did last year when you had the fever?"

"Are you sick?"

She was looking at him again now, smiling. "Oh not really. But don't you see, I can't take you with me in there unless you went in as a patient, and you wouldn't want that, would you?"

He remembered needles drawing blood from his arms, and having to stay for two days in a high, hard, white bed. "Well, couldn't I stay with Dad?"

"Dad is driving me down, don't you see? And who knows, we might go afterwards to a nightclub or something fancy where ten-year-old boys are not

18

allowed, and since we're going to be having all that fun we want you to have a lot of fun, too. You'll have a great time with Dan up in the mountains, taking pictures of animals and birds."

"I don't see why I can't go with you instead."

She was very quiet for a long moment, looking into his face. He squirmed, and she asked, "Would you rather stay next door with Mrs. Palmer?"

"Mrs. Palmer!" Timmy was horrified, objecting now in a far different way. "Mom, she's real old. She doesn't like kids at all. When I cross her yard she yells at me."

"She doesn't want you to make a path in her grass, so you must mind her! But she likes you, and she said you could stay with her."

"No!"

She got to her feet and went back to the sink. Her back was carefully toward him so that he could no longer see her face.

"Go on out and play, Timmy," she said. "And take your peanut butter sandwich with you."

He forgot he wasn't hungry and took another bite out of the sandwich. It tasted like a large lump of modeling clay, hanging in his throat. As he went out the back door he looked around from old habit for Buster. Buster would like a peanut butter sandwich. Buster, though, was gone. For a moment he had forgotten that, too. His old dog, sick and beyond help, put to sleep by the veterinarian, was now buried in the backyard under the pine tree.

He walked on toward the gate slowly, his head down, the sandwich dangling between a finger and a thumb. Was his mother going to the hospital because

19

she was sick and didn't want him to know? No, she would tell him. His parents didn't keep secrets from him. They were actually going on a vacation by themselves for a few days, just as Dad had said. And they would bring him a great gift. What?

Out of the gate, past the hedge of lilacs, he went down the curving driveway and to the shaded sidewalk. The street was quiet. He saw Clarence, the overweight neighbor dog, on the front walk of the neighboring house and threw the sandwich toward him. It was a poor throw and fell at least three feet short of the dog. That kind of pitching, Timmy thought morosely, would never get him on any ball team. Not even a kindergarten team, if the little kids ever got a team going. The dog watched the sandwich for a while before he moved, as though if he waited long enough the sandwich would come to him. Finally, he got up in lazy slowness and sauntered on bowed legs to the slightly battered sandwich. He picked it up gently in his massive bulldog jaws, looked at Timmy, turned and waddled back up the walk to the porch where he lay down again with the sandwich, a bit soggy now, between his resting paws.

Timmy forgot to be unhapppy and laughed at fat, gentle Clarence and went on down the sidewalk at a livelier pace. He liked his neighborhood. It was the kind of place where people seldom moved away, where the houses had porches with roses and vines, and the streets were shaded by huge, old trees. Where you not only knew everyone's name, and they knew yours, but you also knew the names of all the dogs and cats, too. Where church and school and park were within walking distance, and fields of outlying farms came close against it all. Timmy had lived there all his life and didn't want to live anywhere else. He felt good and safe and free. He had multiple choices. As for now, where to go in the hour he had before dinner? Over to the park? Watch the little kids, with their mothers, throw peanuts and other food stuff to the ducks and swans on the little willow-shaded pond? See if Russ or Clark were around? The rest of the gang weren't, he knew, because most of them had already gone on summer vacations.

Clark was going to his church camp. Russ was going to an uncle's farm. No, they were already gone, too. He hadn't seen them around for several days.

Timmy wished he could go with Russ to the farm if he had to go anywhere. He would like to feed baby calves from a bucket, too, the way Russ said he did last year. He would like to swim in the creek, like Russ and his cousin.

But instead, his dad had asked him if he wanted to go with Uncle Dan to his cabin in the Boston Mountains. No. Wrong. He hadn't asked, he had told Timmy he was going.

Timmy sat down on a bench under the shade of a thick-foliaged maple tree and leaned his elbows on his knees, his chin in his hands. He poked at the grass with the toe of his sneaker, adding grass stain to the fraying, drying mud.

Dan wasn't really his uncle, only one of his dad's many friends. And Timmy had no real reason for not much liking him, he just knew he didn't. Much. Certainly not enough to spend a whole two weeks up in the woods with him. Now if his dad and mom would go too, it would be great. Boating, fishing, photographing wild animals. Yeah, then it would be great.

Well, he'd talk to Dad. Mom wouldn't say much without Dad backing her up, so he'd talk to Dad. And maybe Dad would come home early today, this being Saturday afternoon. A day that Dad was just putting in extra, as he had said, to help the boss. Timmy wanted to be there to greet him when he came home, to hold his hand and plead with him.

He kicked once more at the grass then bounced up and ran back the way he had come.

The dog next door still had the peanut butter sandwich between his feet and was looking at Timmy with eyes that said, "Thanks, sort of. I'll eat it later."

The driveway was empty as it was when he had left it. He went through the gate into the backyard, and from there through the small door into the garage. Only his mom's Toyota was taking up its bit of space. It looked like a toy car for sure with all the empty space that was left for Dad's station wagon. He hadn't come home early after all.

Timmy sat down on the steps that led into the utility room of the house to wait for his dad. Minutes dragged in the dim light of the garage, and Timmy considered how slowly time could pass when a boy was just waiting around. Especially when his belly had this tight sense of dread. It was like a morning in school when you were waiting for the lunch bell to ring. When the school year was new and when the teacher was new. When a lot of the kids were strangers. When you felt surrounded by strangers in this place that was familiar only as a past nightmare ish dream is familiar. Time dragged, and you were afraid, a little.

The garage door made a noise and began to rise, and through the growing sunshiny space beneath the door, Timmy saw his dad's station wagon. He got up and moved down to stand just clear of where the car's bumper would be.

His dad leaned out the window and called, "Can't you find a better place to sit than in the garage?" But he was smiling, and when he got out of the car and the garage door was going down again, he put an arm across Timmy's shoulders and gave him a quick hug. "How's my boy?"

"Okay. Dad, Mom said she's going to have a test at a hospital at Shreveport, and it won't take very long. So I was wondering why you can't take me with you, or why you and Mom don't come on to the mountains with Dan and me afterwards?"

"Uncle Dan, Timmy. Uncle."

"But he's not my uncle!"

"You've known him since you were five or six years old and sat on his lap, so you call him uncle out of respect, right? Besides, he likes you, and he wants you to call him Uncle Dan."

His dad opened the door into the house, and Timmy followed behind him, hurrying to keep up, trying to be heard. Both his parents were acting distracted lately.

"Why can't I just go with you and Mom, Dad?"

"You wouldn't enjoy yourself, son."

"Then like I said, why don't both you and Mom go with me and Uncle Dan? We could wait until you got back from Shreveport if I couldn't go there

23

with you.''

His dad was still walking on, ahead of him, and Timmy was hard put to get close enough to see his face. He grabbed at the big hand that swung against him.

"Dad?"

Steve paused and looked down into the troubled face of his son, then, as Connie had earlier, he bent down. "Listen, Timmy. I've already told Uncle Dan that you'll be ready to go bright and early tomorrow morning. You're going to have a great time. And I'm taking your mother out to a fancy restaurant in Shreveport tomorrow night, so we'll be having a great time too, but our time would be not so great if we thought you weren't having a good time. So why don't you be a big boy and think of it as going to camp with the kids or something, only this will be better because you'll have your own camera and you'll see a lot of new things."

"But—"

"Hey, no more, okay? Let's see what your mom has for supper, or if we're going down to the Big Mac. Come on now, don't beg."

"But—"

"Tim!"

When his dad used that tone of voice Timmy hushed. He knew how far he could push them, both of them. And he dared not push too far, not now.

Timmy washed up without being told, brushed his hair back neatly and came to the table with face shining. But he could find no appetite. The pork chop on his plate took on the aspect of a poison toadstool in the woods, and the spinach became the hidden moss, the sodden moss, into which his feet would sink. His parents' voices drifted above him, only partly comforting tonight. He wanted to clutch them and hold them, to keep them from leaving him tomorrow, from sending him one way while they went the other.

Still, his dad had appealed to his sense of pride when he told him to be a big boy. He asked, "What do I have to take? Will you help me pack, Mom?"

"Of course I'll help you pack."

Steve reached over and rubbed his hand through Timmy's hair, sending it from its neat, combed ridges, so carefully put in before he came to the table, into a field of golden wheat that had been tossed and curled by the wind. They both laughed at him, at the unruliness of his hair. He put a hand up and tried to brush it back into place, but he felt the pleased grin push his face from the stiff control of before. He liked the attention they gave him, those times of warm indulgence. And now was a good time to approach them about a new dog.

"Could I have another pup, Dad, Mom?"

They looked at each other, and some kind of silent, affectionate agreement passed between them. His dad was the one who answered.

"Now why didn't we think of that? What say that when you get back from your trip we hunt you up a puppy?"

Suddenly it seemed worth it, the whole thing, the trip into the mountains without Mom and Dad, and two whole weeks with Dan. *Uncle* Dan.

He couldn't sit still. "Oh could we, Dad?"

"Sit down, Timmy," his mother said. "You know

you're not supposed to stand up at the table."

Timmy sat down, one leg up in his chair, bent under him. It made a hard pillow but raised him nearer their level. "What kind of dog can I get, Dad?"

"Whatever kind you get," his dad said, "you have to take care of him, you know. None of this waiting for your mother to feed him."

"Oh I will, Dad, I promise. Didn't I take good care of old Buster?"

"Sure you did," Dad said. "Now, what were we talking about?" he asked, as though he didn't know. But Timmy saw the half hidden humorous turn of his mouth.

"The kind of dog!"

"Oh yes. How about a beagle? They're playful, friendly little guys and need a lot of running around. Then the next time you go with Uncle Dan to the mountains you can take him along."

"Oh, could I Dad? Would Uncle Dan care?"

"Of course he wouldn't care. Why would he?"

"Maybe I could get my dog and take him with me this time!" He could see them now, running together through the woods, wading in the shallow streams, he and his beagle pup. Being with Uncle Dan didn't seem so—so—boring? No, not boring, but—well, scary, somehow. Having Uncle Dan come to the house was different from spending a whole two weeks with him somewhere far away. When he came to the house he talked mostly to Dad and Mom, not to him. To him he just said hello and mussed his hair which, from anyone but his own dad, he hated, and then gave him some kind of little gift. A balloon. A ball. Once he brought a knife, a real neat knife. He

26

liked the knife, but not enough to spend all that time with him. However, if he could take along his pup this trip . . .

"Could I, Dad?"

"Could you what?"

"Could I go get my pup tonight and take him along tomorrow when I go to the mountains with Uncle Dan?"

"No, not tonight. We said we'd get you one when you get back."

Timmy felt the sting of disappointed tears, for now there were two urgent problems, or three. He had to behave like he wasn't feeling; he had to go with Uncle Dan, and he had to go without his pup.

"But what if they're all used up when I get back?"

"Whoever heard of pups being all used up? He'll just be two weeks older and tougher, that's all."

"But—"

His mother got up from the table and took his hand. "Come with me, and we'll get your things ready. Had you thought about a name for your dog?"

"I don't know."

They went into his room, with its stacks of comics and its model airplanes and all the other junk he had collected. His mother was strict about neatness, so that he had to keep the comics in a pile, the airplanes on the shelf when he wasn't playing with them or putting them together, and the other toys in the toy box.

She opened a drawer in the chest and began pulling out underwear and socks. From another drawer came knit summer pullover shirts, and folded, pressed blue jeans.

"You bring down your suitcase from the closet, Timmy, and put it on the bed."

There was a kind of light conversation then, what his mother called small talk. They chose and discarded names for the pup and made other plans for him, laying his life out neatly ahead. He would be a lucky dog.

"Will he have to stay out in the doghouse like Buster did, Mom?"

"That depends on how big he is, and how much winter fur he can put on in the fall, right? Perhaps we can get him a special rug and let him sleep right beside your bed."

"Hey, that'd be great!"

"Don't forget your swimsuit. You'll be wanting that."

"Then he'll be warm all winter, won't he?"

"Sure he will."

The bag was closed, bulging around a lot of clothes, when his mother got up to leave the room. With a sudden and overwhelming sense of loss he clutched her around the waist.

"I'm scared, Mommy," he said, reverting to his baby name for her, his pride gone, his courage gone.

She held him tightly for a moment, then pushed him slightly back and tilted his chin up, her hand cupping it warmly. "Why are you scared, Timmy?"

He tried to find words to describe his feelings, but there seemed to be none. "I'm afraid you won't come back," he finally said. And yet that wasn't right, for wasn't it he, and not she, who actually was going away?

"But we'll all be back, darling, just the way we are

28

now. When you come home, I'll be right here waiting, and so will your daddy."

"But what if you have a car wreck or something?" he asked, one finger touching and fondling a soft blond curl that hung by her ear.

"Dad's a very careful driver." She held him, her hands on the belt of his jeans.

He ventured farther, trying to give substance to his fears. "What if Uncle Dan does?"

"And so is he. In fact, he's kind of a dowdy driver, I'd say."

"What does that mean?"

"Oh—old-ladyish—really slow and careful, you know?" She shook him gently to cheer him up. "Have you ever known Dan to burn rubber when he drives away?"

Timmy laughed. "No." But it was a brief laugh. "I'd rather go with Russ to his uncle's farm."

"That would have been nice, but Russ is already gone. Anyway, don't you think it'll be great photographing animals and other nature beauties?"

"But what if we ran into a bear or a panther?"

"Oh dear! I don't think I like the way this conversation's going. You go on and take your bath and get into your pajamas, then you can watch television for a while. But not long, for you have to be up early."

That was it, he knew. He had lost. They would go their way and he would be sent another, and they would never see one another again. But he wouldn't cry. He'd think about his dog instead and try to think up a really good name.

Three

He didn't think he would sleep at all, but the first thing he knew it was daylight again in his room and his dad was calling, "Timmy, your uncle Dan is here. Are you awake? He wants to get an early start. It's six o'clock, Tim. Come on, wake up."

Timmy felt his stomach sink sickeningly. This was it. After a few more minutes there would be no turning back. He would be in Uncle Dan's van headed north. He didn't answer his dad's calls. If he pretended to be asleep maybe they would decide not to wake him. Maybe it would change everybody's plans. But his dad came on into the room, got him by the shoulders, and pulled him to a sitting position in the bed.

"Come on now, Tim, wake up. Uncle Dan is here."

Timmy stirred, stretched his arms over his head. "Dad, can I—"

"No more of that. Get your pants on and brush your teeth. Your breakfast is waiting."

In the bathroom Timmy could hear the voices of the adults from the kitchen if he brushed his teeth quietly, strained his ears, and left the door open. He wanted to hear. In his heart hope was drowning, and in going down became a kind of desperate, unspoken prayer as he listened for his mother or his dad to make a change in plans.

· Connie was saying, "It's good of you to take care of Timmy for two weeks, Dan. I doubt that a ten-year-old boy will be much company for you."

"Certainly all I want, Connie, when I'm sitting on a hillside waiting for a deer to come by. I just hope he won't get too bored and homesick."

"He's never been away from us for more than a couple of days at a time."

"We'll do okay. I'll keep him entertained. I'll turn a Polaroid over to him so he can see instant results of his photography."

Uncle Dan's voice today sounded a lot like Mom said he drove: slow, careful, dowdyish. It was as though he was thinking every word carefully before he let it out of his mouth. Timmy stood still, listening. Toothpaste began to dribble down his chin, tickling, and he bent over the sink again, running the water for a moment. When again he could hear the voice belonged to his dad.

"You know where to reach me if you need me, Dan. But where can I reach you?"

"I'll have to do the calling, Steve. My cabin is isolated, and several miles from a telephone. Those old hills are large and rugged, with endless forests and no real roads at all—just old logging trails. You'll all have to go with me sometime. But I'll call you after a couple or three days, don't worry. We may do some camping out on the way up, and not get there until mid-week. I hope all goes well with—"

Somebody shut the kitchen door, and the voices faded away. Timmy ran back to his room, dressed, and gave one last look around. With his small suitcase in his hand he went slowly down the hall to the kitchen.

They sat at the table, two dear familiar people, and Dan. Not that Dan's face wasn't familiar, too, but Timmy could find nothing dear about it. The face was too fat, too full in the cheeks, too round in the mouth. And the eyes were narrow strips of dark reflections in their folds and flaps of flesh. There was something about those eyes that he never had been able to look directly into, comfortably. Sometimes, when Dan—*Uncle Dan*—gave him a gift, he felt sorry that he didn't like him more. But he couldn't help it.

"Hello there son," Uncle Dan said now. "Looking forward to a jaunt in the mountains?"

Timmy didn't look at him. "I guess so," he said, and slid onto a chair at the table where a place was set for him. He drank the orange juice and started on the milk. "Dad's going to get me a pup when we get back."

"A pup! Now that's something to look forward to," Dan said.

Connie got up from the table, from her cup of coffee, and went to the stove to bring back a plate of toast and scrambled eggs for Timmy. "Steve, why don't you give Dan the money to buy a pup for Timmy? Would it be too much trouble, Dan, to look

33

for one in the mountains on your way back to your place? Don't those mountain people sometimes keep beagles?''

"Oh sure they do. And it wouldn't be too much trouble at all. But keep your money, Steve. I'll get him the pup, if I can find one.''

Suddenly the trip with Uncle Dan took on a more favorable aspect in Timmy's eyes. "Oh, could we, Dad? Could we?''

His dad looked at him and laughed. "I don't see why not, if Dan wants to bother with it.''

"No bother," Dan said, and rose from his chair, stretching his body up and chest out, so that his pants drooped and bagged from the removed weight at the belt. He adjusted the belt, and let his belly fall back onto it. There was something soft and pillowish about the front of Uncle Dan's body, like in some ladies Timmy had seen, with stomach too large and hips too wide for a man. Nothing he wore, Timmy thought fleetingly, looked good. But that didn't matter. What mattered was the other—the feeling that had no real reason for being. The look in his eyes, sometimes. The subtle changes that were like different shades of gray.

Uncle Dan's hand settled warmly and stickily on Timmy's shoulder. "Ready?''

Timmy slid out from under the hand by getting up on the other side of his chair. He didn't look at either his mom or his dad. He picked up his suitcase and started out the door.

His mother said, "Hey wait, Tim. No kiss?''

He turned toward her but closed his eyes as he waited for the kiss. If he looked at her, he'd cry, he

34

knew for sure. And he didn't want to start crying now. He'd think about the dog, about driving into the mountains and seeing a sign that said Pups For Sale. About stopping there and getting one, or maybe even two. A pup needed company on those days when his master had to go to school. Two pups would keep each other company.

"Dad, could I get two beagle pups instead of one because when I go to school one would get lonesome. I'd take good care of both of them."

All three adults laughed.

Uncle Dan said, "I think that boy's got the makings of a con artist."

"One's enough," Steve answered. "Go on now, and have a good time."

Steve had come to stand in the doorway to watch them leave. Uncle Dan's hand was back on Timmy's shoulder, and there seemed no way to get out from under it without dodging and running, so Timmy walked quietly, but with an effort, beside the soft presence of Uncle Dan.

Connie and Steve stood together on the front walk and watched the van move slowly out onto the street and away. From the right window the thin, bare arm of their son waved back at them from far down the street.

The quiet that was left was too quiet, an uneasy stillness that Connie felt with growing anxiety. She frowned, shaded her eyes from the brightening of the sky overhead and watched the van, seeing it for the first time in a different light. The major color was deep purple, with paintings, murals, on the sides depicting a kind of pictureless intermingling of scarlets and blacks and strange, sensual blues. From this far away, and with the light and shadows thrown like a child's blocks, the formless colors became a picture, for a moment clear and distinct: fat, naked babies, small children, like cupids, flying around a central body that was grossly swollen and fat, with a head that had no real face, a huge blob with a mouth that dripped scarlet blood from one corner, and from the other corner dangled the cherubic arm and leg of a fat baby.

She blinked in a sudden spasm of horror, and when she looked again the picture was gone, replaced once more by the formless colors.

She was going nuts. Her eyes had deceived her, or the light, or the simple fact that she felt like hell. It had been months since she had really felt optimistic about life, or even like getting out of bed in the morning. And this was early. Too early. She closed her eyes and opened them again expecting to see the van in its usual ugliness and simplicity, but it had turned a corner, and the paintings were hidden by the dark trunks and drooping leaf-hung branches of the trees.

She said musingly, "Did you ever notice those paintings on the side of his van, Steve?"

Steve's arm drew her comfortably close against his side. "What paintings? There's nothing but a blob of colors. I think somebody was experimenting when they threw the paint at that old van."

"I don't know. I thought I saw pictures, murals.

36

But even the colors—aren't they kind of wild for him?"

"He probably bought it secondhand from some kid."

"Oh. Yes, probably."

They went back into the house side by side, but Connie's anxiety did not leave. The house was pulsatingly empty and depressing.

"It's lonesome here without him, Steve. Let's hurry and go, before I start out down the road to bring him back."

"It won't be long, Connie, before we're all back. All three of us."

She said no more. Nothing that came to her mind would have sounded anything but depressing, and she could see in Steve's face a kind of strain she had never seen before. And this time she knew for certain she was not seeing something that wasn't there. For his sake she tried to act as though she had more energy than she felt, more optimism, more faith. But, like Timmy, she was scared. Deep down scared. And she wanted both her men, one on each side of her. She wanted to feel her arms around them.

Only then would she feel really secure.

But this, too, was caused by her illness, she knew. This need not to be left alone. She had never been a clinger before.

What would they find Monday morning, with her lying unconscious on the surgical table? Would it be alive, in its strange and frightening life form, cells dividing and consuming, moving into other parts of her body so that eventually all her life would be consumed? What would they find?

Whatever it was, it would have taken with it her last hope of ever having another child.

She had never longed for anyone so much as she now longed for Timmy, to hug him one more time, to tell him they would manage somehow to take him along.

But no, of course he was much better off with Dan.

Four

The van lumbered along, slowly. Timmy could no longer see his house. He watched the park move by, but there was no one in it this early in the day. In the east the sun was just breaking through a low bank of rosy clouds and beginning to warm Timmy's arm. He looked at his companion, saw the streaked blond hair stirring in the wind. It was styled in a formerly modish cut down to the collar, with a few waves, almost like a girl's hair. The side of his face was girlish, too, in an ugly way, Timmy thought, because the cheek rounded out. And the lips looked warm and red and wet.

Timmy moved his eyes away in revulsion and looked over his shoulder into the back of the van. There were things lying around that looked like different sizes of cameras. There were a few boxes. At one side was a bunk bed, and on the other, a tiny wall cabinet like a kitchen.

Dan noticed his absorption. He smiled. "What do you think of my house, Timmy?"

Timmy jerked back. His mom had told him not to gawk around at other people's houses and things when he was a visitor, and he guessed that was what he was now. A visitor. "Uh—okay," he said. And then, "Your house? You mean you live in this all the time? You don't have a real house to live in?"

Uncle Dan reached toward him, and Timmy thought he was going to put that pudgy hand on his knee. He automatically jerked his leg away, and the hand faltered and raised to the radio knob instead. The smile on Uncle Dan's face remained as it was—undisturbed.

"I can't take a house along on the road with me, now, can I? I travel around most of the time, so this van is my house on wheels. It's even got a little kitchen sink back there. Did you see that?"

Timmy looked over his shoulder again and spotted the tiny sink in the middle of the cabinet. "Oh, yeah."

"It doesn't have running water, it's just an outlet. I carry my water in a can."

"But you've got a real house in the mountains, don't you?"

"Yes, that I do. A real house. A cabin, I call it. And I've got an apartment back in town. It'll take us about fourteen hours to get to the cabin. It will be pitch dark by then, and you'll be fast asleep. What kind of music do you like, Timmy boy? Country-western? Rock? Gospel?" He laughed, as though he had made some kind of private joke.

Timmy shrugged. The radio zipped from one kind of music to another and finally settled on acid rock.

"There," Uncle Dan said. "How's that?"

"I don't care. I don't listen to the radio much."

"You mean you haven't gotten to the stereo stage yet?"

"I guess not."

Uncle Dan was still smiling, and Timmy wished he would stop. He turned his face and looked out the window so he wouldn't have to see. Trees slipped by faster now, houses were moving back and fields opening up. His small hometown was being left behind.

"You're in the puppy-dog stage," Uncle Dan said. "What kind of dog are you planning to get, Tim?"

"A beagle, Dad said. Just as soon as I get back, if we don't find any before then." He turned his eyes straight ahead, saw they were going up the ramp onto the interstate highway north.

"I guess you're pretty anxious to get back then, aren't you?" Uncle Dan said as though he had already forgotten his offer to get Timmy a pup.

In a way, Timmy didn't care. He would rather have his dad help choose their new puppy. Uncle Dan's smile wasn't so obvious now, and Timmy figured his jaws had gotten tired. Timmy understood that. His own jaws always got tired when his parents took him visiting and he had to do a lot of silly grinning.

"Yeah," Timmy said. And then, "I had a dog once. Buster. Mom and Dad got him before I was born. I think he was Mom's dog at home, you know, when she lived with her folks on the farm. And when she got married she brought him with her, and when I was born she let me have him for my dog. That is, she said, *he* claimed me for his, and she kind of lost him to me. He was a great dog. He was big. Part collie.

41

Maybe whole collie, I guess. Anyway, he got real old and he got sick and would never be well again, so Dad had to get the doctor to put him to sleep."

"Ah, yes. I remember Buster. He was a fine dog, Timmy. But I'm sure all your dogs will be fine."

"Yeah," Timmy said, stretching his legs more comfortably ahead of him and almost forgetting that he didn't really like Uncle Dan. "I want him little enough so I can carry him in my jacket when it rains, you know? Until he's grown, that is. He'll be about this high." Timmy measured with his hand above the seat. "And he'll be tough and will run a lot like a boy needs, you know? Mom said that's the kind I need. No little lap dog for me. But even if I had a tiny dog, a lap dog, I'd take care of him. I'd never hurt him, would you?"

"Oh no, certainly not." Uncle Dan looked full into Timmy's face. "It certainly is good to hear you talking, Timmy. You usually don't say much when I'm around."

Timmy shrugged. He didn't want to be put on the spot about that. "My parents always told me I shouldn't monopolize a conversation when adults are present."

"My, that sounds very grown-up."

Timmy shrugged again. He didn't like the turn of the conversation. He'd rather talk about dogs. "It was them that said it, not me."

He pointed his face out the window again. Stretching far away were freshly plowed fields, black soil open to the rising sun. In the distance a line of trees looked like a tiny, solid wall of dark green. Also breaking the horizon far ahead was a small town with silos stretching against the sky like round, tall buildings. Not so far ahead he could see a fenced pasture with green grass and fat, grazing cattle. Someone was on horseback on the other side of the pasture, riding toward the cows. In the field behind it a tractor moved, looking with the distance no larger than a toy tractor. Timmy wondered if his friend Russ was the one on the horse.

Timmy sighed. "My friend Russ is spending his vacation with his uncle on his big farm. His real uncle. He's got cousins too, and an aunt. He wanted me to go along, but my Mom and Dad wouldn't let me. I don't know why they wouldn't let me."

"Maybe it was because I asked for your company in the mountains. Did I spoil other plans for you?"

"Well, I don't know why they didn't want me to go to the farm. Mom said she was afraid I'd get hurt, but that's silly. I'm ten years old now. I'm not a baby anymore. Russ never gets hurt. He left right after school was out. That's been almost a month already."

"I'm glad they let you come with me, Timmy. It will give us a chance to get better acquainted."

Timmy made no comment. He looked out the window to see what the horse and its rider were doing. They weren't doing much. They had ridden into the edge of the grazing cattle and were just watching, it seemed. Timmy wished he were the rider on that horse.

"Do you have a lot of friends, Timmy?"

Timmy continued to watch the horse and its rider. If he were the rider he would be feeling the rising sun on his back, and breathing deep the sweet clover of

43

the lush pasture. And when noon came he would check his pocket watch, which was just like his grandfather's gold watch that he would inherit on his sixteenth birthday, and he would ride back across the field to the stockade fence and leave his horse there and go into the big, warm kitchen of the white farmhouse hidden among the trees and sit down to a big dinner of barbequed ribs and chocolate pie. And nobody would tell him he'd had enough pie now.

Uncle Dan said again, "Do you have a lot of friends, Timmy? Tell me about your friends."

"I play with a lot of kids," Timmy said, wishing he'd call him Tim or Timothy instead of his baby name of Timmy. He had just ridden in on his horse for a big dinner at the heavily laden kitchen table. In his fantasy he was too big and too old to be called Timmy.

"How about Russ?" Uncle Dan asked. "Is he your best friend?"

"I don't know. I guess so. We live closer together than me and the other kids. We're on the same block. But Clark is my friend, too."

The van was moving faster now, and the pasture of cattle was left behind. The horse and its rider left behind. Another small town moved into view ahead, dominated by a tall silo, or grain bin, or something as equally removed from Timmy's firsthand investigation.

Farms and towns and hours passed by, and Uncle Dan drove mostly in silence, sometimes tapping his fingertips against the steering wheel in time to the music. Timmy gazed out the window, dreaming his dreams of horses and dogs and clear blue skies. Once

44

or twice he noticed that the speedometer needle edged past seventy, and he remembered what his mom had said about Uncle Dan's driving. She had not known him very well at all. But it didn't matter to Timmy. The miles were still slow miles, and left a lot of time for dreaming.

Uncle Dan said, during a pause in the music, "What about girlfriends, Timmy? Don't you have a girlfriend? Or girlfriends?" His voice slid silkily over the S in girlfriends. "A boy as good-looking as you should have a lot of girls."

Timmy didn't like the sound of Dan's voice. He sounded half asleep. And besides, why were grown-ups always so interested in girlfriends? Everybody but his dad and mom. Every time he was forced to visit a distant relative the first thing they asked him was how many dates he had with how many girls. He knew they were teasing, and that made the question sillier than ever, as though the adults didn't know how to communicate with a boy ten years old.

"Girls are teacher's pets," Timmy said, hoping to end that question forever.

He saw a boy on a bicycle waiting to cross the adjacent two-lane road at the edge of a tiny hamlet and thought of his own bicycle at home. He didn't mind riding through new country in a car, or van as the case was, but he thought it would be more fun to be riding down his own quiet street on his bicycle, shaded by the London plane-trees and maples that lined his street. Especially if his new pup was running beside him. Maybe he could even train his pup to ride in his bicycle basket, especially when he got tired of running.

"Teacher's pets?" Uncle Dan said, slurring the words into one hissing sound. "I don't believe you're much of a ladies' man, Timmy. And that's good, for you're just a little boy." Dan reached over and tapped Timmy's knee with his fingers. "*My* little boy for the next two weeks. Well, looka there. Are you hungry, Timmy?"

Timmy saw a sign ahead, down in a field to the right, that claimed Drive-In in big flashing neon letters that looked a bit sick in the sunshine.

"I'm kind of thirsty," he said, and remembered to add, "Uncle Dan."

Dan reached over again and clasped a hot palm over Timmy's thigh. Timmy pulled, edging toward the door, but the heavy hand pressed down, the ends of the fingers digging into his flesh. It hurt, but Timmy bit his lower lip, holding back the involuntary cry that almost slipped out.

"You're just about all skin and bones, aren't you, boy?" Uncle Dan said, a sudden frown pulling down his eyebrows. With his left hand he steered the van down the exit toward the drive-in. "Haven't you been eating? We've got to fatten you up. Little Mother likes her children plump."

Timmy frowned, puzzled, but he didn't ask Uncle Dan what he meant. Adults had a way of saying things that had meaning only for themselves.

The hand lifted, and after a moment Timmy put his own hand over the bruised area of his thigh. He felt a little sick to his stomach, and wished they weren't stopping at the drive-in.

Uncle Dan drew up close to the side of the building and dug into his pocket for money. He handed a fistful of change to Timmy.

"Now you get yourself a hamburger and fries and a malted milk."

Timmy stared at the face of Uncle Dan. The smile was entirely gone now, and the face that was left looked cold and stern. Timmy felt himself shiver in the warm morning sun.

"I'm not hungry," he said.

"You have to eat. What do you want, your folks saying I didn't feed you? Get it. You can take your time eating, if you want, while we drive on. Order anything you like, but eat."

Timmy had never felt so intimidated. "Yes, sir," he murmured. "But can I have onion rings instead of a burger and fries?"

"Yes, that would be all right, this one time. It's not a balanced diet, though."

"What do you want me to bring you?" Timmy asked.

The corners of Uncle Dan's mouth twitched slightly, and Timmy thought he was going to smile again, which is better than not smiling, he could see that now. But the smile didn't come. Uncle Dan's voice grew silky again.

"I'll wait," he said. "Just bring me a malted. You might do that."

Five

Timmy began to feel better as he waited for his order, even to gaining a touch of hunger at the food fragrances wafting from the screened windows. The sun was bright and hot, and he moved under the wide overhang of the roof for shade. Under umbrellas that rose in the center of round tables people sat eating, or waiting, like him, for their number to be called. Cars pulled in on the other side, and parked in the spaces allotted them under a long roof. They called in their orders from individual speakers.

By the time Timmy's number was called, he was ready to eat. He received his order at the drive-in window and paid for it rather grandly. He wasn't used to handling more than his dollar a week allowance. When he went to the fast food places with his mom and dad, which he enjoyed thoroughly, he always went to the window or the pick-up counter with his dad to help carry, but his dad always paid.

He wondered where they were now. Were they in the station wagon going toward Shreveport, or were they in Mom's little gas-saving car? The thought of them going anywhere without him made him feel a little sick, and he wished he hadn't ordered so much food.

He walked slowly across the graveled lot toward the van, the tray balanced carefully. He went to the driver's side, his eyes glued to the security of tall paper glasses that could so easily spill.

"Uncle Dan? I'm here. I didn't spill a thing."

"Good. Good boy." The voice almost sang as the door opened. Dan's slightly bloated hands reached down and took the tray. His diamond ring glittered with miniature rainbows in the sunlight. "Want to eat in the van, Timmy, or hunt up a picnic table?"

"I don't care."

"All right, the van. Come on, hurry while it's both cold and hot." Uncle Dan laughed merrily, but it sounded rather forced and unnatural to Timmy.

Once he had started eating his onion rings and chocolate milk shake, Timmy was glad he had ordered so much. And further, he was almost glad Mom wasn't along. She would have made him eat a hamburger, too. She would have said, "Onion rings and no meat sandwich? No way, Timmy. Whoever heard of a diet of onion rings?"

He liked hamburgers okay, but he liked onion rings better. He liked to slip them over his fingers like outsized rings before he ate them, and Mom thought that was a ridiculous thing to do. He liked to eat them off his fingers, sometimes.

Uncle Dan asked, "Is that all you're eating? Onion rings?" He sounded almost like Mom in her continuing amazement at her son's likes and dislikes.

"I've got a shake, too."

"Oh, so you have. Tonight we'll cook our own dinner on a campfire. How does that sound, Timmy?"

Timmy considered that, and found it good. He even managed some enthusiasm. "What'll we have?"

"What do you want?"

"I don't care. Hot dogs and potato chips maybe?"

"If that's what you want, that's what you'll have. We'll stop at a grocery store later and you can pick it out. I guess one day of junk food is not going to hurt you. The important thing is that you eat plenty, right now. Do you have plenty there?"

"Yes sir."

"Now that you're with me, you can forget about the rules you've learned. You can do new things, be a new little boy."

Timmy directed a long, puzzled look at Uncle Dan. "Huh?"

"I mean—what I meant was, you can do just anything you want, today, within limits, of course. Is there anything you've kind of wanted to do and didn't because someone had told you not to?"

Timmy thought about that. Uncle Dan had a strange way of putting things. He still wasn't sure of what Uncle Dan had meant. "Well, yeah," he said. "Lots of things."

"Well, you can forget all those rules. You're my responsibility, and I'm going to take very good care of you, Timmy, but I want you to have fun, too."

"Okay," Timmy said, and blasted apart one of the old rules by eating an onion ring off his finger, and sucking up the last of the milk shake noisily. It always made a neat sound coming up through the straw, a gurgle and a slurp with a lot of little bubbles bursting in his mouth. But even as he broke that rule his mother had been so adamant about, he felt a little guilty. And he knew he couldn't break any more of her rules. If she told him he was not ever to do certain things, like climb the water tower—that slim, steep little series of ladders that went all the way to the top, practically into the clouds—then he would not climb the water tower no matter what Uncle Dan said. And if his dad told him, as he certainly had, not to ever go boating on a river or lake without a life jacket, then he would not, even though they were hot and bulky.

"Now that you're with me," Uncle Dan said, "you can take off that hot sweater and those heavy jeans and be comfortable. You can strip right off, if you want to, and be naked—"

Timmy's face jerked toward him in astonishment. "Why would I want to do that?"

"You don't want to? We'll be finding creeks soon, and you might want to take a dip."

"No," Timmy said emphatically. "I've got my swimming trunks with me. Only little kids like to go naked."

Uncle Dan smiled a bit to himself, nodding, his head tipped back, chocolate malt on the corner of his mouth. Timmy turned his eyes away, toward the people at the drive-in windows.

"That's right, Timmy. Little children have no self-consciousness about their bodies. They shed their diapers whenever they can." Uncle Dan patted Timmy's arm. "And you're just a little boy yourself. I wouldn't be bringing you along if you were any bigger. A family needs little ones."

Timmy looked out the window. He felt shivery suddenly. But milk shakes always made him feel a little cold, for a little while. What was the matter with Uncle Dan? Sometimes, it seemed to Timmy, his crazy talk made no sense. But then, wasn't that one of the reasons he didn't hang around very long listening to adults talk? They would sit around in little groups and talk about the weather, or the prices of things, and never notice the way the blackbirds flocked like great drifts of leaves lifted into the sky by errant puffs of wind, or they'd call the stray dog that lived from door to door worthless and ugly, and never see how he trotted sideways, as if his four feet were trying to keep out of one another's way, or how soft and brown his eyes were. Yeah, adults could be funny, sitting in little groups around the table, playing cards, and hollering and laughing or moaning and groaning. Even his own parents were guilty of those shortcomings. So for two weeks he was going to have to listen to Uncle Dan, and the best answer to that, he guessed, was to think of something else. Remember the pup, he reminded himself, and the two weeks will go faster. Grown-ups don't know how to talk to kids anyway. And kids can't talk to grown-ups, because they take plain words and turn them into something else, with meanings not intended. Timmy knew. He'd gotten in dutch with more than one teacher, just because he tried to say what was on his mind.

Timmy spotted a little dog bouncing happily at the end of his chain as he followed his lady-mama up to the drive-in window. "Look at that little dog!" he exclaimed. "What kind do you think it is, Uncle

Dan?" One good thing about adults, Timmy had to admit, they always knew the answers. Ask them anything, and they knew.

"I believe that's a bull terrier puppy."

"If I can't find a beagle pup, wouldn't one like that do?" Uncle Dan grunted noncommittally, bringing Timmy to add, "I guess not. Dad said a beagle. I guess I'd better get a beagle. Are you going to watch for pups for sale, Uncle Dan?"

The man drew a long breath, placed his hands on the steering wheel, and dragged himself upright. "Take the tray back, Timmy, and put the stuff in the trash can. We've got a lot of road ahead of us. Little Mother would not like a dog in the house."

Timmy obeyed quickly, taking the tray and climbing backwards down out of the van. But he wondered, what does he mean, *Little Mother*? Was his mother or someone he called Little Mother, at the cabin, or was it just an expression, a kind of byword? Like someone swearing a little, for instance, the way his grandma used to say something that sounded to him like, "*Mother Matree!*" when things didn't go right for her, when she burned her finger at the stove or made a wrong stitch in her embroidery.

Timmy returned to the van and settled himself close against his door, his elbow pointing out. He watched the landscape move by as they returned to the northbound interstate.

Late in the afternoon they left the interstate and proceeded on north on a smooth, wide highway that roped into growing hills and mountains and deep green valleys, with tantalizingly cool, clear, lively streams of water that Timmy would have given a month's allowance to go wading in, or swimming, or fishing. But he didn't express his wishes to the man behind the wheel. Uncle Dan seemed to have forgotten what he had said earlier about taking a dip in a creek. But the mountain air seemed to revive him, and he lifted up, as if he had been half asleep behind the wheel all afternoon.

"Oh my," he said, breathing deeply of the cool, moist air. "See these mountains, Timmy. Round and high and covered with trees. And down under those trees is another world, Timmy, a dark and mysterious world where anything can happen, where all kinds of dangerous creatures live."

Timmy looked and saw more trees than he'd ever seen before in his life. He didn't know about the mysterious world beneath the trees, or what kind of creatures lived there that could be dangerous. It looked to him like a moist, dark world, very interesting all right, and probably filled with all kinds of little animals, frogs, beetles, chipmunks. But none of them dangerous. It looked like a good place to play. Unless—

"Are there bears here?" he asked.

"Sure. And deer. And mountain lion. You must never stray too far away from me. Your parents would be very unhappy if something grabbed you and ran."

Timmy made no comment. He was looking hard, hoping to see a bear or a mountain lion from this safe distance. They drove now through shadows, a narrow valley shaded by the rise of hills to the west. Although the sky was still a clear and brilliant blue, sunlighted, darkness seemed to be invading the hollows that went ever deeper among the hills.

"The sun will soon be going down, Timmy. We'll stop at a campsite I know and see what we can find to eat. We'll rest awhile before we go on."

Timmy didn't bother to remind him that they were supposed to stop at a grocery store for hot dogs. It didn't matter that much. "Are we going to look for animals to take pictures of?"

"Not tonight, Timmy. I'm tired tonight, aren't you?"

"I guess so."

"After we eat you can crawl into the bunk and go to sleep."

"I'm all right. Are we in the Boston Mountains now?"

"Pretty close, Timmy, pretty close."

A few miles farther on the van edged off the highway and toward a bare spot beneath the trees where there were two picnic tables and at least one grill.

Timmy alighted from the van with pleasure. His bottom felt as though it had turned to plastic, and his legs to silly putty. He jumped around to bring them back to life.

"You just run along and have a look around before it gets completely dark, Timmy, and I'll fix our supper."

"Okay!"

Timmy investigated the campsites, found them unusual, hidden as they were in the crowding forest. He climbed the hillside to the first small section of bluff and, by crawling on his belly under the bluff, discovered a tiny cave, its entrance no more than a foot wide. It had been swept clean, as though it were the home of a tiny woods creature who used a broom to clean his house. There was not even a pebble on the hard-packed clay floor of the entrance. Timmy thought about reaching in, and perhaps finding a furry little nest with furry babies, and then decided against it.

He swung around a couple of slim-trunked young trees.

He stopped and listened to the nearby, loud call of an evening whippoorwill, and the answering far-away cry of two more. He shivered, a little scared, a little cold in the evening dampness.

He heard Uncle Dan's voice calling him to supper.

He ran back, ate a sandwich and drank from the tall, cold, plastic glass.

"That's good for you," Uncle Dan said. "I prepared it in my blender. It's eggs and milk and pineapple juice—plus a few more things. Do you like it, Timmy?"

"Yeah, it's good."

"Come sit by me, Timmy." Uncle Dan patted the bench beside his spreading hips.

Timmy hesitated, then driven by a compulsion to obey the authoritative figure of an adult, he reluctantly sat down. Uncle Dan put his arm around Timmy's waist and pulled him closer on the bench and held him so that leaning away was impossible. Timmy could feel Uncle Dan's breath in his hair, hot and close and unpleasant. So different from the feel of his mom's or dad's breath stirring his hair when they held him. With them he felt like burrowing closer. With Uncle Dan, he strained away as much as he could without being impolite.

"I've always wanted a little boy just like you, Timmy my son."

Timmy pretended interest in the darkening hillside that hovered above them. "It's getting real dark," he said. "I used to be scared of the dark sometimes."

"Oh my. And you should be. Many things walk only in the dark." Uncle Dan's arm gathered him closer. For a moment Timmy was afraid the man was going to kiss him, just as if he were a baby that needed protection. "Would you like to come up and sit on my lap?"

Timmy swallowed air. "I'm all right," he mumbled. "It's not really so dark."

"Are you getting sleepy, Timmy boy?"

Timmy nodded. He was getting very sleepy suddenly, as though the damp, dark fingers of these strange mountains were reaching out for him, claiming him, drugging him with their deep mysteries.

Uncle Dan picked Timmy up, and although Timmy stiffened in revolt, he carried him into the van and laid him on the lower bunk. It was hard and narrow, but the thin foam rubber mattress, with its single, smelly blanket, was balm to Timmy's soul as he curled away from Uncle Dan's arms into the dark comfort of his nest.

The van bounced and jerked through the black leaf-draped road tunnel following the twin beams of light that tried, at times futilely, to find the tracks that were hardly more than a long dead logging trail. Timmy's head cracked against the paneled guts of the van as it jolted sideways, and he woke. The van

58

tilted back toward the left and Timmy rolled on the bunk bed and almost fell onto the floor. His body felt bruised and beaten from the tossing, and he needed urgently to go to the bathroom.

Now nearly forgotten fragments of nightmares edged in and out of his mind, a bit grasped before it was lost forever. He had dreamed of lions and bears, but not the kind found in zoos, not real lions or real bears, but hideous caricatures of them. It was good to be awake, to lose all of the bad dreams in this more urgent business of reality.

He pulled himself to his knees and clung for support to the pole at the head of the bed. "Uncle Dan? I got to go to the bathroom."

The van moved on for awhile as though its driver had not heard, but then slowed, and stopped, and the driver turned. One side of his face was outlined by the faint light of the dashboard like a thin sliver of new moon in a black and starless sky.

"Are you awake?"

"Yes sir. I need to go to the bathroom."

"Hurry it up then. We're almost there."

Timmy went out to the side of the van. Leaves from the foliage at the crowding hillside brushed his face. He wondered how long he had slept in the rough-riding van. He still felt as though he weren't really awake, as though his head had grown to enormous weight, and his eyes had lids made of lead. From somewhere in the black woods came a dreamy-faint unknown animal cry that chilled him to the bone and sent him scurrying back into the safety of the van. He zipped his jeans with some difficulty after he was in the seat.

"Was that a mountain lion?" Timmy asked.

Uncle Dan did not answer his question. He started the van forward at a slow and torturous pace. "Go on back to your bunk, Timmy. It's another seven or eight miles."

Obediently Timmy crawled through the cluttered space to the bunk. He had wanted to sit up in the seat and watch the road. He had wanted to see the cabin as soon as they reached it, but his thoughts were yawned into oblivion.

Timmy dreamed he was walking through a jungle where black foliage of twisted, thick-trunked trees curled grasping fingers toward him, and when he tried to run from evil faces that looked out from among the foliage, vines tripped him, and ground soggy with hidden pools of black water sucked him down, down. He tried to scream and could not.

Suddenly he was no longer in the jungle, he knew, without being able to see his new surroundings. His eyes felt glued, too heavy to open, but he became aware that he was being carried. He was cradled in the arms of someone huge and strong, and he was naked. No, not completely naked. He was wearing something bulky between his legs and around his hips, and he knew suddenly and with a helpless sense of embarrassment that it was a diaper, three ends brought together over his stomach and pinned with a large safety pin. His eyes came open, and as though peering through a gauzy curtain he saw that the man who carried him was Uncle Dan. They were coming through a door, and into a room that smelled old and closed for many years, a room where things had died and had not been cleaned away. Through the gauzy slit of his eyes he saw a wall with old floral paper that was a faded pink and gray, and on the wall was a framed needlework, like Timmy's grandma used to make, that read, Home Sweet Home.

Uncle Dan's arms held him out, as though offering him to someone else, and he said, "Here's your new child, Little Mother . . . Little Mother . . ."

Little Mother, Little Mother, Little Mother . . .

Uncle Dan's voice went on and on, like a chant in Timmy's ears, like an echo fading away into the distance.

Timmy tried to see whose arms were waiting for him, but his closing eyes glimpsed only a wood chair arm, unadorned, and a scrap of material, of tiny blue flowers on white background that could have been a cushion in the chair, or the skirt of someone's dress.

His eyes betrayed him and closed completely, and he was lost once more in darkness.

Six

A whimper, as of a lonely animal, brought Timmy
from his exhausted sleep. He lay still and tense,
staring upward into total darkness. Fear closed
taloned fingers on his throat, tensed his muscles
against movement, against making any sound that
would draw attention to him. Where was he? This
was not his room at home where a soft night light
burned on the chest across by his closet door. This
was—yes—Uncle Dan's cabin? From somewhere in
the pit of night silence came another sound that was
more familiar than the one that had awakened him.
Hooo-whoo-who. An owl in the night. Soft, close.
An owl's voice just outside the window. Shivers crept
over his body, and he realized he was still wearing his
clothes. Even his shoes. He was lying on top his bed,
not in it. And he was afraid to move, to undress and
crawl under the blanket that was soft against his
hands.

Again, the sound, the whimper, so near, so soft and
helpless. Someone crying out in dreams?

He turned his head slowly, noiselessly, toward the sound. Gradually objects in the room took shape from the scarce gray-black light of a night-shrouded window. The darker bulk of a bunk bed, and another. Was it Uncle Dan crying in his sleep? No. No. A man would not sound like that.

The whimper stopped suddenly on a long, soft gasp of breath. A sigh, then, as though the dreamer had risen from a nightmare, and recognized it as only a disturbing dream. Bedding stirred. A body tossed with a faint squeak of bedsprings, then another long sigh of relief as the body settled into its new position.

Timmy waited, but there was nothing more. Against his will he slept again, but lightly, fitfully, as though his mind was sure to keep its third eye open in this strange place. He heard the hoot owl in his half-sleep. He heard footsteps going past the wall. He heard his own heart beating in its sleeping terror of these unknown surroundings. He gripped the blanket instinctively and wadded it around his cold, bare arms, and covered his face with it. He brought his knees up painfully tight against his chest and lay curled in that fetal position.

And then he woke to the unexpected sound of children's laughter.

One eye peeped out from the blanket and saw a finger of sunlight on the board floor. A shadow fell across the sunlight, and a boy's bare foot flashed across his narrowed vision like a pale-bellied fish leaping briefly from a pool of water. Timmy opened both eyes in astonishment. A boy, with tousled, shaggy hair and laughing face, threw a pillow. But not at Timmy. At someone across the room. Timmy's glance followed the pillow and saw another boy, this one smaller, dodge the pillow. It fell to the floor at the side of a bunk bed against the wall. This boy's face was sour and disapproving of an early morning pillow fight.

"Cut it out, Rex," he growled. "Leave me alone. I'm trying to get my shoes on."

The boy called Rex had a long, freckled face, straight reddish brown hair that needed cutting, and the devil in his eyes. "Whata you think, you screwball, you gonna take all day? Come on, hurry up."

His eyes swung to Timmy and settled like red wasps. "Hey! When did you get here? Hey! You don't even have your pajamas on. Did you sleep in your shoes?"

Timmy sat up on the side of his bed and looked about the room in pleased surprise. He had thought he'd have to spend two weeks alone with Uncle Dan, but there seemed to be boys everywhere. Rex, the tall, freckled one. The smaller dark-haired boy who was grumpily getting out of his bed, and above him a third, starting to crawl down the ladder from the top bunk. And then he noticed another, smaller figure that huddled back in the corner of a lower bunk. This one had saucer-round blue eyes that looked scared, and long, tangled blond curls. The hair was so snarled it looked like a pony's tail that was knotted with burrs. Timmy stared without meaning to, unable to stop for a moment, even though he knew it was impolite. He knew suddenly who had cried in her sleep, for this was no boy at all but a girl.

Rex edged toward him, like a rooster in a barnyard

strutting for a fight. "I asked you a question, kid," he threatened in a deepened voice, "and you're supposed to answer when I ask."

Timmy was too glad to see them to be intimidated even by this obvious bully of the group. "I got here last night. Have you been here all the time? I mean who—"

"All the time? What'a you mean, all the time? We're at this screwball camp same as you, kid. Hey! What's your name? Or do you just want me to call you tadpole."

"Camp?" Timmy said. "But I thought this was Uncle Dan's cabin."

"Cabin, camp. What'sa difference? We're here, ain't we?"

"You mean this is a regular boys' camp?" He glanced, remembering the little girl. "I mean, a kids' summer camp, or something?"

"Sure, it's a boys' camp. What'a you think?" Rex snorted in contempt. He glanced at the girl, grimaced in distaste. "Her, I don't know what she's doing here. She was already here when me and the boys come."

"When did you come?"

Rex shrugged. "Me, I ain't keeping time, but—"

The grumpy little boy said, "It was three days ago. We—"

Rex's face swiveled toward the little boy with a dark frown. "Hey, punk, I was telling the story, eh?"

"You said—"

"I know what I said. When I need your help, I'll ask for it. Meantime, you can just hold your breath and let's see how blue you can get. Okay?" He turned his scowl back toward Timmy. "Like I was saying, we got here three days ago, and then this creep he went off and left us again, so now we wake up and you're here. I guess that means he came back too, eh?''

"You mean Uncle Dan?"

"Hey! Uncle whose?"

The boy who had refused the pillow fight, and had corrected Rex, now said, "Uncle Dan, goofy. You know Uncle Dan. It was him that brought us up here." He frowned at Timmy, but Timmy could see it was a friendly frown. "Rex knows Uncle Dan. It's his house. He's doing us a favor by getting us off the streets for the summer."

"Yeah, so *he* says," Rex claimed. "And then the old shit goes off and just leaves us here by ourselves." He appeared to think a second thought and jabbed a thumb toward the girl. "Except for her."

Timmy glanced at the girl and saw her shake her head slightly, her eyes pinned on Rex. But the boys were talking again, and he had no chance to ask the girl what she meant.

"Well you know his name is Uncle Dan," the little boy said.

"Oh, well, him." The red-haired Rex shrugged a careless shoulder. "I thought his name was probably something else, that he was just feeding us a bunch of bull. I know these old guys that call themselves uncle. I know them, oboy, do I. They can't fool me."

"Uncle Dan—this Uncle Dan ain't like that. This one wants us to be happy here. He might even keep us and make us his family," the boy said earnestly.

"Who told you that!" Rex demanded.

"He did, that's who. Uncle Dan did, hisself."

"I don't listen to adult people. Not what they say nor their names. What are they anyway, but shit?"

Timmy glanced hastily at the little girl to see how she reacted to the naughty word, but she didn't move or change her expression from its extreme timidity. His mom had said, "Don't use naughty words, ever, not in a group of boys and certainly never in front of a girl. Not anywhere. If I ever know of you doing so, I'll squirt your mouth full of gentle Ivory and let you spit on that for awhile." That had been told to him sharp and clear the last time he brought a puzzling four-letter word home, and then instead of asking what it meant had used it at the wrong time. Just the thought of a mouth full of Ivory soap was enough to make him disinterested in what his mom called naughty words.

Timmy took a deep breath. He felt his face spread with an impulsive grin of welcome. "Boy, I sure am glad you kids are here."

Rex turned and stared at him with suddenly changed eyes. Instead of the bright hostility glistening in the orange flecks in the velvet brown irises there was a softening, a vulnerability that made Timmy know he would never be afraid of Rex anymore, not even for a second, no matter how he blustered.

"You are?"

"I sure am! My name is Tim." He paused, then added, because it was an important point at his age, "And I'm ten years old. I'll be in the fifth grade this fall."

Rex sniffed, wiped his nose on the back of his freckled hand. "Well. I'm Rex. I'll be thirteen next

December. I'm the oldest. I don't go to school much. This here is Dale, and that one that sleeps there on the top bunk is Joey. Joey's seven, and Dale's eight. They're just a couple of runts. And her—that's a girl. Her name's Susie. She don't talk. She's chicken-shit scared all the time. She's a baby, three or four—"

Susie made a move and held up her hand, her fingers spread. The count was five. Rex shrugged.

"Like I said, she don't talk. She just hangs around. Come on, let's go eat. We have to cook our own. Might be some corn flakes left. And there's plenty of canned milk."

"Yuk," said Joey, climbing down from the bunk. He had slept in his clothes, as had the others, not only one night but several, so they appeared. Little Joey was several inches shorter even than Dale, very little taller than Susie, but he made up for lack of height with added weight. He looked more like a baby, to Timmy, even than Susie, with his plump arms and legs. "I don't like canned milk," he said, when at last he stood among them.

"For somebody who don't like something, you sure can eat a lot of it," Rex said, but his voice sounded as though he was tolerant of Joey, at the least, even though he might be a complaining eater. A little boy who obviously liked food, but who had definite tastes. "We been livin' on corn flakes and canned milk, and pork and beans."

Dale said, "Maybe Uncle Dan brought some groceries."

"I don't think so," Timmy said.

"He don't have to. The cabinets are full of canned stuff," Rex said. "But nothing I like. Just beans and corn and garbage like that. Come on. I'd rather have a bag of chips and a hot dog or hamburger, but corn flakes we get."

Rex headed for the door, and Dale, still trying to get shoes on his feet, hobbled in Rex's wake with one shoe on, the other dragging on his toes. Joey came barefoot. Timmy started to follow, and paused, pointing.

"What about her? Susie?"

Rex shrugged his shoulder. "Forget her. She won't creep outa there until we're gone. She's afraid someone is gonna see her buns."

Timmy glanced back at her with silent apology in his eyes. She stared at him in dumb fear, it seemed to him, the dreams of last night, of all her nights past, in her rounded eyes.

He wanted to tell her he wouldn't hurt her, but he turned instead and followed the boys from the room.

The cabin, Timmy observed, wasn't really a cabin at all. It was just an ordinary house, older than most, maybe, but still a house. There was a hall that stretched darkly through the center, opening into a big room at the front that had a fireplace with an ancient cracked hearth, and a body of rough, varied stones that looked as though they might fall out at any time. It was the kind of fireplace that would have crickets in the autumn and winter, like the fireplaces in Charles Dickens's stories. The hearth now, so far as he could see from the hallway, looked cold and uncleaned, with bits and ends of blackened logs that hadn't quite burned up, and lots of old gray ashes.

At the opposite end of the hall a door stood partway open, and smells of food came from the room that must be a kitchen.

"Hey," said Rex, "is that coffee I smell? And maybe even bacon. He's cooking!" Rex stopped and stood in the center of the long and narrow hall as if he couldn't believe the smells and was afraid to go see. He blocked the way for a moment, then started on slowly.

Halfway down the center of the hall was a closed door on the opposite side of the house from the bedroom they had just come out of. It was the only door on that side of the hall. Joey pecked on it lightly with his fist as they passed it and glanced over his shoulder at Timmy.

"This room is locked. I think it's haunted, or something."

Rex snorted supremely. "That's shit, Joey. He keeps it locked because he don't want snoopy kids in there. *I* know what's in there."

"What!" Joey demanded, as though he didn't believe Rex knew, and was in no way going to be convinced otherwise.

"He keeps his cameras and stuff in there, that's all. He doesn't want kids messing around with his cameras."

Timmy followed the leader and did as Joey and Dale had done and touched the door when he edged past it in the narrow hall. He liked Joey's idea the best, especially now that he knew he wouldn't be alone in this house with Uncle Dan.

Dale paused in front of Timmy and leaned against the wall long enough to finish pushing his foot into the half-on half-off shoes. "How do you know so much, Rex? You ain't been in there, I know. Joey and me have been here just as long as you have. Nobody's been in there."

"I didn't have to go in." Rex had stopped again and was looking back in their direction. But the certainty in his voice was missing from his eyes. "It's got a keyhole, ain't it?"

They all stopped and the look passed among them. The agreement was made in silence. Joey bent first and put one eye to the keyhole. It was, after all, his ghost. Dale peeped next. "Hey yeah," he said in an awed whisper, eyes rounded.

"Be careful," Rex hissed, looking over his shoulder toward the kitchen where there was the clink of plates and flatware against a tabletop. "If he wanted us looking in his old camera room he wouldn't lock the door, so don't let him see you."

The boys waited for Timmy to take his turn at the keyhole, and even though he ached to look and to see whatever marvels they had seen, he could not. That would be spying, and he knew his parents would not approve.

"Well," hissed Rex, "do it."

Timmy shook his head. Rex's lips curled in disdain, but instead of saying anything he stooped and took another squint-eyed peep through the keyhole as though to reassure himself on what he had seen the first time. He came up with a look of smugness on his face.

"Well, he moved it, that's all. But I saw it yesterday, so I know."

No one challenged him. Both Joey and Dale looked as though they had seen Joey's ghost, but neither of them elaborated on it.

Timmy wished they would talk about what they had seen, and he wanted to take his turn at the keyhole so badly that he almost decided that Mom and Dad wouldn't care after all, but he just couldn't make himself move toward it.

Rex gave him one more chance, then said, "Piss ant, miss ant. Come on, follow me. At least we don't have to eat corn flakes. Maybe."

They pressed on toward the kitchen, grouping into a tighter knot. Timmy looked behind and saw Susie was coming along the hall, but when she reached the locked door she looked at it with her fear-filled eyes, acted for a moment as if she weren't going to pass it at all, then saw Timmy watching her. As if his eyes gave her courage, she pressed against the opposite wall and slid swiftly past the locked door. Within another moment she was close behind Timmy. He heard her draw a long breath of relief.

He wanted to ask her why she was so afraid of the room but decided she wouldn't tell him anyway. Also, it looked as though Susie was simply a little coward, maybe afraid of everything.

The kitchen was a brighter room than the other rooms Timmy had seen. It had a window at each end, and one at the back. A long plank table in the center of the room, with wooden ladder-back chairs on each side, was set with six plates. At a stove against the interior wall was Uncle Dan, but he looked different.

He looked bigger here in this low-ceilinged house and held a small spatula in his hand. Also, he was wearing a small flowered apron that came up over his bulky shoulders and crisscrossed over his back. The ties barely reached around his middle so that the bow

73

in back was tiny. The apron was edged all around with ruffles.

But there was more than the apron that made him look so different.

It was, Timmy decided almost immediately, while still in mild shock from seeing Uncle Dan wearing a ruffled little apron that wasn't half big enough, the look on his face. His lips were tucked in at the corners, almost like a grin, but not quite. His hair was slicked back, as though just combed neatly and laid back with water. His eyes looked a bit squinted, with deeper lines at the corners, again almost as if he were smiling.

And too, he was humming as he worked. It was a high-pitched hum and sounded like a woman's voice. He didn't look at the kids as they stood knotted just inside the door staring at him.

In the middle of the table was a platter of pancakes, steam rising from them. There was a bowl of butter and a pitcher of syrup. The table had been spread with a cloth and was as neatly set as if Timmy's own mother had set it.

Rex moved, went to the table, paused, and looked at the man in the apron. "I guess we set down," he said slowly, indecisively.

Uncle Dan looked at them with his tucked-in mouth and crinkled eyes. Timmy saw that it did look like a kind of smile from the full-face view. And when Uncle Dan spoke, Timmy's chin dropped, for he spoke in a falsetto voice that didn't sound like Uncle Dan at all.

"Children," he said, sweetly, "you must go outside and wash."

Susie had already slipped past them and was going out the back door into the yard, as if she knew what was expected of her.

Timmy followed the boys out the back door, so aware of the man in the apron, of his voice and his strange facial expressions, and so aware of being watched by him that the hair on the back of his neck prickled.

At a hand pump in the backyard they stopped. A pail of water sat on an old wood table beside the pump. Hanging over the low limb of a sheltering tree were a couple of towels.

Rex silently poured water into a pan and shoved Joey forward. "You first," he said.

He stepped back to stand close to Timmy, his back toward the house, his mouth dipped sideways for a conspiratorial whisper that was loud enough for Dale's ears, too.

"What's with that creep? Does he think he's a woman or something?"

Timmy shrugged. He only knew that he was even more glad that he was not alone with Uncle Dan.

Dale spoke up defensively. "He's cooking breakfast. What's wrong with that? Would you rather eat them old cold corn flakes like we been doing?"

"He's wearing an apron, wise-ass! What man'd wear an apron?"

"Lots of men wear aprons, when they cook."

"How do you know so damned much?"

"I seen'm on television."

"That's when they're in the backyards doing a cookout thing, with steaks and hamburgers! And it's not aprons like that."

"I don't see anything wrong with that apron. I think it's pretty."

Joey whispered, "I saw that hanging on the wall in the kitchen. On that nail by the stove. Between it and the winder, and that rocking chair. It hangs there."

"Yeah," Rex agreed. "I did, too, I guess. But I thought it belonged to a woman that used to live here maybe." He giggled then swaggered back and forth in exaggerated effeminacy. "I didn't know it belonged to Uncle Dan."

The boys all giggled, and Timmy found his own grin remaining. Uncle Dan in an apron like his own mother wore when she cleaned the oven or something? It really was funny.

"Look," said Rex, pointing to a small wood building back in an overgrown area behind the yard. "You want a bathroom, Tim? That's it out there in the brush behind them Christmas trees." He gave Timmy a shove toward the wash pan from which Joey withdrew with dripping face and hands. "You can wash now, I'll wait."

Timmy looked at the half-hidden old toilet. It had a door standing partway open that had a little hole cut near the top. "That's a bathroom?"

"Just partly. We wash here. It's called a toilet by rights. It's wild. Wait'll you see it."

Timmy washed his face in fresh, cold water and dried on the towel that Joey handed him. With the other boys he visited the curious little house hidden by the cedars. Another interesting thing about it was the three holes cut in the long seat in the nearly dark interior. The center hole was only about half as big as the other two, one of which was almost large enough to fall through. But Rex had it all figured out.

"You see, a long time ago a family lived here. A pioneer family. They didn't have electricity or running water or anything. Just like now. So they built this. And that great big hole is for papa and mama, and the little hole in the middle is for baby. So he wouldn't fall in. The other one is for regular people. Grown-ups. Big kids. In them days people hunted their own meat with their own musket rifles and growed their own vegetables after they cut down the trees and cleared some land, and because they worked so much, and et so much, they all had to go to the toilet at the same time. So they had community holes." He grinned wickedly. "How about that? I'll bet they done a lot of screwin' around in here, too."

"How do you know that?" the skeptical Dale demanded.

"I read it in my history book, runt. How do you think?"

"You didn't read that last part!"

Rex laughed. "You don't know the kind of history books I read, runt. We better go," he added seriously.

They wound their way back along a path that was nearly crowded to nothing by blackberry briers and the tickling, sticky ends of the cedar limbs. Before they had reached the end of the path a male voice shouted, "You boys get in here to breakfast, right now!"

Uncle Dan stood on the stoop just outside the kitchen door. His apron was gone, and his face no longer held the tucked-in, effeminate expression. His eyebrows had lowered, and he was glowering about the backyard, looking for them. Then he spotted them at the end of the path.

"Breakfast is getting cold!"

He disappeared back into the kitchen. The screen door slammed like an exclamation point laid down heavily at the end of his statement.

Rex had no remark. He led the way hurriedly.

The little girl was already at the table, looking even smaller than she had when huddled on her bed. The plate in front of her held one pancake swimming in syrup. One bite was gone from it. She chewed slowly and automatically, her round eyes never leaving the face of the man who sat at the end of the table.

Timmy took the chair across from her. On the plate at his place was syrup with a pancake in the same state as Susie's. A big glob of butter had been dropped in the center. There was nothing else.

He saw all the other plates were the same.

But Uncle Dan held a large, white platter in his hands that was rounded with runny eggs and slices of fried meat that looked like a luncheon meat taken out of a can, sliced and fried, rather than bacon or ham.

He waited until all the boys were seated, all the chairs scraped into place and still. Then he passed the platter to Rex.

"Take as much as you can eat, my boy," he said. "Show Little Mother how much you appreciate the food she cooked for you."

Rex looked up straight into Timmy's eyes, and for a moment Timmy was afraid both of them were going to burst out laughing. Little Mother? He was calling himself *Little Mother*?

What, Timmy wondered, would his dad say about

Uncle Dan when he told him that!

The grin that almost tugged at Rex's lips faded swiftly away when he looked down. As well-behaved as if he were at a church dinner, Rex used the spatula on the platter to scoop one egg and a slice of meat onto his plate.

"Take another one," Uncle Dan said, smiling, watching, "Little Mother likes to see her children eat." His gaze switched to Susie and darkened, as if night had fallen in the back of his eyes. "Doesn't she, Susie? Little Mother is very displeased with Susie, because Susie is a bad, bad little girl."

Susie swallowed, a long gulp that almost convulsed her throat. Syrup oozed onto her lower lip, two drops like tears. She stared directly at the man, without so much as a blink to break the stare. She seemed hypnotized, unable to break her gaze away. Her hand holding the fork over her plate trembled, and the tines of the fork made a clinking noise against the plate, for a moment the only sound in the room.

Timmy wondered why Susie was so scared. Uncle Dan, even calling himself such dumb things as Little Mother, didn't seem so bad that a little kid even as young as Susie would be so scared of him.

"If Susie doesn't eat, doesn't mind and do as Little Mother wants her to, she's not going to get to go in and see her."

Rex raised his head and looked into Timmy's eyes again. Now there was a silent question there that Timmy could not answer. Rex's eyes lowered almost immediately to the platter, and he slipped another egg and slice of meat to his plate. He passed the platter on to Joey.

Joey's hand slipped, his wrists twisted, and the platter almost spilled. All the food slid to one end and piled, and Timmy found himself squeezing the edge of the table. What would Uncle Dan do if the food spilled?

"Careful, Joey," Uncle Dan said. "Little Mother doesn't like her nice clean tablecloths messed up."

Joey said, "I didn't spill anything." With both hands he carefully set the platter down. Glancing at Uncle Dan for approval, he took as much food as Rex had.

Uncle Dan smiled. "That's a good boy. Now eat it all up. I'll tell Little Mother what a good boy you are, and maybe you can go in to see her right away."

Susie suddenly lurched over her plate, her mouth opened and a gush of pancakes, half chewed, spewed forth into her plate and onto the tablecloth. Before she had finished vomiting she was crying, great sobs that made Timmy hurt to hear.

Uncle Dan shoved his chair back from the table and came with great, long steps around to Susie. He jerked her out of her chair by one arm, dangling her as if she were a doll, and slammed her to the floor.

"I don't know why I keep you around here! At this rate you're never going to do anything right, don't you know that, Susie? What does Little Mother think of you? I'll tell you what she thinks of you!" He went toward the kitchen, dragging Susie by the arm while she stumbled, trying to keep up. At the door he paused long enough to look back at the boys. "Eat! If I come back in here and find that you have not eaten, you're going to get the same as Susie!"

Joey was eating desperately, bent over his plate, scooping in the food and swallowing without scarcely time to taste.

Dale only sat with his syrupy pancake, unable to move. Rex looked at him and at Timmy.

"You're not eating," he stated flatly. "Neither of you."

"I can't," Timmy said.

Dale shook his head in silence. His wide dark eyes looked as if they would burst into tears of sympathy any moment.

Rex got up and scraped the food from his plate back onto the platter. "I'd rather have corn flakes," he mumbled, then went on around the table taking up Dale's plate and Timmy's and scraping them out. He carried it all to the window at the end of the room where the glass was raised to let in summer air, but the screen was latched. He slid open the latch, leaned out, pushing the screen open, and poured the food into the dark privacy between the house and the shrub that grew beneath the window. He latched the screen and came back to the table where he sat down and folded his hands.

Outside there was silence now, only the morning birds calling out their territorial songs, and chirping messages that only they understood. Timmy did as Rex and Dale were doing and simply sat, stupidly watching Joey clean up his plate of food; but he was thinking of Susie and wondering why she was no longer crying.

The back screen door opened, and Uncle Dan came in. Susie was following behind him, her face scrubbed clean, the front of her dress freshly laundered and wrung out. She was white and trembling as she followed in the shadow of Uncle Dan, but her tears were gone.

"Now," Uncle Dan said, smiling, his eyes sweeping the table with approval, "see, Susie, the boys cleaned up all the food. They're good boys, aren't they? You come now and be a good girl and let Uncle Dan comb your hair. Little Mother will want to see your pretty curls all combed out. Gather round, children, and watch Susie get her hair combed."

He pulled a wood rocker out from the corner and placed it by the north kitchen window. Timmy held his breath, hoping that none of the food Rex had scraped out had spilled and remained there on the windowsill where Uncle Dan could see it. Rex cast Timmy an apprehensive glance, but obediently went near the rocking chair and waited.

Uncle Dan sat down heavily. The chair squeaked in several different pitches, and Timmy saw that it had been wired together at one place. Uncle Dan had in his hand a hair brush and comb, and he sat waiting, with knees spread. Susie went hesitantly to him, as though she had done this many times before, turned her back and sat down on her heels, her knees against the floor. Without turning her head, she looked with her big eyes from one boy to the next, ending with Joey who was still at the table, then dropping so that she stared at the floor.

Uncle Dan motioned to the floor. "Sit down, boys, gather round us. Come on away from the table, Joey, you have finished your breakfast and I'm really proud of you. Little Mother will rejoice when I tell her."

Timmy watched the other boys and did as they did, sitting down on the floor with legs crossed and drawn up, in a half circle around Uncle Dan and Susie. The man looked down at them with a pleased smile.

"There. Oh my, what a nice family. It reminds me of my own family when I was a youngster like you. There were four of us boys, too, and one little girl, like Susie. And that's why we chose you, you know. I always knew I'd have four boys and a girl, just the perfect family. When I was small, like you, we'd gather round the knees of our grandpa and hear stories about every imaginable thing. It was better than television, much better." He combed a tangled strand of Susie's hair gently, and Timmy watched in fascination those thick fingers with the silken strands. How could a thick, huge man's hand like Uncle Dan's, that had only a few minutes ago dragged Susie out of the kitchen, now be so gentle with her hair? Timmy felt he didn't know this Dan. He watched the thick fingers comb the hair bit by tiny bit and curl it around his finger, slipping the finger out then and letting the hair fall down Susie's back in a long, silver-blond tube.

"Now children, I want to know, how did you get along while I was gone? Did you take good care of each other and of Susie?"

Rex said, "Yes sir."

"You didn't bother Little Mother?"

There was silence among the children. They sat looking up into Dan's face as though mesmerized, and a glance sideways at Rex showed Timmy that

83

Rex's freckles were standing out again on his sensitive skin that could look as white as paper, or as pink as a wild rose petal. Timmy had never seen it so white as now.

Susie lifted her head and shook it slightly.

"No," she said in a loud whisper. "we didn't bother her."

Seven

". . . And deep in the woods there are strange animals such as you have never seen before, and at night ghostly things rise out of the hollows and curl among the trees. My grandpa knew all about these things, and we children were very careful not to go alone into the woods. So you, too, must be very careful. Now there," Uncle Dan said, smoothing with his thick-fingered hand the crown of Susie's head. "You're beautiful, Susie. Isn't she beautiful, boys?"

"Yes sir," they mumbled, and she was, indeed, with her hair shimmering on her back and curling softly around her small face.

She had relaxed as Uncle Dan talked, his tone droningly monotonous and increasingly comfortable as he stopped referring to the mysterious Little Mother and talked instead of a childhood that sounded like fun, and told stories his grandpa had told.

Timmy had seen the boys relax as Susie relaxed; he

85

had noticed that even Rex had appeared to become enthralled.

But Timmy was aching to move. He searched his mind for an excuse to escape from the kitchen and came up with it on the next thought. "Can I be excused, Uncle Dan? I need to go—out."

"Of course, Timmy. Run along."

Timmy got up with his feet tingling from sitting on them so long and hurried out the back door.

Mists rose from the hollows that fell away from the ridge on both sides, drifting about the tree trunks and rising toward the blue sky. Now that he was alone he was more aware of the grayed boards and logs of the old house, the deep varied greens of the thick, surrounding forest, the calls of morning birds.

He stared toward the toilet but couldn't bring himself to go alone into that shadowy wilderness. What if Uncle Dan was right about the strange animals? And the ghosts that disguise themselves as mists from the hollows? Timmy's logic told him it was not so, especially about the mist, but his skin grew tight and shivery nevertheless, as if somewhere within him the truth was hiding, and he agreed with Uncle Dan that the mists were ghosts and the animals strange and dangerous.

He wandered back to the pump again where with sunlight spilling upon him made him feel less shivery, and he made a big show of washing his hands, just in case Uncle Dan was looking out the window toward him.

He didn't mind so much being here now that he knew he would have company, even though he would have preferred being with Russ at his uncle's farm. Or with Mom and Dad in Shreveport. Or better yet, at home, with both his parents and with his new pup.

A keen happiness gripped his heart at the thought of home and puppy. "Now," he speculated aloud, a habit picked up early from being an only child, "what'll I name him? Captain? King from *King of the North?* Kazan?" He nibbled his lower lip in deep contemplation, trying not to think of Uncle Dan and the increasingly mysterious Little Mother. *Was* there a woman somewhere in the house? But no, Uncle Dan had said she cooked the food, but he knew for certain she had not. Uncle Dan had. But, back to his puppy. A name was important. It had to be worthy of the dog. "Buster? After my old dog. He'd like that, I bet. Buster. Buster Junior."

A soft sneeze, close by, jerked his attention back to the present surroundings. He whirled. The little girl sat within five feet of him, beneath the wash table, her back pressed against a rough wooden leg that leaned crookedly inward. She could have reached out and tripped him when he was washing his face. Now she had one hand, still dimpled with baby plumpness, pressed against nose and mouth as if to stifle the sneeze that had just escaped. Above her hand the full-moon eyes stared at him.

Timmy looked around for the boys, but Susie was alone. He hadn't seen her come out of the house. Her hair was already beginning to look ruffled, as if the smoothed curls could never stay confined.

"Hi," he said, and shuffled his feet uncomfortably and shoved his hands into the pockets of his jeans because what did you say to a girl as quiet as Susie

87

except just, oh, hi?

He started to move away when her hand lowered abruptly and her whisper came like the soft wind in the boughs of the pine tree.

"Kazan."

"Huh?"

She whispered again, "Kazan is a pretty name."

He looked closely at her and wondered why she acted so afraid. Had she thought she would be here alone, too? Or was she afraid because she was the only girl? Or maybe there was something else wrong with her. He stepped closer and squatted on his heels.

"Can't you talk out loud?"

In answer she merely closed her lips tightly, and her gaze passed beyond him to the silent, gray, moss-touched house. And suddenly he knew why she had spoken in a whisper. She was afraid of someone in the house. Someone who might hear.

He reached out his hand but did not touch her. "I won't hurt you," he said. "I was afraid, too, when I first came, but I got over it."

Her eyes widened sharply and moved back to his face. Her lips parted as though she might speak, but she didn't.

"Of course," he admitted importantly, "I'm older than you. I'm ten. That's twice as old as you are."

"I'm five," she said in her soft whisper.

He waited, but she offered no more.

"Did Uncle Dan bring you up here, too? How come you're the only girl here?"

She only stared at him, and he stared back at her, trying to understand this situation of finding kids at Uncle Dan's cabin when he had thought there would be no one here at all.

"When did you come?" he asked.

Susie's shoulders lifted slightly in a wordless answer. Her eyes drifted away from his face and back again. She didn't know, she couldn't remember, or something. He was trying to figure it out but was getting nowhere.

"Were you here before Rex and the little boys?"

She nodded vigorously.

"Have you been here all the time?"

She shook her head, and her gaze drifted downward again.

"How long are you going to stay here?" Timmy asked, and her shoulders raised and dropped again. He added, "I only have to stay two weeks."

He had her full attention again, and she whispered, leaning toward him, "Where are you going then?"

"Home," he said, surprised. "My dad's going to buy me a puppy. Uncle Dan said he would, but I don't think I want him to now. I'd rather have my dad and mom help me pick him out."

For a moment Timmy thought Susie was going to smile. Her eyes flickered slightly and looked less afraid.

An idea popped into Timmy's mind. Although it didn't fit her behavior it at least explained what she was doing here. "Is one of those boys your brother? Or is Uncle Dan your real uncle?"

But she shook her head, and he remained as puzzled as ever.

"How come your mom and dad sent you up to a kind of boys' camp with Uncle Dan?"

She pulled a long breath that sounded as though it had climbed a stairway in her chest. "I don't have a mom and dad."

"You don't!" Timmy was quiet a moment, trying to assimilate that information. "Then you must be an orphan."

"What's an orphan?"

"That's a kid with no mom or dad. You know, like Little Orphan Annie."

She stared directly at him, then whispered, "I don't know her."

They were silent. Timmy was still trying to take it all in. He couldn't imagine not having parents. He knew some kids whose parents were divorced, who lived with only one parent, but he had never met a real orphan before.

She said suddenly, "I had a mama once."

"Did she die?"

Her shoulders raised and lowered again without spoken comment. She didn't know.

"What happened to her?"

The same silent, unknowing answer.

A soft sound came from the house, a thud somewhere within, as if a door had closed. Susie jumped, looked toward the house, and then huddled farther back under the table. Timmy could understand why she might be afraid of Uncle Dan. He had been good to her when he combed her hair, but he had been bad to her when she vomited in her plate. But she was more afraid of something else, he was sure. He leaned under the table toward her and whispered his question.

"Susie, is there a woman in the house somewhere?"

Her face seemed to freeze, her round eyes staring at him, her lips tightening as if she refused to talk to him anymore. He leaned closer, persisting.

"Is she real? That person Uncle Dan calls Little Mother?"

Susie nodded, a quick series of nods. And then she was crawling away, around the table leg, past the water pump, and into the thick undergrowth where she disappeared. Timmy sat back on his heels feeling as if she had thrown cold water on him. He looked toward the house. Then he shrugged.

"She's crazy," he muttered aloud. "Uncle Dan's crazy, and so is she."

He got up, but he stood looking toward the house. All those other windows, those rooms he hadn't been in, and the one with the locked door—were they her rooms?

But no. Little Mother hadn't cooked their breakfast like Uncle Dan said she did; he had cooked it himself. With *her* apron, perhaps.

He felt confused, and he didn't want to think about it anymore. He just wanted his two weeks to pass in a hurry so he could go home.

He heard the gentle closing of a door and got to his feet so he could see. Rex, head and shoulders above the two younger boys, came out of the house first. Joey and Dale followed behind him like a short train of ducklings.

Timmy went to meet them.

"Where you guys been?"

91

"Talking to Uncle Dan," Rex said, with no belligerence.

They stood together, all silent. Then Timmy said, "What'll we do? Anybody got a ball? We could play ball."

All three heads wagged negatively, but Joe said, "We could climb a tree."

"No," Rex said. "I don't want to climb no dumb trees. We could shoot marbles." He dug deep into his pockets and gazed off toward the hollow. "Anybody got any marbles?"

"I don't."

"Me neither."

"I'd rather climb a tree anyhow," Joey said.

Timmy looked toward the table and saw that Susie still had not come back. She had disappeared, perhaps to blend into the landscape as effectively as a hiding fawn. He looked around for her.

"Where'd Susie go? We ought to play something she can play, too."

"Why?" asked Rex. "She wouldn't want to shoot marbles anyhow."

"We don't have any marbles to shoot," Timmy reminded him.

"Maybe," suggested Dale, "we could find some if we looked around. Maybe them pioneer kids left some marbles." He stooped and eyed the ground among the thick, smooth cover of pine needles.

Rex looked at him with contempt. "That's dumb. Where'd pioneer kids get marbles?"

"How should I know?" Dale replied in grumpy concentration, going down on his knees to explore beneath the pine needles with his hands.

"What if you dig up a snake, runt? The kind Uncle

92

Dan told us about, with fangs at one end and a stinger at the other?''

They stood around, watching Dale lose enthusiasm for his job. The small boy finally sat back, his legs bent under him, and started doing things with pine needles, sifting them through his fingers, putting them in small piles, making clean little roads among the piles.

Joey, watching him, said, ''We could get some rocks and play cars and trucks and build roads and things.''

Rex sneered. ''With rocks? They don't have no wheels.''

''Then let's go climb a tree, like I wanted to all the time.''

''*You* go climb a tree. Me, I'm gonna do something else.''

Timmy suggested, ''We could explore.''

''Explore what?'' Dale said as he continued to make roads in the pine needles.

Timmy motioned vaguely in all directions. ''Everything. Maybe there's a cave on the hillside. We could walk down the road, too.''

''Not my road, you don't,'' Dale said, leaning over his playground protectively, his arms spread like a mother bird's wings. ''You'd ruin 'em.''

''I wasn't talking about your road. I was talking about the big road, the one the van came up.''

''That thing?'' Rex said. ''That's just a trail, that's not a road. And it's real rough and straight down the hill. Big rocks sticking right out in the tracks. If I'd knowed it was so far up here I'd 'a stayed back in own.''

''Not me,'' Joey said. ''There ain't no trees there.''

93

"Well, who needs a tree?"

"I do! I like trees. I like it here at camp. I never been to camp before in all my life."

"Well, I have, asshole," Rex said. "No big deal."

"When did you ever go to camp?"

"When I was in my next to last home, that was when. The church took a bunch of us for five whole days. We stood around, just like now. No big deal."

Timmy said, "I almost got to go with my friend Russ to his uncle's farm. He feeds baby calves and rides horses and tractors, and goes swimming in the creek."

Joey breathed an awed, "Gosh," his eyes almost as round as Susie's.

"Hey!" Rex said with unusual enthusiasm. "How come you didn't?"

"My mom and dad told Uncle Dan I'd go with him. So I did. But maybe next year I'll go to the farm instead." He had their attention, totally. Even Dale had stopped building roads and was watching and waiting. Timmy squared his shoulders. "But when I get home," he said, "Dad is going to buy me a pup."

Joey cried, "A real honest to goodness pup of your own?"

"Sure."

Rex said, "You got folks." A curiously flat statement.

"Sure."

Dale went back to his solitary play but more slowly.

"Your real folks?" Rex asked.

"Yeah." Timmy thought of Susie. "Susie doesn't, she's an orphan."

94

Rex turned away, put out a foot and deliberately destroyed a section of Dale's roads. "What are folks anyway but shit. Just shit. Nobody cares anyway whether they got folks. All they do is screw around and get bombed on something. Nobody cares about havin' folks."

Timmy's definitive "I do!" was lost under Dale's cry of rage. The smaller boy attacked Rex's leg with fury, wrapping his arms around it and sinking his teeth into the calf. Rex shouted, grasped Dale's dark hair in both fists, and yanked. Dale came up swinging, head down and used as a battering ram into Rex's groin. Rex yelped out a string of swear words while Dale emitted an ear-splitting sound that was half sob and half scream.

"Boys! Boys! Boys!"

The shout came from behind them and was accompanied by the sharp slapping of palm against palm. The two boys stopped fighting instantly. Timmy whirled toward the clapping of the hands to find Uncle Dan coming toward them.

A camera hung on a strap from one shoulder, and Timmy recognized it as a movie camera he had seen in Uncle Dan's possession before. Another bag, made of canvas and bulging with things hidden, swung against it.

"Come on now, boys," Uncle Dan said. "No fighting. What's the trouble?"

Timmy waited for Dale to tell on Rex, but both boys remained silent, standing now side by side and facing Uncle Dan.

"Well," Uncle Dan said after a quiet moment of waiting, "how would you children like to take a walk down the path to the swimming hole?" He patted the canvas bag. "We're taking a picnic lunch along. How does that sound? You can swim and play as long as you like."

They came alive, out of their waiting trances, joyously. Voices mingled and overlapped in confusion.

"I didn't even know there was a swimming hole here in the mountains!"

"Is there a town down there?"

"Wait'll I go get my swim trunks. They're in my suitcase!"

"A real pool?"

"A swimming hole, he said. A creek, I bet."

"Don't go until I get my swim—"

Uncle Dan caught Timmy's arm as he ran by and jerked him to a halt. "Now, Timmy boy, the others don't have swim trunks, so why don't you leave yours where they are? This is a secluded hole in the creek in the hollow down there. No one is going to see you."

"But—"

"Hey!" Rex shouted. "We get to skinny-dip. Come on, chicken-shit."

"Don't you call me that!"

Uncle Dan said mildly, "He's right, Rex. Keep your tongue in your mouth."

"If my mom had you for awhile she'd squirt your mouth full of Ivory soap and let you spit on that for awhile!"

"Hey! No, she wouldn't! I can say whatever—"

"Come on! Come on!" Uncle Dan slapped his hands together again sharply and the sound came back in a faint echo.

"Hey! Did you hear that? What made that?"

"That was an echo, dummy." Timmy still felt angry at Rex. "There's a cave somewhere, that's all. Didn't you ever hear an echo before?"

Uncle Dan was looking around. "Where's Susie?"

Timmy looked up at him. "She's not going, is she?"

"Well of course she's going, Timmy. We're not going to leave anyone out."

"But she's a girl!" Timmy was thinking of skinny-dipping in front of a girl, and no way was he going to do that! "She's not going to swim with us, is she?"

"Yes, she certainly is."

Timmy set his chin firmly and stalked out and around Uncle Dan, out of his reach, and toward the house. "Then I'm going to get my trunks."

He heard Uncle Dan laugh, and the laughter, low and chuckling, followed him into the dim, silent house.

Uncle Dan called, "We're not going to wait for you, Timmy boy, if you don't hurry. We'll leave you to find your way alone through the forest and the ground cover that hide all kinds of horrid creatures. They reach out and twine around you, and you're gone forever, and no one ever knows where you went. Like a spider paralyzes its prey by injecting a venomous poison, so do they, and they eat you over the next months even though you're still alive. You don't want that to happen, do you?"

Timmy muttered to the cracked and uncaring walls, "I don't care. I'm not going to skinny-dip with a girl. Not even a little one like Susie."

Timmy dug through the untidiness of his suitcase,

but there was no swimsuit. He sat on his heels, a small furrow of thought between his eyebrows. He remembered definitely his mother telling him to get his trunks, and he thought sure he had. But they weren't here now, so he must have forgotten after all.

He got to his feet slowly. They would be gone, Uncle Dan and the kids, and he would be stuck here alone in the house with the strange, dank, fetid smells, and the creakings that sounded as if . . . as if someone were walking, very slowly, trying perhaps to keep her presence unknown, for some strange, unnatural reason, perhaps to watch the children through the cracks in the walls, the knotholes that held blackness in their depths, the—

A door closed softly somewhere in the house.

He could stand it no longer. Feeling strange eyes looking at him from the dark silences of the old house, feeling long, clawed fingers reaching for him, Timmy ran.

His footsteps pounded on the old boards of the hallway. The house trembled when the back door slammed.

He caught up with them where a narrow deerlike trail disappeared into heavy, hanging limbs and lush, dark vines. Uncle Dan led the procession. He held one hand behind him, clasping Susie's dimpled little paw out of sight beneath palm and blunt fingers. She trailed him carefully and awkwardly even though his pace down the hill was slow.

Timmy took up the end, sliding into place behind the short, chubby little figure of Joey.

"So you decided to come with us after all," Uncle

Dan said jovially. "Did you find your swim trunks, Timmy?"

"No."

"So then what will you do, since you're so grown-up you've become modest? Just wade?"

"No."

"Ahha. That explains how deep your modesty goes." And he laughed, the kind of sound that belonged in the dark, damp, slimy undergrowth beneath the ground vines and the mayapples and other thick, green vegetation.

The path turned and dropped, going deeper into the dark green toward the faraway hollow, and became steep and at times treacherous. The boys emulated Uncle Dan's methods of staying on his feet and grasped the tender limbs and necks of saplings for support. Their progress was hot and sticky and slow.

"You must never come down here alone," Uncle Dan said, pausing for breath and dragging from a hip pocket a large handkerchief with which he wiped his steaming face. "There are snakes, terrible, poisonous snakes, rattlesnakes that lay coiled by the side of the path and, contrary to popular opinion, don't always give a warning rattle before they strike. And, if one of them should catch you on the head or neck you'd be dead before you reached the top of the hill and the house. And you wouldn't like that, would you? And the copperheads! Oh my. They're the same color as last winter leaves, and they like to hide in leaves, and when you walk by, zip, it's got you, so fast and so silent—"

Susie whimpered, a frightened little animal sound

that reminded Timmy of her sleep cries.

"Oh now," Uncle Dan crooned, "did I scare you? Well, it's important you know the dangers of being away from the house. And the snakes aren't all, you know, and the rattlesnakes and copperheads are the nicest of the poisonous snakes."

"The nicest?" Dale said in his skeptical grouch. "How can they get any worse than that? Besides, I don't see any snakes."

"Of course you don't. You never see one until you're bitten," Uncle Dan said.

Joey asked, "What snakes are worser, Uncle Dan? Tell us about them."

"Oh, I don't know if I should. Come on children, easy now—and don't fall into the undergrowth at the side of the path. We've a long way to go yet."

Rex said, "It's hotter'n hell here. Where is that creek anyhow?"

Timmy saw him looking to right and left as he followed behind Susie, and even though Timmy could almost feel the lethal gaze of the snakes' eyes, he was careful not to look at their hiding places.

"In the hollow, Rex, in the hollow," Uncle Dan said as if he were growing tired of the snake game. "Susie, your hand is wet and slippery as a snake's belly, let me hold your arm instead—come on, don't pull back." He gripped her carefully just below the elbow and started them moving again.

Joey asked, "What snakes are worser, Uncle Dan?"

"Oh yes. What snakes are worser. Well, I'll tell you, Joey. It's the water moccasins."

Several voices at once, including Timmy's cried, "*Water* moccasins?"

"Yes. And it's just like it sounds. They live in the water, and at the edge of the water, and in the wet, boggy ground near the creek. They're very quiet. When you get close they open their mouths and the inside is white, like cotton, and they have long fangs in the upper jaw to bite you with. Only you'll hardly know a thing about it—you die so fast."

"Is there them kind of snakes where we're going swimming?" a hushed awestricken boy's voice asked.

"I'm with you today, Joey—or Dale—who said that?"

"Joey," Rex said.

Uncle Dan grunted. "When I'm with you, I'll watch the water. If you be sure to stay away from logs and deep, still holes, and to play where the water is clear, you'll be all right. But you must never, never, come down this path without me. If I'm not with you, you must not leave the yard."

"Except," said Dale authoritatively, "the road. You can walk down the road."

"Oh no," Uncle Dan cried in horror. "Never the road. There are much worse things in these miles and miles of mountains than the snakes!"

"What?"

"Well, that's a story for another time."

Questions began flying, hushed sounds in still air. The only voice that remained silent was Susie's. Answers came back, from boy to boy, as hushed and fearful as the questions.

"Are there goblins and spirits and things? And ghosts?"

"No, goofy, them things lives in fairy tales and old houses. There's bears and panthers and wild Indians that nobody's ever seen—''

"Are there vampire bats and werewolves?"

"You saw that in a movie!"

"I didn't either. They live here in the woods, Uncle Dan said so."

"When did he? I never heard him."

"Are there monsters and witches?"

"Now!" Uncle Dan said at last. "You got it right. There *are* monsters and witches."

There was a pause, breath held, and it seemed as though the very heart of these possessed forests stopped beating for a long, still minute, its secret slipping away. A voice whispered, *"Where?"* Susie had spoken at last.

Uncle Dan stopped on the downward path again to wipe his face, to look slit-eyed deep into the tangle of woods where black tree trunks rose out of the green growth and stretched through the still, hot shade to the forest roof.

He answered her whisper with one of his own, a loud, slow hiss that reached clear back to Timmy and further pulled the hair at the back of his neck and made him wish he weren't at the end of the line.

"Who knows?" were Uncle Dan's words, as he peered slowly about. And then, "Perhaps the monster hides behind one of these trees. And the witch? She lives in a log cabin over that ridge." He paused, turning. "Or is it *that* ridge? I really can't remember. Of course she doesn't bother grown-ups, like me. But children? Ah—that's another thing."

A half-brave voice squeaked, "Hey! There's witches, all right, but there ain't no such thing as real monsters."

Uncle Dan glared over his shoulder at Rex. "Are you disputing my word, boy?"

"Well—"

"Now listen here. You've heard of Bigfoot, haven't you?"

"Sure. But that's out West."

"Yes, that one is. But *here* there are monsters that's been known to carry a boy right out of his own backyard. Don't you ever read the newspapers?"

Timmy said, "I heard about that one! The little boy's mother ran out and chased the monster away!"

"Now there's a boy who listens, and reads, too. You're a bright boy, Timmy."

Joey asked, "Did he get the little boy?"

"No," Timmy said, excitement making his voice echo loud. "He dropped him, and then the monster ran off into the woods. He—"

"*These* woods?"

"He was great big—maybe ten feet tall—and he had hair all over him! And he growled like nothing ever heard before. It was horrible. Isn't that right, Uncle Dan?"

"What'd he want with the little boy?" Rex asked.

Uncle Dan said ominously, "I expect he wanted to eat him."

A long shudder built to a crescendo in Joey's body.

"I don't want him eatin' me."

"I'd eat him first," Dale growled, hissing out his nose in derision.

"Oh you. You couldn't eat a frog."

"I don't want to eat no frogs. Frogs never hurt nobody. But I'd eat a monster."

"He couldn't either eat no monster, could he,

Uncle Dan?" Joey yelled, forgetting to be quiet, forgetting to be anything but exasperated with the bull-headed Dale.

"Oh no, Joey. The monster would eat him first without a doubt."

"See?"

"Then," Dale said, "I'd turn into a monster myself and come back and eat *you*."

Joey's voice became tearful. "He wouldn't either, would he, Uncle Dan? He couldn't do that."

"If you two don't hush you'll draw the attention of every monster in the mountains, to say nothing of the witch, who can put a bad spell on you even from faraway. All she has to know is that you're here, and she's got you in her power, if she wants you. Besides, there's Little Mother. And she watches all around, all the time. She watches the road and the paths. You don't want to displease Little Mother, do you?"

Susie began whimpering and pulling back, trying to struggle her arm free from Uncle Dan's grasp. His fingers readjusted on her arm and tightened.

"Here now, what's wrong with you? See what you've done, you boys? You've frightened little Susie. Don't worry now, dear, Uncle Dan will protect you." He raised his head and sniffed the air, enough said now to keep the children in line behind him like obedient ducklings. "Oh I smell the water. Smell the water, children? We're almost there. Come on now, let's hurry."

"I wonder," said Joey as he slid half sitting down the steep and narrow path. "If Dale really could turn into a monster at night."

Rex seemed to like the idea. With a whoop he said,

"Hey! When the moon is full, I bet Dale grows whiskers and everything."

Uncle Dan laughed. His belly shook above his belt, trembling under his tight, sweat-soaked, clinging knit shirt. "Oh you precious simpleminded children. Such innocents, as if you were born yesterday. You're going to be perfect for Little Mother and me. At last, we've found our ideal family." His laughter had stopped now, and he sounded as if he were talking only to himself. "We're going to be so happy here, with the dark woods closing us away from the world. I knew the minute I saw you children that you were the perfect ones. That at last, after all my trial and failures, I was going to succeed."

They didn't understand what he was talking about, and the tone of his voice had changed so drastically from the jovial and good-humored one that had marked the progress down the hill, that they were silenced now.

The smell of the water at last reached Timmy's nose, and he sniffed toward it. There was a slightly fishy smell, too, and he thought he heard a fish jump in the water with a cheerful splash.

The path dipped even more steeply and became a narrow bed of slippery, black slate. Timmy's feet slid out from under him and he sat down with a grunt, almost causing a falling domino effect among the others. Vines were yanked from roots as hands grabbed and clung. Uncle Dan's large body stopped the fall. He looked back at Timmy. His mouth had the tucked-in look it had assumed when he wore the apron.

"Poor Timmy. Did you hurt yourself, son? Little

Mother will heal you."

"I'm okay," Timmy said, getting a foothold again on solid rock.

The wet, sweet smell of the creek tickled his nostrils. Coolness, fishiness. And now, below, at last, twinkling and reflecting like a strip of bright mirror beneath trees and sky and rising hillsides, the water beckoned. Timmy wasn't the only one who saw, who forgot the witch, the monsters, the snakes of Uncle Dan's warnings, and Little Mother.

Eight

Steve sat in a ground floor waiting room of the large hospital with others who were waiting also for something to happen to someone they loved, someone they were concerned about. Surgery had begun at nine o'clock on Connie, and time moved by incredibly slowly. No one paid attention to anyone else. Occasionally someone picked up a magazine, but it was soon laid aside. Smoke filled the air. Ashtrays overflowed. People paced and stared at the wall and sometimes the ceiling. Steve found himself reaching into the shirt pocket where he used to carry his cigarettes. But that was two years ago.

He wondered what was going on in the surgery room. He didn't even know where it was, upstairs or down. What did they call it? He didn't know that either.

Occasionally the loud speaker spoke someone's name, and one of the people who waited, and sometimes more than one, got up hastily and went down the hall to the nurse's station where, presumably, they received the news they had been waiting for. But so far Steve's name had not been called.

He checked his watch again. Nine Forty-five.

He thought of Timmy. Saw him in the mountains sitting on a bluff that overlooked a valley, and a river, such as they had seen on a vacation once. The drop below the bluff was sheer and dangerous. If Timmy edged too close would Dan notice? If Timmy clumsily stumbled, would Dan grab him in time?

Dan was always talking about how much he loved kids, and he often brought Timmy gifts, but did he really know much about taking care of a little boy only ten years old? Did he know that Timmy could get his mind set on some kind of adventure and wander absentmindedly and walk right into a puddle of water, or probably right off a bluff?

Steve moved with the agitation of the thought and got up to pace the floor. In the corner stood a potted palm. In the soil around it were several cigarette stubs. He went over and looked out the row of windows, but the view was not especially comforting. There was smoothly cut lawn and carefully planted trees, all in a row, and the beginning of the cement parking lot that was loaded with cars from whose tops the sun glinted brightly.

He came back to his chair.

An elderly woman said to him, "Waiting can become very hard to take sometimes, can't it?"

He gave her a grateful smile. Talking would relieve some of the tension.

"Very hard."

"Do you have someone in surgery?"

"Yes. My wife."

"My husband is having a minor surgery. A hernia. That is, minor as compared to some. The doctor said it would be similar to an appendectomy, and that he can go home shortly. Do you have children?"

"One son, Timmy. He's ten years old."

"How nice. Thomas and I never had children. So unfortunately, we don't have grandchildren. I expect your son is with a grandparent?"

"No, he's not. Both my parents and my wife's parents are gone. Dead. He's with a friend of the family. He was going on a trip to the mountains so he offered to take Timmy with him." Steve rubbed a hand over his chin and mouth. "I suppose he's better off. I'm sure he's better off. But it will be great to get my family together again. I mean Connie, my wife, and Timmy. That's about all there is of the family anymore. I've got a couple of sisters, and so does Connie, but they all live in other states."

"Yes, families do scatter now. My relatives are scattered from coast to coast. You were fortunate that you had a trusted friend with whom to leave your son. Some aren't so fortunate. I was just reading this morning in a newspaper someone left over there on that table about a child that's missing. A small boy, from the slums, you know. People usually don't seem to know just how many children are missing in those places, but someone reported this one being picked up by a man."

Steve said, not liking the subject, "Too bad. I always hate to hear of a kidnapping."

"They aren't really calling it a kidnapping. No parents reported him missing, but some playmates saw the van stop and saw the child get into the van,

109

and the child hasn't been seen since. It was just a small piece in the paper—very small—"

The loudspeaker said, "Mrs. Thomas Webster. Mrs. Thomas Webster."

The lady jerked up, grabbing her purse, her knitting bag, and hurried down the hall, out of sight. Steve stared at the hallway, at the point where she had disappeared.

Van.

Steve twisted in his chair. It was red plastic and very uncomfortable. He reached again for cigarettes and looked longingly at the cigarette machine. But no, stopping the habit once had been too hard to have to go through it all again.

. . . Playmates saw the van stop and saw the child get into the van. . . .

The newspaper, handled by many, pages separated into three groups, lay across the room on a black plastic table. Steve stared at it for a long while before he abruptly got up and gathered it together. He began searching, page by page, for that tiny piece of information the lady had read. Far over in the paper he found it:

A young child, perhaps seven or eight years old, was seen getting into a purple van that was described as having an indistinct mural on the sides in blues, blacks, and reds. The driver was not seen. A playmate of the child was unable to give further information. The child, Joey Fulton, had been living with distant relatives.

Steve looked at the date of the newspaper. July 10.

And today? July 16th.

A purple van with an indistinct mural?

Steve put the paper aside. It was a coincidence. There were probably a lot of purple vans with crazy psychedelic paintings on the side. Dan was a good old joe.

He liked kids. He might stop and give a kid a lift somewhere. But he would have no reason to pick one up off the street, unless he just took him down to an ice cream place for a cone or soda. But if he did that, he'd bring him back, for Christ's sake. He'd bring him back.

The world was full of vans. Red. Black. Blue, green. Purple. *Purple, with an indistinct mural on the sides in blues, blacks, reds.*

Steve got up and went to the window again and stood there, thumbs hooked in back pockets. He stared out over the cars until the colors glazed and blended together and shimmered in the heat.

There was no way now that he could keep from thinking of Dan. Dan Walker. What did he know of him? What did he *really* know of him? They had met three or four years ago, maybe five, at a party given by . . . who? Yeah, George and Sheila. A backyard thing with grilled burgers and beer. It must have been four years ago, for Timmy was starting first grade that fall. He recalled that part vividly because Dan had given Timmy a plaid canvas and leather book satchel. A fairly expensive one. Dan sold cameras then, too. He lived in the Southgate Apartments. Said he and his third wife had just divorced, and he wanted to get away from the memories and the town where they had lived. But he had never said just where that was. They had respected his wishes to put the past behind, and no one questioned him.

Sometimes he disappeared for a month or so, and when he reappeared he didn't say much. That was acceptable. Why pry into a man's private affairs? Everyone knew he had this hobby of taking pictures all over the country. He had kept them entertained a couple of times with his pictures of deer, elk, birds, and even a chipmunk that had delighted Timmy. Dan gave that picture to Timmy. A small chipmunk with his cheeks full of nuts, or some other goodies people had fed him. Little beggar. Unafraid. Coming right up to the parking lot on the mountain road to take a handout, Dan had said. Dan always went to mountainous areas, it seemed.

The loudspeaker said clearly, "Mr. Steve Malcolm, Mr. Steve Malcolm."

Steve jumped alert, just as others before him whose names had been called, and hurried toward the hallway and news of Connie.

Nine

The path ended in a three-foot drop at the bottom of the hill, and below it lay the strip of gravel between washed bank and sparkling creek edge, white and gray in the spotted sun and shade, clean and cool from past spring floods. Willows at creek banks on the far side dappled the water like the sides of a speckled trout. Boy voices lifted, shouted, echoed in keen pleasure. Even Susie's solemn little face took on a pleased pucker around the mouth as she stood at the shallow water edge. She bent and pushed small sneakers off her feet as around her, unnoticed, the boys flung clothing from hot and eager bodies and went splashing into the deceptively clear stream. They found water that appeared shallow, with pebbles magnified clearly on the bottom, deeper than it looked, and colder, so there were shouts of surprise echoing as water washed high on naked bodies. Timmy kept his brief white undershorts on, and the soft knit soon plastered in wet and transparent wrinkles to his body.

Uncle Dan sat down on the gravel, eased his feet into the cooling water, and watched the children's movements with absorption. They flitted in and out of his vision like water bugs skimming the surface. And then he noticed the little girl, Susie, standing in the shallow creek edge a few paces down. He beckoned to her.

"Come here, Susie, let Uncle Dan help. You can go swimming too, you know."

She looked at him and slowly shook her head.

Anger, swift and consuming as it could be with him, tightened the muscles in his face, causing his jowls to quiver.

"Are you disobeying me?" he said.

She shook her head again, her lower lip drooping, the pleasure going out of her eyes.

"Can't you speak?" he demanded. "Answer me!"

Her lips formed the words in a whisper, "I don't want to go swimming."

"Come here, Susie, come here I say! This minute!"

She approached him reluctantly, fear and confusion jerking her along. He took her small, plump arms in his hands and smiled into her face.

"There now, does that hurt so much? I told you, Uncle Dan is here to take care of you. To keep the snakes away, and the monsters, and the old witch on the hill. You trust Uncle Dan, don't you, Susie?" He shook her gently, and her head nodded. "There, that's my girl."

He pulled her close between his bent legs and cuddled her for a moment in the crook of his arm. Her small body remained tense against him.

"You don't want to get your dress wet, now, do

you? You're not afraid to go swimming, are you?"

She nodded vigorously and whispered, "Yes."

"Why?" He held her more loosely in the enfolding arm and felt the gradual relaxation of her body, the trusting lean against him. "See how pretty and clear the water is? You can even see the rocks on the bottom."

She pointed across toward the underwater bluffs on the far side. "But there it's deep. There are snakes in those rocks."

"Perhaps," he agreed. "But I don't want you going over to that side anyway. It's much too deep for you. Why, I'll bet even Rex would drown over there if he couldn't swim so well. But you can swim on this side where the water is nice and shallow. You would like that, wouldn't you, Susie?"

She inclined her head, and the movement became a nod of affirmation.

"Good. I want you to enjoy yourself, Susie girl," he said in satin smoothness as he drew her dress gently over head and arms. "And we don't want to get our panties wet either, do we, like silly Timothy is doing."

His fingers slipped under the elastic at her round middle and swept the panties downward.

Timmy heard the scream just as one of the boys splashed a mountain of water into his face. It tore through the happy shouts of the boys in anguished terror and silenced them as effectively as though they had been struck speechless. Timmy turned toward the cry instinctively, blinded by the water that stung his eyes and flattened his hair down across his forehead. He brushed at it wildly, pushing hair back to uncover his vision, blinking water from his eyes. Susie stood between Uncle Dan's heavy thighs, bent slightly forward, her hands gripping the top of her panties in a desperate attempt to keep them from being entirely removed. Her screams came in gushes now, one after the other, and Timmy saw in a dreamlike trance that Uncle Dan was laughing, a soundless laughter drowned under Susie's fear.

Suddenly the man released Susie's panties, and the upward strain of Susie's arms ripped the thin nylon upward, almost to her armpits, so that she was covered more at the top than at the bottom. Her screams stopped on a gasp, and Uncle Dan's laughter bellowed forth. He pinched one of her small, revealed buttocks, leaving two red marks with an angry white dividing line.

She ran, still holding her stretched panties high under her arms, their crotch a mere broken strip that neither concealed nor protected. She ran downstream, her bare feet splashing droplets of water into the air. Still entranced, Timmy watched her, watched too the sparkling water drops in the air and the reds, blues, greens, and yellows that flashed like winking lights within them. It all seemed in slow motion, from Susie's escape to the droplets suspended in midair behind her. They formed a rainbow halo above her, a veil of protection between her and the real world.

Uncle Dan's sobering voice called, "Where are you going, Susie? Down where the snakes and the monsters can get you?"

She slowed to a stumbling walk among the rocks and boulders in the knee-deep water.

116

Uncle Dan laughed a little more and then drew from the bulging canvas bag that hung beside his camera a cigarette for himself and several lollipops that were as colorful as Susie's rainbow had been.

"Come here, Susie girl, Uncle Dan has something nice for you."

She stopped still and turned, but looked at him with round, hurt eyes and drooping mouth.

"Well, anyway," he said, "we sure know Susie has a voice, don't we boys? And oh my, what a voice. My ears are still ringing."

"Mine too," Joey said testily with a forced smile that was half grimace.

"And we know she doesn't like to have her panties taken off. Not even to go swimming."

"Yeah," Rex said, with a failed attempt at his usual derision. "She's afraid somebody'll see her buns. Some buns! Who wants to see them?"

Uncle Dan grinned broadly through his cigarette smoke.

"Watch that language, Rex, you're talking in front of a lady. A very particular lady who doesn't like to be looked at. However, she might not object so much if one of you boys tried it. She might even like that real well. Would one of you like to take off her panties?"

They moved as if released from puppet strings, caught with embarrassment, each to his own reaction. Rex flipped water with the heel of one hand toward the far bank. Joey ducked down to his chin and made awkward attempts at swimming. Dale began to pay close attention to the tiny, silver minnows that nibbled at his body. And Timmy looked at Uncle Dan and thought how nice it would be if he could become a double bionic boy and lift the whole creek full of water and dump it on Uncle Dan's head. He had treated Susie mean. He was still treating her mean. He was so strange and so changeable, and Timmy decided he liked the tucked-in mouth and the apron better.

The man saw Timmy's intense gaze and misinterpreted. He extended the hand holding the lollipops.

"Look pretty tasty, don't they, Timmy? I'll tell you what, you can have choice number two. Susie gets first choice because she's a girl."

Timmy shook his head. Even though his throat constricted with a sudden desire for the sweetness of candy, for the comfort of sweetness, he didn't want it from Uncle Dan after the cruel way he made the little girl scream and run.

"What? Don't you like suckers, Timmy boy?"

"No," Timmy lied stubbornly and faced downstream. Susie had sat down and was looking toward them in her watery and timid isolation. The creek swirled round her, leaving only her head above its cool and murmuring embrace. He began to wade toward her.

"Take her one of these, Timmy," Uncle Dan said, calling out to her, "Which color do you want, Susie?"

She didn't answer, and Uncle Dan separated one of deep red from the yellow, the orange, and green.

"Here, Timmy, take Susie this one. It will go nicely with her temper."

Timmy started to refuse, for to take anything from him now would mean that it didn't matter if he had made Susie run away. But then he saw her face, the pucker of near tears, and the look of longing for something that would comfort her. She was alone, held only by the creek that eddied past her in uncaring, ocean-bound destination.

He retraced his steps and picked from Uncle Dan's fat fingers the red sucker with the clear wrapper.

Uncle Dan lay the rest of the candy on the rocks beside his flattened rear and focused the camera on Susie. "Damn," he muttered clearly so that Timmy heard even though the words weren't spoken to him, "I sure missed some good stuff when Susie took off." Then, louder, "Better tug your undershorts up, Timmy boy, if you don't want your naked bottom in a movie." And he began laughing again.

Timmy didn't look back at him, but his free hand automatically reached down and yanked his water-drooped shorts closer to his body. He remembered now why he had never liked Uncle Dan even though his mom and dad said he should. It was the teasing. He used to get fighting mad when Uncle Dan teased him, grabbing the seat of his jeans when he was still littler than now. And Dad had said to stop getting so mad, that was just Uncle Dan's way of showing affection, and he was only teasing. Well, Timmy didn't like being teased by Uncle Dan. And he didn't like the way Uncle Dan had teased Susie. When *he* loved somebody, he never teased them. He never teased old Buster, and he would never tease his new pup, Kazan.

She didn't try to run from him, as he was afraid she might. He stopped several feet short of her and stretched his arm full length, offering the red sucker.

"Here," he said.

She didn't move. Her own arms stayed under water, and he could see them clasped tightly around her bent knees. She would have to reach, and maybe move forward, to take the candy. And she wasn't moving.

He stepped closer and leaned, so that all she need do was raise her hand. "Go on," he said. "Take it." And then he heard his dad's words coming from his own mouth. "And don't mind Uncle Dan. He was only teasing. That's the way he shows he loves you."

Her gaze faltered and dropped, and her arms came loose from around her legs, but her movements were slow and undecided. And still she didn't accept the red sucker.

Timmy squatted in the water so that his head was almost on a level with hers. He carefully kept the candy above water. "Sometimes he teases me, too," he said.

She raised her eyes to his.

"Yeah," Timmy said, encouraged. "When I was littler than I am now, about like you, he used to give me a quarter every time he came to our house, and he'd shut both his hands and make me guess which one it was in. And when I got close enough to touch the hand I thought it was in—he wouldn't let me just guess out loud—then he'd grab me and kiss me. And he'd laugh, like today. Dad said he was just teasing Because he liked me. But I didn't like to be teased, so I stopped playing his quarter game. And that made him laugh too, because I didn't like the game." He proffered the red sucker again. "Here, Susie, don' feel bad."

Slowly her hand rose and she accepted the candy

He sat in the gentle current of the water and silently watched her remove the wrapper and discard it to float downstream. He wondered if it would go all the way to the ocean or perhaps be swallowed by a fish or get caught in a willow limb on the creek bank. He watched Susie taste the sucker, and he knew she was feeling better.

He began wading back upstream toward the other boys and Uncle Dan, and he saw the camera eye watching him and Susie, like one huge, bulging eye in the center of Uncle Dan's face.

Timmy turned abruptly toward deeper water and dived in, swimming under the surface among the darting minnows. When he finally came up for air he heard his name called from the boys to Uncle Dan, one voice echoing another, "Timmy." "Tim." "Timmy boy."

He swam in where his feet touched the ground. "What?"

"We're going," Rex said, and Joey added, "Upstream."

Uncle Dan was standing, the camera dangling against his belly so that the protruding eye was now on his side, like a black growth. The other boys splashed through the water toward the clean-washed, narrow gravel beach.

"We're going up to a waterfall," Dale called over his shoulder to Timmy. "A real, honest-to-goodness waterfall."

Joey said, "I'm going to ride over it in a barrel."

"Hah!" Dale snorted. "Where you gonna get your barrel? There ain't no barrels out here in the woods."

"I'll make me one."

"Outa what?" Dale shouted above the splashing of his advance toward the bank.

"I'll cut me down a tree, that's what. And I'll take my knife and carve me a barrel and I'll get in it and go over the waterfall, and you can't go along. You'll have to stand on the beach and watch."

"I'm not either. I'm not going to watch you. I'm going to make *me* an Indian canoe and I'm not going to let you ride in my canoe either—"

Uncle Dan picked up Susie's small dress and called downstream to her, "Come on, Susie girl, you don't want to be left behind. Here's your little dressy. Come on, be a good girl and you can wear it in the water. Wouldn't you like to stand under the waterfall?"

Timmy and Rex climbed into their jeans and shirts, and Dale and Joey quarreled their way out of the water and to their tossed heaps of clothing.

"Come on, boys," Uncle Dan said, noticing them. "Why are you putting on your clothes? Don't you want to play in the water anymore? Just carry them along."

"Already got mine on," Rex said, pulling his zipper. "Besides, there's skeeters."

"They won't kill you." Uncle Dan turned his attention back to Susie. "Come on, or we'll leave you here with the snakes and the monsters, and Rex's mosquitoes."

She rose from the water and came slowly, the red sucker protruding from her mouth like a pacifier.

Timmy pushed wet feet into uncooperative sneakers and hurried to catch up with Joey and Dale who were splashing upstream in the edge of the water their white, naked bottoms shining with dampness and sunshine, their clothes dangling from their arms. Uncle Dan raised his camera again, and it swept evilly from Susie to the boys running ahead. Timmy felt a sudden and fierce hatred of that camera, and wished vaguely that something really dreadful would happen to it, like the huge, hairy hand of a monster reaching out from the lusty, green undergrowth behind and snatching it away.

Instinctively, he got behind Uncle Dan, so that the camera could not easily find him.

The creek curved around the protruding finger of the high, tree-covered hill, and the beach became an almost impassable rocky strip between swift, flowing water and the impenetrable growth on the steep bank. Dale and Joey led the way, followed by Rex, Uncle Dan, Timmy, and finally, Susie in her short dress and the red sucker drooping from her mouth. Timmy offered to let her go ahead of him, but she hung back and shook her head.

At one point along the trek, where sweeping water had washed out the bank and the only way by was up through the ground ivy and tree limbs and roots, Dale stopped and demanded crossly, "Why are we going up here, anyway? Why didn't we just stay where we already wuz?"

Uncle Dan said, "Where's your sense of adventure, Dale? Either go on, or get back behind Susie like the little coward you are."

"I am not! I am not either a coward!" And he plunged up the bank, his short legs stumbling, his arms reaching, hands grasping for woody support. "Hey! There's a little path up here," he cried in pleased surprise when he was safely above the clutching water. "Somebody's been here before us, I betcha."

"Of course," Uncle Dan said, "How otherwise would I know where the waterfall is?"

They clamored up and over, one at a time. Timmy reached back and offered Susie his hand, but she ignored it, and came up the steep six feet of washed bank on her belly, hands grasping exposed tree roots to aid her climb. The front of her dress came up black with mud and soil, and her sharp little knees carried dark caps of mud. By pursing her mouth and tilting her face up she kept the stick on her candy free and clean.

The sound of the waterfall, rushing, falling, came to them first. Then followed the sight, and for the length of a stilled heartbeat, a held breath, they were motionless. It fell from far up the mountainside, a hollow in the crowding hills, sparkling and gleaming in the bright sun rays. A full sheet of water swept down a flat rock as wide as the front porch of the house on the hill above. It ran smoothly over the rock floor to settle into a still pool at the base of tiered rocks, reflecting the blue sky above and green foliage on each side. And here too, a few paces away, was a larger, smoother beach than the one they had left.

"Oh wow," several voices breathed at once, and then there was a laughing scramble like a bunch of lively pups loosed from a cage.

"Wait!" Uncle Dan called. "We're going to play games this time—ah, it's more than a game. It's protection from anyone who looks at us. We're all going to wear little black masks, so that we'll look like racoons. Okay? Come on, here's one for each o you." He laid out small black masks that had holes for eyes, and beside them, a stack of sandwiches and cookies. "And this is our lunch—to be eaten whenever you're hungry."

Joey reached for one black mask and adjusted the rubber band at the back of his head. "Hey, this is keen! What kind of game is this?"

Uncle Dan laughed. "Well, let's call it, 'guess who the boy is.'"

Rex said, "Sounds dumb to me."

"I don't want to wear a mask," Timmy said. "It'll just come off in the water."

"No it won't. Don't be a spoilsport, you boys. Look at that little boy there in the mask. Who is he, anyway?"

Joey snickered in secret delight, but Dale said crossly, "Everybody knows that's Joey."

"They do not!" Joey shouted. "Uncle Dan didn't know."

"Uncle Dan did too know. He knows everything there is to know."

Uncle Dan chuckled appreciatively.

Rex turned his back in disgust. "Jeesh," he said. "Stupid assholes. Them boys," he added carefully, as though to make Timmy understand he hadn't meant Uncle Dan.

"Come on," Uncle Dan demanded less playfully. "On with the masks. We want some nice entertaining home movies to show Little Mother. Since we've moved up to the cabin she doesn't have television to keep her entertained. She'll love seeing these movies."

Rex said low to Timmy, as he slipped the narrow

mask into place, "I still think it's dumb shit, but I guess we better humor the old boy. Hand me one of them there sandwiches."

Timmy handed a sandwich to Rex and took one for himself. He stood impatiently in the edge of the water, stuffing half a peanut butter sandwich into his mouth as fast as it would go, the mask hot and bothersome on his face. He wondered why Uncle Dan couldn't make home movies without the masks. And then he wondered more about the home movies, and he wondered about Little Mother. Why was she so silent? Why did she never come where the others were? Was Uncle Dan only teasing?

Of course, that was it. He was teasing. Adults had strange ways of having fun, some of them, and for Uncle Dan it was the teasing, and being one way one minute and another way the next.

The best thing to do, Timmy decided, was to ignore him. He had only thirteen more days and his two weeks would be over.

His meager appetite was gone. Thirteen days seemed forever. He tossed the last bite of the sandwich far out into the smooth, deep pool and watched small fish dart upwards and wage a tiny war over the crumbling white bread.

"Go on in," Uncle Dan shouted above the roar of falling water. "It's perfectly safe. You can stand right under the fall and breathe. Did you know that?"

Timmy found to his amazement that it was so. Water struck the top of his head and split, cascading, and he not only could laugh and breathe, he could even see through the holes in the mask, through the water. The trees beyond shimmered. The sheet of water was a thick, sparkling wall between him and the outer world. Beside him he could see Susie, even, her dress plastered wet to her body, and a smile on her face below her mask.

That was great, he thought. Susie was having fun now, and maybe Uncle Dan wouldn't tease her anymore.

Timmy was enjoying himself so much that he didn't even mind the eye of the camera that followed every move they made.

It was over too soon. Uncle Dan called them out, his shout competing with the rush and roar of the water. "Come, children! Time to go, time to eat. Dale, Joey, you haven't eaten any of the lunch Little Mother made for you."

Dale said suddenly, unexpectedly, "Why do you say it's made by her when you made it yourself? I saw you making it."

There was a tense, brief silence, filled only by the sounds of nature, of water falling down the mountainside, of birds singing in the trees.

Uncle Dan said, "Ah, see, my water babies, Dale doesn't believe Little Mother made the lunch. I'll have to take him in to see her, so he'll know, so she can tell him herself."

They moved out of the water, fingers and toes wrinkled, and into clothes crumpled and damp and stuck with sand. Timmy sat on the rocks and pushed water-bleached feet into sneakers that seemed to have shrunk several sizes.

He saw the other children shivering, the shadows

of the trees and the spray from the waterfall turning the air cold. Susie's lips had turned blue, and Dale's lips too were pinched and blue.

There was fear mixed with the cold, and Timmy could feel it as palpably as he could feel the moisture in the air.

Ten

The man kneeled suddenly in front of Timmy and took over the job of squeezing tight canvas shoes onto Timmy's sandy feet and lacing them snugly, against Timmy's protests.

"I can do it myself," Timmy dared to say, too uncomfortably aware of the other boys and what they might think of Uncle Dan's putting shoes on him as if he were a baby. Too aware of their opinion to be afraid of repercussions from Uncle Dan himself. "I almost had them on by myself," he insisted.

"Little Mother wouldn't like it if I didn't take good care of her children," Uncle Dan said.

Timmy almost shouted that he was not one of Little Mother's children, but bit back the words just in time. He pressed his lips together and reminded himself that Uncle Dan teased, and his dad had told him that when anyone, big kids or older boys at school, teased him, to pay no attention. "They're trying to make you mad, Timmy, to make you fight them because they know you're too little to win, and they only think it's funny. Big boys like to annoy little boys sometimes when they don't have anything better to do." Timmy supposed that applied to Uncle Dan as well, even though he wasn't a boy anymore.

Uncle Dan stood up and put his camera into its case. "Are you all ready to go?"

He received a couple of unenthusiastic answers. They milled about, dressing, looking longingly back at the water.

Rex picked up a couple of small, flat stones and spun them leaping across the water. Dale and Joey stood still, watching. It looked like a very neat trick. Timmy looked for a flat stone. Dale grabbed up a rock as large as his hand and plowed it into the water. Rex laughed. Timmy decided to try later, when Rex wasn't watching, and tucked his rock out of sight into his pocket.

"Come along, children. It's going to get dark before long. It gets dark very early in all these trees and hollows. There's a path going up the hill right here, so we don't have to go back to the one where we came down."

Timmy looked up into what seemed to be a hillside of impenetrable forest. The treetops reached skyward, where the sun had gone somewhere beyond them in the west. He wanted to go home, to start walking and not look back, but ahead of him was already the coming dusk, as though the hills were closing in upon the narrow hollow with its suddenly threatening stream of swift, harsh water. Ahead of him, too, were the night sounds that tightened his skin and made the backs of his arms and neck tingle with warning.

Waiting behind him was Uncle Dan, but also waiting were the other kids. And in them he found companionship against the unknown dangers of the mountain nights.

Once again Timmy followed at the end of the line, but in subdued slowness, just managing to keep the others in sight up the long, steep hill. Homesickness had overtaken him, making him feel isolated and crushed by the weight of it. The others slipped away, Rex's heels disappearing around a curve in the path, and Timmy began to hurry. In a strange way they were like his classmates or even closer, like brothers and sister. It helped to make him feel less alone.

When at last they reached the tall pine trees behind the house it was a weary group that collapsed upon the gentle bed of pine needles.

Uncle Dan began to hum, a high-pitched sound that made chills curl down Timmy's spine. He looked at the man's face and saw that the lips were tightened into small rosebuds again, the corners pulled in. Timmy sat up and watched Uncle Dan, half afraid and yet fascinated by this abrupt change.

The man walked prissily away, disappeared into the house, and after a moment the dark windows of the kitchen lighted softly, a pale, golden light that was not made by electricity. When he came back out he was wearing the ruffled apron and was carrying a tray filled with buns, frankfurters, relish, catsup, and mustard.

"Children," he said, his voice in its falsetto of the breakfast voice, as if he were mocking the voice of a woman, "Little Mother has decided that we will forget nutrition this evening, since you have been such good babies today, and have a treat that she knows you'll love. Here, let me put these things down, then I'll build a campfire. Don't you just love a campfire?"

There were no answers. Timmy saw there was no teasing light in Uncle Dan's eyes and no true mockery in his voice. In some strange way this was real. One by one the boys sat up from their sprawling postures beneath the pine trees and watched without comment. Susie had snuggled into a knot back in the shadows beneath the table. Uncle Dan appeared not to see her as he went to the table and put down his tray.

In a blackened place in the backyard, where campfires had been built before, the man scraped together a small pile of pine needles and a few sticks, humming all the while. Around them he placed three stones, blackened with the soot and smoke of earlier fires. From his pocket he took a small lighter and flicked open a flame.

In the growing darkness behind him the fireflies were beginning to sparkle in the night, like falling stars.

The humming notes from Uncle Dan were ghostly fingers reaching into the back of Timmy's neck, barely touching, moving like whispery breaths around the edges of his ears.

Rex said under his breath, "I wish he'd stop that damn music."

Joey drew a long, long sigh, his chest rising and falling with it.

They watched Uncle Dan put more sticks on the fire and the flame rise into the night, toward the stars that were coming out, and the fireflies that flew unknowing into it.

Uncle Dan peered across the fire toward the children, his eyes squinting to see them, his round face firelighted and red, like a jack-o-lantern. From one side he picked up a stick that had many points up and down its length, lateral twigs that had been cut off and sharpened.

"Don't you just love a fire?" he minced, smiling.

Onto the sharpened end of the stick he poked a frankfurter, and then down each side, until the stick looked like a very long and skinny hand with pudgy fingers. Uncle Dan kept peering through and around the flames at the children, kept grinning, kept humming. He held the stick of frankfurters over the flame and suddenly they were sizzling and turning dark with their skins blistering. From broken skins something oozed, dripping into the fire.

"I'd druther have peanut butter sandwiches," Rex whispered to Timmy.

Timmy understood the feeling. He had always liked hot dogs, but he had never seen them roasted over an open flame before. And there was something about that soft sound, *sssss*, like insects frying in a flame, that, mixed with the humming, made Timmy wish he could just go on to bed instead.

"There now!" Uncle Dan said, drawing back the stick of blackening frankfurters. "Come on, children, grab a bun. Come, come, don't tell me you're too tired to move. If that's the case, you can't go swimming anymore, can you?"

Timmy and the boys got up and held open hot dog buns for the frankfurters, and humming again,

133

Uncle Dan prissily and daintily picked the hot dogs off the stick and handed one to each child. The fifth one he laid down on a paper plate.

"Now where's Susie? Susie come on and eat. You don't want Little Mother displeased with you, do you?"

Susie came out from under the table.

"That's a good girl, a very good girl. Here's your hot dog my infant, with a dab of relish, oh yum, yum. You can tell Little Mother how very much you appreciate all these nice things she does for you, can't you?"

With the hot dog clasped close against her chest, Susie slid off into the darkness beyond the fire. Timmy's eyes had to adjust to looking into the dark before he saw her, with her back to the trunk of the pine tree.

Uncle Dan went into the kitchen, and the light in the kitchen window dwindled away to a faint glow, and then disappeared.

"He's taking some supper in to Little Mother," Joey said.

"Naw, shit, there ain't nobody there," Rex said, but he raised his head and looked for a long while toward the house.

"Little Mother's there," Joey said, and Dale nodded, his shadow thrown upon the grass looking eerily long and pointed.

Rex's head jerked back. "D'you ever see her?"

"No, but I know she's there."

"How do you know?"

"I just know. I heared her breathing in the night once."

Rex giggled. "Breathin'! You're as crazy as the old man."

"I did too!" insisted Joey. "I woked up and she was leaning down over me, and she had long hair, like Susie's, and she was wearing a long, white dress. She had just finished kissing me."

"Bull shit," Rex muttered. "Why would she kiss you?"

"Because I—she—just because." He added, bashfully, "She was lookin' to see if she wanted me to be her little boy."

"You was dreamin', Joey," Rex said with a note of sadness in his voice, the derision gone. He drew a long sigh as if he were tired and leaned back on one elbow in the grass, his long spider legs crossed in front.

Dale said, "If you don't believe Joey, ask Susie. She's been here a long time. I bet she's seen Little Mother a lot of times."

"Oh yeah?" Rex challenged, his tiredness and brief sympathy gone. He sat up and yelled back into the shadows beneath the tree, "Hey, Susie, come here."

Susie didn't move. She was but a small, pale form against the dark trunk of the pine tree, huddled motionless, her face a round, ghostly blur.

"You want her," Timmy said, "you got to go there where she is."

"Okay, come on, all of you. I bet you she's gonna say no. I bet you—" Rex dug into his pockets. "A washer and two pennies, and ever' thing else I got in my pockets."

"You ain't got nothing," Dale said.

"I got more than you have."

135

"You don't either!" Dale yelled. "I got a hundred yards of string, and a diamond I found on the creek bank, and a snake's skin—"

Rex had started to demand proof concerning the diamond, but it was eclipsed into a grunt. The snake skin was more important. "Where'd you get a snake skin?"

"I got it this morning, in the pine needles under the tree!"

"I don't believe you. Let me see it."

"No."

"That's what I thought. You don't have one."

"I'm not going to let you see it. You'd want it, and you'd take it away."

"No I . . . listen. We had a bet on, didn't we? I bet you ever' thing I got in my pockets against ever' thing in yours that Susie says there ain't no Little Mother around here."

Dale considered. One by one the boys got to their feet until they were standing face to face in a loose huddle.

"All right," Dale decided. "I bet you that she says yes."

"I'll make her tell the truth," Rex said as he stalked into the darkness beneath the tree.

The hair on the back of Timmy's neck tingled and rose slightly. Rex sounded as if he meant business, and Timmy already knew what Susie was going to say. Not that he believed her, but she had told him Little Mother was there. She was like the other little kids, ready to believe anything. But nevertheless, he hurried to keep up with Rex, to see to it that Rex didn't do something mean to Susie.

Rex bent over the slightly more visible figure that hunkered farther down at his approach.

"Susie," he said in surprisingly gentle tones, as if speaking to a baby who barely understood. "We want to ask you a question that's very important. Will you tell the truth?"

Susie's head nodded. Her big eyes looked from one face to the other. Firelight threw faint, reddish flickers across her face, brushing up and down like scarlet feathers from forehead to chin.

"How long you been here, Susie? At this here camp of Uncle Dan's."

She shook her head, then whispered, "I don't know. A long time."

"Then you know for sure there ain't no Little Mother, don't you?"

She shook her head again.

They bent over her, watching her face closely, and one of the boys accidentally placed himself between her and the firelight, and once again she was a shadowy, ghostly figure against the tree. Rex reached out and shoved Dale over, and Susie's face was palely visible once more.

"There," said Rex, "did you see that, guys? Susie shook her head, which means no. No, there ain't no Little Mother."

Susie suddenly was nodding vigorously. She whispered, "There is! There is too!"

"Hah!" Dale said, reaching a cupped hand toward Rex. "You owe me. Pay up."

"Now wait," Rex said, shoving Dale's hand out of his way. "Don't lie, Susie. If Uncle Dan knew you lied, what would he do to you?"

"I'm not lying," she whispered and pointed toward the house. "She's in there."

"Where then!" Rex demanded. "Where is she?"

"I don't know!" Susie's face puckered, visible even in the pale, reddish light from the fire. Tears rolled, gathering light like diamonds. "I don't know where."

"Hey," Timmy said, tugging at Rex's arm. "Come on and leave her alone."

"Shit," Rex said, allowing Timmy to urge him away. "She don't know nothing. She's just like Dale and Joey, she's just guessing. That ain't worth shit. I don't owe you nothing, Dale, till you prove to me there's a woman in that house."

From somewhere in the black depths of the trees and hollows came an unearthly cry. It quivered in the air and fell like shivering talons on the flesh of the children and stopped them where they were.

"That's her!" Susie cried in a shrill whisper. "That's her. At night she goes out of the house. And she sounds like that. She's everywhere. All the time."

But Timmy had heard that sound before, and even though he shuddered, hearing it, he was not really afraid. "It's an owl," he said. "A screech owl."

"Yeah, sure," Rex said hesitantly. "Just an old owl."

"No." whispered Susie.

"Yes," Timmy said and turned back to her and found that she was now standing, no longer finding the tree adequate protection. "It's just an owl, Susie. It'll fly away now and cry its song somewhere else."

"That was a song?" Dale asked.

"What's an owl?" asked Joey.

138

"An owl is a bird, that's all, that is awake at night instead of in the daytime. This kind of owl, anyway. He hunts at night. And when he cries out that means he's telling other owls that this is his territory and for them to stay over in their own territory."

"How do you know that?" Dale asked grumpily.

"My dad told me."

"Your dad?" Dale said.

Rex offered, "Yeah, he's got a dad, and a mom, too."

"I didn't know that."

"Sure," said Timmy. "Everybody does." And then, too late, he remembered that Susie didn't.

"I don't," said Dale, "and neither does Rex and Joey."

"We're going to have a dad now," Joey said. "We got folks now. A dad and a real mother, all our own."

"Oh yeah," said Rex with his usual derision, "Who?"

"Her. Little Mother. And Uncle Dan."

Rex shrugged. "You're a dreamer, Joey."

"Then why else did Uncle Dan want us?" Dale asked.

"He just brought us up to this here summer camp, that's all, and when summer's over we'll be going back to the foster homes and the people at the trailer park. If they're still there. And Joey'll go back to wherever he came from, and Tim will go home to his mom and dad."

"I'm not going to stay that long," Timmy said. "I'm only here for two weeks."

The light swelled in the kitchen windows again, rising from a flicker as of softest candlelight to a full, soft yellow, like a Halloween jack-o-lantern glowing on a dark night. The light came from the open back door and fell long and diffusing across the yard and outward toward the toilet lost in darkness. The campfire, burning down to sparkling embers, cast small competition.

Uncle Dan's figure suddenly filled the doorway, blocking the light from the door so that only the windows helped dissipate the darkness in the backyard where the children stood, gathering now instinctively into a small group, each lending security to the next. Even Susie stood close behind Timmy, in his shadow.

The back screen door opened, and Uncle Dan came on out into the yard. He stood in the light from the doorway and clapped his hands, peering ahead into the darkness like a half-blind man.

"Children? Come children, I have good news for one of you tonight, and for the rest of you, it's bedtime. Come on in now."

Timmy felt someone grasp his shirt in the back, and he glanced round to see Susie peering past him. Her eyes were full-moon huge, and her lower lip drooped away from the upper and trembled visibly even in the shadows of the night. He felt her fear and absorbed it, so that the house suddenly looked like a dangerous candy-crusted cottage lost in the woods, and the man in the door the wicked witch in disguise, But then with the clarity of a different aspect, of a boy older and less fearful than the girl, he saw how silly that was. The house was just a house, built partly of boards and partly of logs, with low ceilings, a peaked roof, and ordinary windows and doors both front and back. And Uncle Dan was . . . Uncle Dan. Now he was smiling, his eyes crinkling, his teeth gleaming in his shadowy face. His voice sounded happy. He was himself once again, the man to whom Timmy's dad had entrusted him. But then he said, "Little Mother was delighted with our play in the creek today. She thought it sounded just lovely. And she wanted to know if you had a good time."

None of the children said anything. Still knotted, they waited as if needing a shove forward. Even Rex, though he stood a head taller even than Timmy, stood waiting without answering Uncle Dan. At last a small voice spoke up.

"Yes," Dale said.

"Ah, my boy, Dale. Such a good boy. Maybe Little Mother's favorite. Come on now, all of you. Come to the house."

He came out to meet them and scooped an arm around to the rear of the group, guiding them toward the house. They filed through the door, and Timmy saw that the dim yellow light in the kitchen was coming from a kerosene lamp, similar to the lantern that his dad took along on camping trips. It sat in the middle of the table. Beside it was a bucket of water and a wash pan and cloth. Uncle Dan took Dale's hand and drew him close to the table.

"Let Uncle Dan get you all cleaned up, my boy. Little Mother wants to see you tonight. Isn't that marvelous?"

"Little Mother wants to see *me*?" Dale sounded awed. His eyes had grown almost as large as Susie's, but not with fear.

"Yes, she wants to see you. She called your name

141

specifically. She said to me, 'Bring little Dale in tonight.'"

Uncle Dan pulled out a chair by the table and sat down. He drew Dale close and began to scrub his face, neck, and ears with the washcloth.

"And tomorrow night, who knows? Whoever is the nicest boy, I'm sure. Susie is hardly ever nice enough to get to go see Little Mother. Maybe one of these days she'll be chosen."

Uncle Dan dried Dale's face, scrubbing it again with the terry cloth towel until Dale's skin glowed. He straightened his shirt and smoothed the small collar.

"Did—does—will Little Mother like me?" Dale asked, almost stammering in his excitement.

"We certainly hope so, don't we?"

Dale laughed a little. "Yeah! M-maybe she'll—she'll keep me?"

"Maybe. Maybe."

Uncle Dan dipped a comb in the water in the pan and carefully parted Dale's dark hair with it. He combed part of it to one side, then used the heel of his hand to urge a wave into it. Dale was beginning to look like a little boy whose mother had gotten him ready for school.

Uncle Dan happened to notice the other kids were grouped in the center of the kitchen watching as Dale was being groomed for the visit.

"Go on, go on to bed, all of you. I want you in bed and quiet within ten minutes. There's a light in your room. I'll come in later and blow it out. Go now. You're staring so much you're making Dale nervous. And we don't want him nervous when he sees Little

142

Mother. You don't want her to get a wrong impression of him, do you?"

"No sir," Rex mumbled, and Joey shook his head. Rex led the way into the hall.

The kitchen light touched only a portion of the hall at the beginning, and the door to the bedrooms were closed. They proceeded into increasing darkness, a tunnel that ended in blackness somewhere near the living room, that fetid air of the interior suggesting unknown horrors of the past.

Rex stopped suddenly and whispered loudly, "Hey look. There's a light on in the locked room. See the keyhole."

Joey whispered, "I'm not going to look in there. I want to go to bed."

"Well, you big baby, that's where we're going. You in such a damn hurry, Joey, you go on. He said there was a light in there so there ain't nothing to be afraid of."

Rex passed the locked door, with Joey close behind. Susie rushed past Timmy, leaving him to bring up the rear. In unaccustomed impulsiveness, just as Rex opened the door and stepped into the bedroom, Timmy bent to the keyhole, gleaming out softly in the darkened hallway like one small, oblong eye. He squinted through the small slit in the old-fashioned lock.

At first he saw only a wall papered with a faded pink and gray floral pattern. Then he moved slightly and a picture frame came in view. He stared, edging a bit farther to his left. The entire frame now was visible, and within its borders was a needlework print, with tiny flowers and vines trailing alongside

143

the words Home Sweet Home.

Timmy jerked back, his throat suddenly dry, his tongue feeling thick and scratchy between his lips.

His dream! The needlework on the wall, and something else—a wooden chair arm and floral material that he thought might be a cushion, or somebody's skirt. He remembered it all clearly, as if it were happening all over again.

It was her room! Little Mother was real, and she lived in the locked room.

And Uncle Dan had carried him to her the first night, so that she could see him.

Like a newborn infant he had been presented, wearing only a diaper.

Eleven

Steve stood by Connie's bed, his hands closed gently over her left hand. It lay as limp in his as though it were a dying bird, its blood still coursing slowly but warmly. The dimmed light was turned away from her. Behind him the hospital window looked out upon a black night. She moved restlessly, moaning in pain. Her face turned toward him. Her eyes opened.

"Steve?"

It was the first word she had spoken since she had come out of surgery that he had heard. Intravenous needles, taped in her wrist, fed a colorless solution constantly from a long, narrow tube that drooped from a bottle suspended above the head of the bed. Hanging low on the side of the bed was a clear bag attached to a catheter. She was pale, but at last she was conscious. He leaned close to her.

"It's over, Connie, and everything is okay. It wasn't cancer, Connie."

She closed her eyes and smiled faintly.

A nurse came into the room with a hypodermic syringe and a cheerful smile. "I'm going to put her to sleep again, Mr. Malcolm, so why don't you go home and get some rest? We'll keep a close eye on her. She's doing fine."

Connie's face turned toward him again. "How's Timmy? Did Dan call?"

Steve kept his face as expressionless as he could, "Timmy's fine. Connie, I'm going home for a few hours. I need a change in clothes and some food. I'll be back later on."

"Yes."

The shot of pain killer had been given and the nurse remained in the room to take blood pressure, as one or another of them had been doing every fifteen minutes all day long. He felt in the way, even though none of them had made the slightest complaint about his presence. All afternoon he had felt desperate anxiety, for his unconscious wife, for his son. He leaned over the high railing at the side of the bed and kissed Connie.

"I'll be here when you wake up," he said.

She didn't open her eyes, and he sensed that she was already affected by the drug, was already drifting into sleep again.

He drove fast, as fast as he dared, through the small towns, the home-light-dotted countryside. He alternated between cursing himself for being so trusting of Dan and for feeling something was not right about the man. Christ, he told himself, he'd known him for four or five years. You can't know a man for that long without knowing what kind of man he is. So he hadn't called the hospital as he had said he would.

But then on the other hand, hadn't he said it might be a few days? But, since he was supposed to be a friend of the family, wouldn't it seem normal for him to call this day, or this evening, to find out how Connie was?

He knew only one thing for certain: He had to find out more than he knew about Dan Walker. He had to know something about Dan Walker's family connections, where his mail came from, for instance. There had to be connections somewhere, someone he could call and talk to, someone who would reassure him about Dan Walker.

That piece in the paper haunted him.

He reached Carlyle within the hour, but instead of stopping off at his house at all, or stopping to eat anywhere, he drove directly to the apartment complex where Dan had lived since he had come to town. If the manager cooperated, he'd soon have some idea of where his mail came from, maybe. Or, maybe Dan had talked of his hometown and his family to someone. Or . . .

He parked near the door that said Manager and put his finger on the doorbell. The ring was answered promptly, and an elderly little man with glasses dangling in one hand and a newspaper in the other looked out at him.

"Sorry to disturb you," Steve said. "But I'd like to ask you a few questions about Dan Walker."

"Dan Walker? He's not here."

Steve nodded. "I know that, but—"

"He checked out."

There was a silence in which only the summer insects buzzed, cicadas in the trees, crickets in the grass. A whippoorwill far away in the country setting it preferred.

The manager said, "So, he doesn't live here anymore."

"Where did he—when did he leave—move out?"

"A couple of days ago. His rent was due and he handed in the key and said he wouldn't be coming back. He didn't give the two weeks' notice that he was supposed to, but sometimes people don't, so what can I do about it? Can't have him picked up by the police for that. So he's gone, and I'm left with an empty apartment."

Steve felt as though he had been drained of all his senses. Reality had made a complete flip. "I'm—uh—a friend of his. He didn't tell me he was moving."

The manager said nothing. He stood waiting, the light from his sitting room spilling out around him, throwing a long shadow forward on Steve's feet. He wanted to get back to his chair, his television, and his newspaper.

Steve took a long, deep breath. "Where did he move to?"

"I don't know."

"Where—do you know where he might have gone?"

"Nope."

"His mail—did you ever see any of his mail?"

"No, not much. Each apartment has its own box."

"Do you have an address for a next of kin?"

"No, I don't."

"Would you happen to know where any of his relatives live? Someone I could contact, who might know where he is?"

"No, sorry. I knew Mr. Walker only to speak to. I do know he didn't have any visitors to speak of. I never once saw anyone at his apartment, and there were never any complaints of noise. He was a quiet tenant, an ideal tenant, in fact. He was gone most of the time. I think he must have had a traveling job."

"He was a camera salesman."

The man nodded, accepting that his hunch was right. He added, "Sorry."

Steve turned away, murmuring thanks. He was wasting time, but he didn't know where to turn next. Then suddenly he knew—George and Sheila Breck. They were, so far as Steve knew, Dan's oldest and closest friends in the town of Carlyle. It was at their house he had first met Dan Walker.

He drove into an older section of town that was much like his own neighborhood and saw to his relief that lights were still on even though it was close to midnight now.

Their response to his ring took awhile, so that he was beginning to think they had gone on vacation and left the lights on, but the door opened and George looked out with surprise on his features, a silent question of "who the hell is calling at this hour" dragging at his mouth. Then he recognized Steve and smiled.

"Hey! Come on in."

"Sorry to bother you, George, but I'd sure like to talk to you and Sheila for awhile."

"Fine, come in. We were just watching a movie on HBO. Nothing special. I have to watch a dozen to find one I can stay awake through."

They went down a short hall and to a dimly lighted

149

room where Sheila sat on a sofa with her feet tucked under the long, full skirt of a robe.

"Steve!" she said. "Is something wrong?" She straightened, dropping her feet to the floor. "Is Connie all right?"

"Yes, Connie's going to be all right. She was asleep when I left her. She had surgery early this morning."

"Yes, I know. I've been thinking of her and wishing her well. Sit down, please. Would you like something to drink?"

"No thanks. I just want to talk to you about Dan."

The two faces stared at him. George pushed a remote control device and the quietly running television went black and still. Neither of them asked what he wanted to know. Neither of them made the slightest comment, and Steve found their waiting silence unnerving. Of course everything was unnerving today, tonight. Everything.

"I went by his place," Steve said. "He's checked out of his apartment. He left no forwarding address."

Still no comment, but Sheila raised her eyebrows pointedly and looked at her husband.

"The thing is," Steve said abruptly, no longer planning his words, "I'm getting scared, damned scared. Timmy's with him, and I don't know for sure where they are. I thought, since you're Dan's best friends around here, you might be able to tell me where he's gone."

Sheila leaned forward. "He took Timmy? When?"

"Sunday morning. It was supposed to be for two weeks to his mountain cabin, but he hasn't called. I hope you can tell me where the cabin is."

George shook his head. "I've never been there. I've

heard him talk about it a little, that's all."

Sheila was staring fixedly at Steve, and he had a feeling there was something on her mind. But instead of her speaking, George said, "I wouldn't worry about Timmy, Steve. I've never known Dan to be anything but dependable."

"But unpredictable," Sheila said quickly. She cast a glance at George and received one in return. A message was passed that puzzled Steve. Sheila's lips parted as if she were going to say something more, then she leaned back and pressed them together.

"I just began to realize how little I know about Dan's background and family," Steve said. "I know he's been married, but divorced, or something. Maybe she died, or maybe she even lives in another town. I think she's got their kids. I don't even know how many for sure."

"Two, I think," George said. Then frowned. "I hadn't thought of it either, Steve, no reason to. I just thought Dan was a guy around with a family somewhere that he was divorced from."

"Did he ever mention to you where his folks live?"

"There was some kind of tragedy in Dan's life. He had brothers and sisters, but part of them at least perished in a fire when their family home burned down. He only mentioned that one time to me, and never talked about it again. I didn't question him about it, of course. Some people like to talk about tragedies in their lives and some don't. I felt that Dan was one who didn't."

Sheila was looking at George again and at last said, "George, I think we should tell him about Jackie."

151

George shrugged and picked up his pipe from the end table. With his attention focused on tamping tobacco into the pipe and lighting it, he was silent, although Steve had a distinct feeling of only a partial amount of approval from George.

His wife said, "Dan took Jackie down to the drive-in for an ice cream cone one day, Steve, when Jackie was only three. That was a little over a year ago. And he didn't bring him back. Evening came and I began to be terrified, just as you are now. I wanted to call the police, but George said wait, give him more time. We had known Dan three years, and although he had always been very fond of and generous with our little boy, he had never given us any reason to distrust him at all. In fact, I wouldn't have let Jackie go with him if I hadn't trusted him so much. But I was really scared when about nine o'clock that night, here he came. Jackie was tearful. Dan didn't give any real reason, but he looked contrite."

"Where the hell had he been?"

"He said he'd taken him to the park and time just slipped away."

"That doesn't sound like something a sensible man would do."

"No," Sheila said. "It was awhile before I even wanted Dan to come around, but since Jackie was safely home, and Dan never asked to take him anywhere else, I couldn't do much about what had happened. I just told him I thought it was terrible for him to take a child and keep him away, without telling the parents or calling or anything. Phones were available to him. He could have called."

"You don't know what his motive was?"

George said, "I think Dan is lonely. At least that's my guess. I would be if I were in his situation, on the road most of the time with his job, and no family waiting at home."

"That's no excuse for what he did," Sheila snapped. "What was he really going to do, kidnap our child?"

George said, "He said he took a nap and it got dark before he woke up. Maybe he did."

"That's not what he told me! And why would he sleep when he was taking care of Jackie? Was he left unattended?"

"He said Jackie went to sleep."

"See," Sheila said to Steve, motioning angrily at her husband. "Still, he excuses him."

"I can't believe," George said good-naturedly, "that Dan would kidnap any of our children. Not ours, not Steve's. I think if I were you, Steve, I'd give him the two weeks. And I'll bet he's back by then."

"Not me," said Sheila, "I'd call the police. If Dan has checked out of his apartment and left no forwarding address, he's gone. And Timmy with him. No way would I trust him. I'd call the police."

Steve got up, and Sheila and George followed him to the door.

"What are you going to do then, Steve?" George asked.

Without looking back, without slowing his steps as he hurried out of the house, he said, "I'm taking Sheila's advice. I think she's right. I'm going to the Shreveport police though, rather than the local, because a little boy was picked up there a few days ago by someone driving a purple van. Maybe the police there will help me, because I think I can help them. I have to find my son."

Behind him, he heard Sheila cry softly, "My God, George, a purple van? There can't be two just alike in the whole South, not like that one. It sounds like he has kidnapped Timmy, doesn't it? And some other little boy, and there's a whole world out there to get lost in."

Twelve

Timmy climbed into bed and pressed his back against the wall. Another kerosene lamp exactly like the one in the kitchen glowed from a low table near the door, but the clear glass globe of this one was streaked with smoke and the light it gave out flickering and low. Any moment, it seemed, the yellow flame would flicker a last time and go out, leaving the room in blinding darkness. Long shadows danced grotesquely across the floor behind Rex as he removed his shoes. They prepared in silence for bed. Susie disappeared into the shadowy recess of her lower bunk, and Rex climbed the ladder to the one above her, and his shadows played across the ceiling, long and thin and twisting.

Joey asked mournfully, "I wonder why she didn't take me, too?"

Rex shushed him. "Go to sleep, Joe."

They grew quiet, bodies eased into beds and settled. A soft sigh came from Joey, expressing his sorrow at having been left behind, and a moment later a softer sigh of tiredness. A low gurgle rose from Rex's throat, a near snore. In the trees outside the single bedroom window the screech owl quivered out its eerie cry, and layer after layer of chills rippled through Timmy. He pulled his blanket high around his face but felt compelled to leave his eyes uncovered so he could watch the room.

The window was uncovered by curtain or shade, and Timmy felt as though eyes were staring in at him. Was she outside watching? Why did she stay in hiding? Separated from them, just waiting and watching perhaps. But why?

The door opened. Uncle Dan slipped in, peered in the directions of the bunk beds, then cupped his hand over the lamp globe and blew. The light went out. In the lamplight from another room Timmy could see Dale standing in the hall just outside the door, his hair neatly combed, his face scrubbed clean, his shirt tucked neatly into his shorts. He was as quiet as the children who slept.

Uncle Dan left the room, pulling the door shut behind him.

The darkness at first was complete. Gradually the window lightened, a long, narrow rectangle in the wall at the foot of Timmy's bed.

He lay tense with fear, frowning at the pale window, listening hard for sounds in the other parts of the house. He was experiencing his dream again, vividly, seeing the framed embroidery Home Sweet Home, and with growing trepidation the hem of *her* dress.

The owl cried another time near the house, then again farther away. He had flown, casting no shadow on this dark night, with piercing eyes able to see in the darkness so as to avoid all obstacles of the forest. Timmy was not sorry to hear him go, on his silent wings, his cry trailing behind him like a lost soul without sanctuary.

Timmy closed his eyes, squeezed them uncomfortably shut, and tried to sleep. Then suddenly, from another part of the house, Dale cried out. There was a half scream, then a long series of whimpers, then again, silence.

Timmy swallowed a knot of fear and sat up in his bed, the blanket pulled up to his chin. His hair brushed the bed above he sat so upright in the corner. His ears pulsed with straining to hear, with listening again for that sad and sorrowful cry. Had Dale seen something that made him cry out, or had he hurt himself? Or—

Boards squeaked as though from abrupt footsteps.

A shrill cry rang out, an aborted scream of terror, a cry of madness, or denial. But Timmy didn't know to whom it belonged. It didn't sound like any human, not Dale, not anyone. It was silenced almost as soon as it began, as though a hand had been clamped down, smothering the voice. Soft whimpers came again, almost lost in the log walls separating room from room.

Timmy sat listening, wishing he dared cross the room to Rex, wake him, and ask if he had heard. But soft snores coming from Rex gave him the answer.

The house grew quiet. Only the soft settlings of the old logs disturbed the night.

Timmy at long last went to sleep sitting in the corner of his bunk.

*   *   *

Timmy woke with a hand heavy on his shoulder. It shook him, insisting that he waken. He came up, blinking and trying to focus his sleep-dazed eyes. The room was shadowed twilight now, the heavily leafed oak tree outside the window closing out early morning sunlight. Rex stood above him, rust-red hair falling over his freckled forehead.

"Come on, get up Tim, let's beat the little kids out." His voice was an impatient whisper.

Timmy struggled out of bed, leaving his blanket in a tumble, and crawled half asleep into jeans and knit pullover shirt and dirty sneakers. Rex led the way out into the dim, cool hall and down it to the silent kitchen, glancing warily all about like a spy trying not to be seen.

"Where are we going?" Timmy asked, sotto voce.

Rex slapped a finger against puckered lips and uttered a harsh, "Shhh! Don't talk. I'll tell you when we get outside."

Timmy passed the locked door on tiptoes, with the memory of his experience there pushed aside. This was another day. The terrors of the night gone. They moved into the deserted kitchen without seeing anyone.

Rex unlocked the back door slowly with only a soft click, then shut it carefully behind them. "Now. We can talk. Nobody seen us."

"Okay." Timmy yawned. "What'll we talk about?"

Rex shrugged. "I don't know. Whatever you want to. Meantime, what say we look for arrowheads or something?"

"Okay," Timmy answered, waking to the excite-

158

ment of the search. "Where'll we start?"

"How about over there under that tree? If I was an Indian brave I'd get behind that big trunk and shoot my arrow at the white man, and the deers and bears and things."

They dug beneath the pine needles for awhile, then Rex sat back on his heels.

"Do you know what an arrowhead looks like?"

"Sure. It's shaped like this." Timmy sketched a diagram in the soft black soil with a finger. "They're whittled out of little, flat stones. Flint stones."

"I wonder how they whittled a stone? I had a knife once and it wouldn't hardly whittle wood."

"I don't know. I think maybe they used another stone. I don't think they had knives back then."

The back door opened and Joey came into the yard and toward them, where they squatted beneath the tree. His hands were shoved deep into his pockets, his dark hair tousled, his eyes wide and questioning.

"What'er you guys doing?"

"None of your business, runt," Rex said.

"Oh, tell him," Timmy said. "We can all look, and maybe get us a big collection."

"Well, okay," Rex said, "we're looking for arrowheads."

But Joey looked beyond them, eyes searching, thoughts already somewhere else.

"Where's Dale?" he asked.

"Asleep, I reckon," Rex answered.

"No he ain't. He's gone. The ghosts got him after he comed back to bed last night."

Rex snorted. "That's dumb, Joey. Ghosts don't even have hands. They don't have anything. They're

159

like little pieces of clouds."

"Well then where's Dale?"

Rex got up and wiped his hands on his pant legs. "Probably all wrapped up in his blanket like he always is. It's just hard to see him up there on the top bunk. Come on, Tim, let's go show the runt here where his buddy is."

They went leisurely toward the house, Rex leading and talking.

"My baby brother used to tangle himself up in his blanket just the way Dale does. Like a mummy, rolled over and over. I wonder where he is sometimes. I ain't seen him since the welfare people took him away when he was two years old. The didn't get me. I hid. Not that time. They got me later. But they didn't keep me. Now hush you guys. Let's don't wake up Uncle Dan. He's liable to get mad as hell if someone wakes him up. Adults do."

Joey muttered, "You're the one making all the racket."

Rex had no answer for that except silence. They entered the house in a line and proceeded quietly down the hall and into the bedroom.

"I'll get 'im," Rex said, and climbed the ladder to the top bunk.

In the lower bed of another bunk Susie lay huddled into an incredibly tiny knot in the darkest corner of her bed. Timmy thought as he looked at her that she seemed smaller than ever, as though she had shrunk into a round ball and had pulled her skin in upon herself. Then he noticed with a startled twinge that her eyes were open. She stared at him almost as though she didn't know him.

"Hi, Susie," he said, smiling.

There was no answer from her and only a further shrinking into her corner.

"Hey!" Rex said in surprise. "You're right, runt, he's not here." He backed down the ladder and bent to look in upon Susie. "Do you know where Dale is, Susie?"

She only stared at him, too, eyes switched from Timmy with a jerk as though Rex's voice had added to her wordless fright.

Rex continued leaning down, waiting. Behind him Timmy and Joey waited.

"She don't know," Joey finally said in contempt. "She don't know nothin'."

Rex grunted and straightened, turning his back to Susie. "He musta got up and sneaked out real early. Earlier even than us."

"Or the monsters got him," Joey said, adding hastily, "and I *know* they've got hands! Else they couldn't carry off so many people."

"They don't carry off a lot of people, dumbo. Besides, how'd it get into the house? The back door was locked when we went out, wasn't it Tim?"

"Yes. But isn't there a front door?"

Rex thought for a moment, then snapped his fingers. "I know. He went out the front and he's in the toilet. He et too many hot dogs last night. He's got the shits today."

"Hey, yeah! That's what!" Joey laughed in delight at this bit of wisdom, this answer to the puzzle of his missing friend.

"Sure!"

"Let's go throw rocks at him!"

"Hey no, we can't do that. Let's just sneak up behind him and scare him, and make him think something's comin' outa the woods to get him."

"Hey yeah."

"Sure."

"Let's go."

They clamored down the hall, making the walls dance, and out the kitchen door. Rex stopped.

"Now then, be quiet, you guys. You two go around that way, and I'll go this way, and we'll meet behind the toilet."

They crouched through weeds, past briers that dangled ripening blackberries, dodged under cedar limbs, and finally came together again behind the tiny, old building that leaned a bit eastward as though one day soon it would simply settle back upon the brush with a long sigh and be done with the world.

"Now," Rex whispered, "let's rush it all at once, with an Indian yell."

They squared off, then whooping rushed upon the unfortunate old toilet. And then stood in disappointed surprise.

"Well," Joey said, "maybe he didn't hear us."

Timmy rounded the faintly odorous corner and opened the sagging, reluctant door. A big, fat spider had woven herself a web into one back corner, but she was the only occupant.

"He's not here!"

"Maybe he fell through the hole."

"*Yukkk!*"

Together, the three faces peered down into the nearest toilet hole and saw a dark pit with rocks and general sewage. Together they drew away, faces crinkled in revolt and relief.

"Well," Timmy said, "at least he's not down there." A vague memory, like an unwanted dream edging into consciousness, came to Timmy, but he pushed it away. Dale had cried in the night, somewhere in the house, but this was a new day, a bright and sunny day, and Timmy didn't want to think of last night.

They squeezed through the door all at once, and they stood together again, eyes searching from brush and brier thickets to deep clusters of trees and the dark drop into the hollow toward the creek.

"He didn't want to climb no tree," Joey said sadly, looking up into the top of a pine tree. "So I know he ain't there."

Rex said, "Well, the last I saw of him was last night when Uncle Dan cleaned him up to go see her. Little Mother. Maybe he's still with her."

"No," said Joey. "He comed back to the room to go to bed."

"How do you know, did you see him?"

"No, but—"

"Then you don't know."

"Yes I do too! Why wouldn't he go to bed?"

Rex turned away, giving Joey a cold shoulder. In disgust and out of the side of his mouth he said to Timmy, "Like I thought. Like I said. He don't know nothing, he's just guessing."

Timmy had to face his memory at last. "I heard him crying last night," he said.

"Crying?" Rex asked.

"Yeah, like . . . I don't know. Not much. He didn't

cry much."

The eyes of Joey had become round with wonder. "Did Uncle Dan whip him?"

Timmy shrugged. "I don't know."

"Did he do something wrong? When he went to see Little Mother? Didn't she like him?" He ended his questions with a wail, "Ain't she going to keep him?"

Rex said, "Hey, punk, don't cry. Maybe he'll be back for breakfast. Come on, let's do something."

Rex led the way back to the scratched area beneath the pine tree that sheltered the water pump and squatted, his hands digging again into the pine needles.

"What'er you guys looking for?" Joey asked, and they were right back where they had started, it seemed to Timmy.

Kids cried all the time, he reminded himself. He'd cried too, just the other day when he stumped his toe and made it bleed. It had hurt like old Billy Ned. Maybe Dale had stumped his toe, or gotten a splinter from one of the old boards in the uncarpeted floor.

"Looking for Indian arrowheads," Rex said. "You can look too, if you want to."

"Okay." Like Rex and Timmy he squatted and began to sift pine needles and soft, black humus-filled soil through his small hands. "Maybe," he said after awhile, "he'll come out to play with us soon."

"Yeah, maybe," Rex said.

They busied themselves with play, with searching for something that wasn't there, convinced in their hearts they would garner a huge collection of arrowheads. If gold had been mentioned instead they would have searched as diligently and with as much faith and expectation for that gold. They finally stopped sifting soil not because of lost faith but because of attentions drawn elsewhere. A quail somewhere in the blackberry patch by the toilet sang out his bobwhite song and Joey exclaimed, "I betcha that bird's got a nest over there somewheres with baby birds in it."

"Hey, yeah!" Rex got to his feet and dusted his hands. "Let's go see. What kinda bird you reckon it is?"

"It's a bobwhite quail," Timmy said in faint disgust. "Didn't you ever hear a bobwhite before? Everybody knows what a bobwhite is."

"I know about quails," Joey said. "I saw some once." He was taking long slow steps, on his toes, toward the blackberry thicket.

Timmy stood a moment and watched the boys. They were going in the right direction, but their faces were lifted toward the treetops.

"Quails nest on the ground," he said.

They stopped and looked back at him and said in unison, "They do?"

"Sure." Timmy caught up with them. "What are you going to do?"

"Find its nest," Rex said.

"You're not supposed to bother birds' nests."

"Who says?" Rex demanded.

"Yeah, who says?"

"My mom and dad, and besides, everybody knows that."

"Not even to just look?" Joey asked, his brows humped in little question marks.

"No. Not very close anyway. Human scent scares the mama and she's afraid to hatch her eggs."

"Then we could cook 'em," Joey said.

Rex grew bored suddenly, "Oh, let's forget that old bird."

"I'm hungry," Joey said.

"Me too," Timmy said, turning toward the house. "Yesterday he cooked our breakfast. I wonder if he's going to today."

Rex shrugged his shoulders. "Hey! I know. Let's have a race. I'll bet I can beat both of you around the house. I'll bet I can run around the house twice while you're running around it once." He spread his legs and got set to go.

"You cannot."

"Wanna bet?"

"Sure."

"All right, when I count to three. One, two, three, go!"

Joey was gone like a steeple chase hurdler, elbows jackknifed and pumping, legs stretching. Rex paused to shout, "Hey! You cheated!" And then took off after him, and after a moment of astonishment Timmy followed. Over a fallen limb from a knotty old ash tree that hovered over the north side of the house, under the low limbs of a dogwood that grew beneath it. Through drifts of last winter's fallen leaves. Ahead of hard-running Timmy, Rex was long and lean, all bone and growth and freckles. But little Joey was close to beating them all when Rex stretched forth an arm and grabbed him and hauled him to the ground to drop puffing upon his stomach.

He held Joey down. Timmy slid to a stop beside them.

"You asshole runt, you cheated," Rex accused, pressing Joey's arms into the leaves. "You started running before I said go."

"You didn't say to go when you said go, you said to run when you counted three, and I did! And I won."

"You won shit. We're not even halfway around the house."

"I won anyway."

Joey turned his head abruptly and said low and hissing, "Listen. What was that?"

Rex followed Joey's gaze with his eyes, toward a nearby window. "What was that?"

"I heard it too," Timmy said, "somebody said something."

"It was a groan," Joey said. "Maybe it's Dale."

Rex let Joey up and moved in toward the window. "Shhh, you guys. Let's look and see."

"Whose room is that?" Timmy asked, holding back, remembering a time he was playing spy and had peeked into a neighbor lady's window and his dad took away his allowance for two weeks.

"I don't know," Rex said. "Might just be the front room. It's open. Blind's up. Come on."

He waved them onward, and they joined him to hunch beneath the rotting window frame and slowly rise to peep over the edge.

They saw two narrow beds. One was neatly made, and the other was covered with a large, hairy body sprawled sleeping on its belly, dressed only in briefs, arms outthrust and hanging off the bed, legs spread and bent. It moved, grunting. They ducked quickly and squatted on their heels against the boards of the house.

Rex whispered, eyes glittering with silent laughter, "It's *him*. It's Uncle Dan."

"He's got hair all over him, like a gorilla," Joey said in wide-eyed awe.

"We'd better get out of here," Timmy said. "What if he woke up and saw us? I'd lose my allowance for a year if my dad found out."

"Why?" Rex asked. "We're not doing anything except walking by." And he covered a low explosion of giggles with his fingers.

Joey stood up again and on his tiptoes boldly stared through the window. "Dale ain't there," he said, forgetting to keep his voice down.

"Hey! Get down! And keep quiet. You want him hearing you?" Rex yanked on his pants' leg.

Joey obeyed, sitting down again between them, back against the wall, hands on bent knees. "Dale's not there," he repeated somberly.

"Did you see his big fat buns?" Rex asked, whispering and snickering through his fingers. "You can see the hair on them right through the material of his shorts, they're so tight. Hair on his buns even! Ha."

"Let's go back," Timmy said. "Maybe Dale already went outside."

On the other side of the window came another groan, long and drawn out, ending in the clearing of his throat. The bed squeaked torturously, and a board added its own voice as Dan put his feet to the floor. There were more grunts, short and breathy,

168

like a pig, then a long, loud yawn.

Rex turned slowly on his haunches, reached behind him and grasped Joey's shirt. They eased up and into procession, and walking stooped, slipped past the window. When they were about twenty feet along the side of the house, Rex stood up and ran, and the boys following ran, too, even though twigs cracked noisily under their feet, and limbs that were pushed out of the way snapped back and slapped the side of the house.

They came to a huddle in the backyard.

"He heard us!" Timmy gasped. "He couldn't help but hear."

"If he says anything we'll tell him it was a deer."

"Well..." Timmy thought it out. A lie was wrong, but maybe in this case his mom would understand. "I guess we could say that. Cause there are deer up here in the woods, I bet."

"I bet too," said Joey.

"There ain't no bet," Rex said, "when you're both betting the same side. I'll bet you there ain't no deer!" He reached into his pocket and dug around. "What've you got to bet me?"

Joey turned away. "Nothing. You don't pay your bets."

Rex grinned and shrugged, lifting one shoulder laconically and letting it drop.

Timmy lifted his face and sniffed, concentrating on morning odors. An oddly sweetish, sickening smell wafted occasionally from the house, decaying old wood and rotting bones of small animals perhaps: mice, rats, squirrels in the attic; and from the woods came green, damp, mushroomy smells,

169

and a whiff sometimes of cool fishiness, as though the creek, so far, far down the steep hillside, gave up sweet fragrances in fingers reaching to the sun-touched hilltop; over it all was the smell of pine, pungent, fresh, and it, too, suggesting coolness.

"Let's wash up," Rex said, "and go eat. Race you to the pump."

They broke into another race that carried them to the wash table in the rear of the backyard. Rex began to pump the handle, and long squeals of rustiness preceded the belch of water from the spout. Water splashed out onto the ground where a small indentation had long been made in the soil, and mud sprinkled onto Timmy's feet. He jumped back out of the way, and both Rex and Joey hollered with laughter.

Timmy grabbed the empty water bucket off the table and held it under the rushing spout of water. Rex pumped harder, and the gushes filled the bucket. The bucket began running over, splashing into the soft dirt and sprinkling bits of mud onto Timmy's legs again. Joey began to laugh once more. Timmy backed up, holding the over-filled bucket out in front of him with both hands.

"Enough! Enough!"

Rex stopped pumping, and the water stopped with only a few drops falling to the small pool that had been created beneath the spout. Joey jumped into it, bare feet gathering mud as he tromped and splashed.

Timmy carried the bucket to the table and lifted it spilling some down onto the tops of his shoes. Re reached out to help.

"You're kind of a runt yourself," he said, "ain't you?"

"I'm not," Timmy started objecting, and then decided to change his tone. "Well, I'm only ten."

"Oh yeah. Me, I'm gonna be thirteen my next birthday. You wanna wash first?"

"I don't care."

Rex poured a granite dipper full of water into the wash pan and set it at the edge of the table near Timmy.

The back door of the house opened. Uncle Dan pushed Susie out into the yard.

"Children, children," he called in the prissy voice that matched the apron he again wore, "come now, it's time to eat. Wash up quickly."

He went back into the house. The boys, subdued, washed in silence, and Susie, coming quietly up into the group, allowed Rex to help her. He poured fresh water into the pan and placed it on the ground where she could easily reach it, and then, in unusual solicitation, stood over her, watching her splash water into her face and wash her hands. Timmy handed her the towel. When she had finished drying Rex spread the towel over a low tree limb to dry.

They followed Rex into the house.

Timmy was relieved to see that Uncle Dan had removed his apron, and it was hanging on the nail on the wall, a limp and shapeless yardage of white background and many colors of small flowers. The table was set with cereal bowls. In the middle of the table was a box of cereal and a couple of cans of milk.

171

"Little Mother was very tired this morning and asked that you eat cereal. I assured her you wouldn't mind."

They took their seats at the table under Uncle Dan's direction.

"You Susie, you sit there. And Timmy, you there. My, my, isn't Timmy beautiful with his face washed and his hair pushed back? If Timmy were a girl he'd be a heartbreaker, wouldn't he? Perhaps he will anyway. Perhaps he will. There, Joey, you sit near Susie."

There was no place set for Dale, and the eyes of all children fell for a moment upon the empty chair. Rex's voice, when he spoke, sounded unusually timid.

"Uncle Dan," he said, "where is Dale going to eat?"

"Why, with Little Mother, of course, Rex. Where did you think? And, we have decided," he added, smiling paternally at Rex, "that from now on, you must call me Papa."

"Papa?" Rex mumbled, staring at Dan.

"Yes. You see, Little Mother adored Dale, and is going to keep him with her, and she has decided to adopt you children. All of you, if she likes you as much as she likes Dale."

His eyes swept the table and each face around it.

"So from now on, I'm to be called Papa by each and every one of you."

Thirteen

Timmy stared at Uncle Dan. *Not me*, his mind was insisting, *not me*! He doesn't mean me, he means the other kids. They're orphans, all of them, and they can be adopted, but not me!

Uncle Dan hovered for a moment over Susie. "Eat, my child. Little Mother is not very pleased with you. She thinks you need to act more appreciative. Why aren't you more appreciative? Little Mother says you can't come in to see her until you learn to smile."

"I can smile," Joey said, suddenly so excited that he was standing with one knee in his chair. "Look at me, Uncle Dan, I can smile. Will she want to see me?"

Uncle Dan looked up and across the table at Joey. The smile on his own face was gone now, and the look it left was cold and fixed. "What did I tell you to call me?"

Joey, abashed, settled down in his chair. "Papa?" he said meekly.

"Little Mother will be very displeased to hear that you called me Uncle Dan. I am your papa now."

Joey asked, "Does she like me, too?"

"We'll see. We'll see. Later."

Uncle Dan crossed the room to the kitchen stove and the nail on the wall beside it. He took down the apron and put it on, slipping the loop at the top over his head, carefully arranging the crisscrossing sections in back and tying the bow. It barely surrounded him, so that the bow was short, with almost no ties hanging down. The bottom hem of the apron came several inches above his knees in front, the waist fitting just below his chest. He began to hum that tuneless song that mysteriously went along with the apron, and Timmy saw that the corners of his mouth were tucked in again.

He came to the table and opened the cereal box. Going from child to child around the table, he poured the cereal bowls in front of each half full. He ladled a spoonful of sugar onto each bowl and poured in milk from the pierced cans. He kept humming in a high-pitched tone, his strange little smile tucked like a madonna's smile onto his face, changing his looks, changing even the aura that surrounded him.

Timmy glanced at Rex and saw him glance his way at the same time. Just as their gazes collided Timmy giggled. It was a nervous burst of laughter that he hadn't meant to happen. Uncle Dan was funny, but not ha-ha funny, and of all times to laugh, Timmy felt it should not be now.

Uncle Dan kept humming, as if he hadn't heard.

With the children fed, he went back to the area near the stove and the free-standing cabinets, and sat down in the rocking chair by the window. From a

174

basket on the floor he picked up a small garment that looked like it might be one of Susie's dresses. He slipped a thimble on his finger, threaded a needle, and began to mend a tear in the sleeve.

The chair rocked, making a short squeak as it rolled backward and a long squeak as it came forward. Uncle Dan hummed and stitched the little garment.

Rex's sharp elbow dug into Timmy's ribs. "Let's go," he whispered. "I've et all I can, ain't you?"

Timmy looked at his dish. It was a soggy mess; the corn flakes soaked in the yellowish milk unappetizingly. He decided he'd rather have one of Rex's peanut butter sandwiches, however bad that might be, than this; and he would rather wait until noon for that. But to just get up and leave the table without asking to be excused? Mom wouldn't like that, and probably neither would Uncle Dan.

Timmy looked at the man rocking in the chair for a long moment. Rex elbowed him again, and Timmy spoke.

"Uncle Dan, may we be excused please?"

There was no answer. Dan continued to rock and to sew. There was no pause in his humming.

"I guess it will be all right," Timmy said experimentally, watching Uncle Dan for the slightest sign that he heard. There was none. Timmy slid off his chair.

"Hey," said Joey, "did you hear that? It sounded like a door shut. I'll bet you that's Dale going outside to play. Uncle D—Papa Dan, can we go out and play with Dale?"

"I didn't hear no door," Rex said.

"Well I did!"

Rex said, "He's not going to answer you either, so we might as well go."

They filed out, an orderly little marching army led by Rex.

The backyard was not a large place. Weeds had been cut down close to the door with a wide path out to the pump. Trees crowded close upon the cleared area. A washtub hung on the back wall of the house, and a broken down table and two chairs had collapsed into the weeds on the south side, toward the deep, unbroken forest in the direction opposite the creek. There were numerous places to hide, if one counted the clusters of bushes, the thick growths of vines that made a wall from one tree limb to ground, and the corners of the house itself. Joey began to look.

"Dale?" he called. When he got no answer he added, "He's here somewhere, I know. He's hiding. Are you playing hide-and-seek, Dale? Just answer yes if you are."

Joey peeked around the nearest corner of the house and stared toward the other. He stopped. Timmy could see the hesitation, the slight rise of fear at the unknown.

"Maybe," Joey said, "maybe Little Mother went out with him and they're taking a walk. Together. Now that she's going to be his mother, they would do something like that, for mothers and sons walk together a lot. I know, cause I've seen them."

"No," Rex said. "I've got this idea, see. Little Mother can't walk. She's in a wheelchair or something in her room. That's why she stays there all the time. If Dale went out, I bet he went alone."

"Then let's find him," Joey cried, "before he gets caught by the monsters on the other side of the house."

"There ain't no monsters, Joey. Snakes maybe."

"Uncle Dan said there was!"

Rex gazed toward the near horizon of trees and brilliant blue sky, and it seemed to Timmy, observing him, that a different Rex was emerging. The mask he wore had dropped away for that vulnerable moment in time, and the vague worry that Timmy was feeling increased.

"What'll we do, Rex?" he asked.

Rex moved and the mask returned in part. He attempted a nonchalant shrug and failed. "Joey's probably right, he's playing a game with us. And when I find him I'm going to rub his face in the dirt." He put a hand on the shoulder of each boy and gave them a gentle shove in opposite directions. "You cover that part, Joey, and you that one, Tim. I'll go this way. We'll meet right here again when the sun is up there, above that old tree."

"Okay. See you."

Timmy's area was toward the blackberry thicket and into the woods behind the toilet. He found a dead stick fallen from the hovering limbs of an oak tree and used it to prod into the blackberry thicket, to separate brier from brier so that by lying on his stomach he could see into the leafless, dim interior of crossed blackberry stems. A small rabbit leaped and ran, and Timmy's heart leaped and ran in perfect time with it until it was gone and silence was left behind again.

177

He moved on back into the dense undergrowth of the forest, slowly, heat from the still sun-struck day stinging his skin and burning his eyes with sweat that beaded down from his forehead. Occasionally he called out softly, "Dale? Dale? Where are you, Dale?" But he was almost afraid of his own voice, for it seemed the deeper he crowded into the brush, the greater and more numerous the eyes that watched him.

He checked the sun, but it hadn't moved far enough to turn him back.

He circled back toward the toilet, toward where he thought the toilet might be, for his world was narrow here, narrow and still and suffocating. "Dale?" he called more softly and heard a rustling in the leaves. But whatever ran darted and ran too fast and too easily for a boy hampered by the thin arms and fingers and claws of the endless undergrowth. Whatever ran ducked its head and ran through the ground ivy, the heavy green mayapple leaves.

His mind dwelt for awhile on snakes, the kind Uncle Dan had warned them of, and it seemed his keen ears picked up sounds of movement and other snake sounds all around him and behind him. He swallowed against the pressure in his throat and it grew worse, as though a snake had dropped from the trees and wound itself silently and stealthily around his neck.

And then, like a call from beyond this world, came the faint call of his name. "Tim?" He stood still, not breathing, and listened to the pound of his heart, to the wild rush of his blood.

"Tim!"

The call seemed closer, louder, and familiar. And in being familiar, it was a welcome sound. He cupped his hand around his mouth and called back, "Here I am!"

"Come on back, Timmy!"

It was Uncle Dan, sounding like himself again, and Timmy forgot to be afraid of snakes, for the call had to mean that Dale was there too, and there was no need to search further.

"I'm coming!" he shouted, his feet crushing the vines and the large, glossy leaves of the mayapple in his rapid retreat from the strange pull of the unknown and untouched forest that lay mountain upon mountain beyond.

Uncle Dan, without the apron now, stood in the shade of the pine tree near the pump, and close by were Joey and Rex. Timmy slowed to a walk.

"Where is Dale, then, Uncle Dan?"

Dan looked wildly angry, his fair complexion ruddy, his lips loose and trembling with emotion nearly out of control.

"You were told that Dale is with Little Mother, and I won't have you boys bothering her by searching for him! And another thing, Timmy. You left the table without eating the food Little Mother gave you to eat, and you went into the woods without asking permission, indeed, after you had been cautioned against going away from the house! If Little Mother hadn't told me what you were doing, you might have been lost forever. Now, you have to be punished."

Timmy stared at Uncle Dan, then at the two boys who stood so meekly nearby. What kind of punishment? . . . But Dan had taken out a pocket knife and snapped a long blade open. For a moment Timmy had a flash of terror for the knife, but then he saw Uncle Dan was using it to cut a limb from a sassafras bush that grew behind the pump. It was a large, supple limb, and when he had finished stripping it of leaves, it looked like a long green whip.

"Another thing, Timmy," Uncle Dan said, coming slowly toward him. "Little Mother is very unhappy that you refuse to call me Papa. Why can't you be grateful like the other boys, Timmy? You and Susie are bad children. There's no gratitude in either of you. But she, at least, is obedient. She doesn't run away into the forest. Why are you so disobedient, Timmy?"

"Because you're not my papa!" Timmy cried, edging backward away from Dan, away from his strong arms and hands and the fury in his face, away from the long green whip in his hand.

Dan leaped forward abruptly and brought the switch down in slicing swiftness on Timmy's shoulder and raised arm. The end of the whip sluiced a raw mark across Timmy's cheek. Timmy cried out involuntarily and covered his cheek with his hands. The pain was like something alive in his flesh, burning and fierce. He stared incredulously at Uncle Dan and then found his voice and shouted, "You can't whip me! My dad never told you you could whip me!" His scream dissolved to sobs. He stared through a blur of tears at the large man bearing down toward him and dodged back instinctively.

Dan grabbed Timmy by the arm and jerked him upright. "Why are you doing this to my family? You bad, bad boy, you're going to ruin everything! Little

Mother will not like this at all. You must not disturb her, do you hear? You must not disobey! I don't like to do this Timmy, but when my sons disobey I must punish them."

The switch came down again, hissing through the air as if it were alive, slashing into the thin material of his shirt, again and again. But this time Timmy was determined he would not cry, and he closed his eyes against the sight of Dan above him and the arm raising and lowering with such strength, carrying the whip to cut through his clothes into his flesh.

Timmy heard a child begin to sob, but it came from somewhere behind him now, from Joey, or perhaps Susie. It would not be Rex. Rex would not break down into sobs, and neither would he. Not for all the whips in the world would he let Uncle Dan make him cry now, and not for all the punishment Uncle Dan could devise would he ever call him Papa.

He thought about running, making a desperate dash for the road, or going back into the timber again. But instinctual logic told him he would not get far. If Uncle Dan didn't catch him, the endlessness of the woods would take him as its own and he would perish. And the sobbing was still behind him, frightened and choking. The switch might be turned on that one next, on Joey or Susie or whoever it was who cried.

He stumbled to his knees and fell in a hunch upon the ground, his head lowered and covered by his arms, his knees drawn up beneath his stomach. Uncle Dan did not pull him to his feet again but kept beating his back, the switch shredding and becoming shorter and more blunt and more painful. Among all the sounds that reached Timmy's ears, the sobbing, the sound of the stick whishing through the air, was the sound of Uncle Dan breathing. Short, hard gasps of effort and fury.

At last he stopped and stood back, panting and breathless. Then he dropped what remained of the switch near Timmy's head, turned on his heel and marched into the house.

For a moment Timmy remained where he was, feeling the sun scald the painful cuts on his back. Then he pushed himself up to his feet, and in a stooped position ran around toward the front of the house and out beyond the van parked under a cluster of oak trees in the weedy front yard. He stood there at the rear of the van, his arms doubled across his stomach, his back rounded against the pain, and stared down the little track of road.

The road ahead of him was long and dangerous and with no one to help him. He felt his helplessness now as he never had before, and he sat down upon the ground and buried his face in his arms. Then, against all his will, he began to weep.

Fourteen

Steve felt like the invisible man. Men and women in blue uniforms wandered past him as if he weren't there. Someone had told him to wait, and so he stood with an elbow on a scarred counter that divided one area of the long, narrow room from the other and waited. His impatience revealed itself in the soft, rhythmic snap of his fingers.

They carried papers back and forth across the room, in and out of doors. They answered phones that seemed to be ringing constantly. And finally a woman in blue uniform who appeared to be ambling by with papers in hand just happened to stop and look across the counter at him. It all appeared to be accidental, yet the woman said, "Are you the one wanting to know about the little boy who was supposedly abducted by a person in a purple van?"

Steve straightened. "Yes ma'am."

She looked at the papers in her hand. "It was a false alarm. The boy, Joey Fulton, was simply picked up and taken to a boys' camp for the summer." She smiled at Steve. "It wasn't a kidnapping case, it was a case of getting one child off the streets and into a clean environment."

"Oh." But the ease of anxiety did not come, and he asked, "How do you know that?"

She checked the papers again. "A Mrs. Keena Price, with whom the boy was staying, said so. She, herself, gave permission for Joey to go."

"Would it be all right if I go talk to her?"

"Certainly." She looked again at the papers and read to him the address.

"Do you happen to have a description of the van?"

She smiled. "Purple."

"That's all?"

"Well, with a painting on the side of red, blue, and black." She smiled at him again and began walking on, clearly through with him. Her smiles had begun to seem forced.

Steve had to find a service station that sold city maps before he could find the obscure address, which no one he asked seemed to ever have heard of, and the city was just coming awake as he drove into the steaming slum district and parked warily among all the other vehicles and trash cans that spilled onto the narrow street. The buildings rose straight toward the sky here, with no room for grass or trees. Faded signs hung out over the sidewalk, announcing places to eat, or drink, or sleep. The address he wanted was tacked to the top of a door beyond which he could see a flight of stairs going steeply up. On the bottom step an old man slumped sleeping off a drunk, or, perhaps, an illness. Steve stepped over him and climbed upward into early morning darkness. One low-watt bulb burned above the landing. Smells of cooking came from all directions in the depressing building, coffee, bacon, other smells all mingling into a nauseating and sweetish odor. Beyond the walls, too, came the sounds, voices, abruptly, in the middle of sentences and phrases as though televisions or radios were being turned on.

He knocked at door number six and began another wait. He knew he had come too early, but this night had been a long one, shortened only by a two-hour nap in the back seat of his station wagon. He had to work as fast as he could. He wanted reassurance. He wanted to know if this purple van had any connection to Dan Walker. He wanted to know a lot of things before he went back to the hospital. Anxiety ate at him like acid.

After his fifth pounding on the door it opened and a sleepy-eyed woman looked out. Clearly she had just gotten out of bed and was clutching a robe around what was probably nakedness.

"Whata you want?" she demanded. "Man, it ain't even daylight."

"I'm sorry," he said. "Actually, it is, the sun is up. But I apologize for disturbing you. I need very much to talk to you."

"What about?"

"A little boy named Joey Fulton was reported kidnapped by a man in a purple van, and—"

"Ah! That shit again?" Her free hand slapped at the air between them in dismissal. A deep frown cut into her young-old forehead. Behind her skirts, peeping out like chickens, came two small faces. Other noises picked up in the room behind her:

running footsteps, a man cursing at a child. "They ain't nothing to that, man! I told them police so. That little brat down the street yelled before he knew what he was talking about. This here friend of ours offered to take Joey to his camp for the summer, and so we let him, that's all. And the first thing we know the cops are out here asking questions."

"The friend—would you tell me his name?"

She shrugged. "Sure. It was Charlie Smith."

"Charlie Smith." The relief did not come, not yet. "Would you describe him to me, please?"

She reached down and shoved backward on one of the small faces, and it disappeared. She shrugged. "Heavyset. Fat faced. Light haired."

"Blond? Streaked blond, and worn rather long?"

She nodded.

"Does he sell cameras by any chance?"

"You know him?"

Steve nodded. "I think I might. How long have you known this Charlie Smith?"

She motioned vaguely. "I don't know. Six months. A year. He just comes around once in awhile."

"Was Joey Fulton your son?"

"No. He just lived here already when I moved in." She glanced over her shoulder and moved aside, disappearing behind the door, and in her place stood a young man with long, greasy hair.

"Howdy, man," he said. "You looking for old Charlie?"

"I am. Do you know where he's gone?"

"Sure. Up to the mountains for the summer."

"Could you give me an address, or directions to his place?"

"Naw. All I know is he likes to get back in the sticks every now and then. I only been here a coupla months myself, and don't really know the territory. Just drifting through."

The young man leaned against the door and lighted a cigarette. He had a friendly, carefree face. He was willing to talk, but Steve doubted that he knew anything. And the anxiety was swelling, coming alive as it hadn't before.

"This Charlie, he's the one with the purple van?"

"Yeah. A camera salesman. That kid, Joey, didn't seem to have any folks around. I think his old lady skipped out last winter and just left him living here with whoever was here, and old Charlie felt sorry for him, you know? Keena knew he was taking him up to this mountain camp, but the other little kid didn't know. The one he played with, you know? Anyway, Keena was burned all to shit with all the questions. But it's simmered down now. The cops were even gonna get out an APB, but I guess they didn't."

"Thanks for your information," Steve said, and went back down the stairs and over the old man at the bottom. The street outside was beginning to crowd now with moving vehicles, wandering people, as he got into his car and drove back toward the police station.

He was given several *oh you again* looks from calm unhurried faces. The uniforms were still walking back and forth along the room, all beginning to seem like robots to Steve, all dressed alike, but of varying sizes and different races and sex, all wearing the same non-expression on their faces.

"Could you help me," Steve demanded of the first

187

one who wandered close. "I'd like to report a missing boy. I'd like to have that purple van stopped, found."

"What purple van?"

"The one that was supposed to have abducted little Joey Fulton. I'm pretty sure it belongs to a man I knew as Dan Walker, but which seems to be an alias. He has my son, as well as this other boy, and I need desperately to find him."

"If you'll just wait here a few minutes, sir, I'll see if someone can help you."

And again he was left waiting, while the uniformed robot with the expressionless face moved on.

Fifteen

The touch upon Timmy's shoulder was soft and light, but he jerked away from it and cried out again, new sob upon old. Susie's face was close, shimmering and blurring in his flooded vision.

"Don't cry, Timmy," she whispered. "Don't cry."

The laughter rose behind them, and they struggled up, together, and stood close. Uncle Dan watched them from the front fender of the van. "Now that's more like a happy family. Children comforting one another. Little Mother will be pleased when I tell her. How very touching."

Timmy tensed to run, to take his chances with the world of monsters, endless dark woods, and a road that was long miles of no one to help him. But the small and defenseless body of Susie pressed against him, so near and so hard her trembling became his trembling. With a will of its own, Timmy's arm went around her shoulders, and his sobbing stopped.

"Don't you hurt her!"

Uncle Dan motioned upward with open palms. "I

wouldn't think of doing such a thing, Timmy boy, I wouldn't think of it."

Timmy held him with his eyes as he moved, slowly and warily, toward the weed-grown side of the house, his arm pulling Susie along step by step beside him. Uncle Dan leaned against the van fender, folded his arms across his chest and smiled as deceptively as the movements of the snakes he had told them about. He wore many faces, but this was the old one, the one that teased and tormented in adult fun. The one with which Timmy felt most comfortable. When Timmy reached the corner of the house he called back, "I'm going to tell my dad and he'll—he'll—come after you."

"No, he won't Timmy," Uncle Dan said. "Because you see, I'll get to him first, and I just might kill both him and your mom, Timmy, if you ever say a word to anyone. And you know I will, don't you, Timmy boy? If you try to run away, or *anything*, I'll go right to their house and kill them, and no one will ever know who did it. So you had better stay close, Timmy, and keep quiet."

Susie's hands clutched his shirt, pinching into his skin beneath. "I'm afraid," she whispered. "I'm afraid."

He pulled her into the weeds against the house, then gently loosened her fingers and took her hand in his. "Come on, Susie. You stay close to me and Rex and Joey. Come on." There would be some kind of security in numbers, if not safety.

They crept in around the house to the back corner, Susie's hand getting sweaty-slippery in Timmy's. They paused at the corner, but Uncle Dan had not gone around to the backyard. Only Joey and Rex stood there, Joey with his fists pressed hard against his eyes, Rex with his hands plunged so hard and so deep into his pockets they made little bags against his thighs halfway to his knees.

Timmy, pulling Susie, cut across the yard to stop near them.

Joey took his fists out of reddened eyes and looked at Timmy and Susie, and looked at them again, one to the other. "You're back," he said, and let out his breath. "You're back, and I'm glad."

"Me too." Timmy released Susie's hand and wiped the wet from his palm and onto his shirt.

Rex dug one toe into the soil beneath the pine needles. "Joey cried," he said with no hint of derision. "He was afraid he would hurt you really bad. Did he?" He watched the soil make a little hill in front of his toe.

Timmy remembered Uncle Dan's threat in every pore of his cold-sweating body. His mom and dad. They wouldn't know not to let him into their house. They wouldn't know what that laugh meant, nor the slit of his eyes. They would laugh with him, like always, thinking he was their friend. And they might even invite him to spend the night in the guest room, and when they were asleep . . .

"No," he said hastily, the words coming with bitter spit into his mouth, "he didn't hurt me bad."

"I don't like him anymore," Joey said.

Rex slapped his hand over Joey's mouth, and Joey accepted it with widening eyes that followed the larger boy's darting glance toward the house.

"Don't talk like that," Rex said, "if you don't want

the same as Tim got. They might be listening. Let's go play something just like always. Just like nothing ever happened." He removed his hand from Joey's face and placed it companionably on his shoulder.

"What'll we play?" Timmy asked, with no interest in any possible game. "We have to keep Susie with us. We ought to play something she can play, too."

His back burned in pain still, but it was lessening with moments of blessed relief. Timmy bit his lip and tried to forget that his back felt hot and raw and bleeding, with his shirt sticking to it in places, and the sun scalding the wounds right through the shirt. He felt an instinctive need to run to the creek and lie down in cool water, but felt a deeper, social need to pretend his back didn't hurt at all.

"I guess we ought," Rex said in answer. "if she wants to play with us. She never did before. I guess we could look for arrowheads again. Susie, you can help us look for arrowheads."

They sat together under the tree, in silence. Rex half-heartedly lifted pine needles and dropped them. His eyes raised often to sweep the house, and a tiny furrow of thought settled on his forehead.

Susie sat with her back against the tree, and Timmy squatted near her feet. The heat of the day droned around them with the rising buzz of June bugs in the air and jarflies and katydids in the trees. Joey lay down, curled, and rested his head on his arm. He was the first to speak.

"I wonder why Dale don't come out and play?" His lower lip drooped in a pout. "He likes to play with me."

Rex stared in silence at the house.

Timmy had nothing to say. He wished he could ge

to a telephone and call his mom and dad and warn them about Uncle Dan, but he hardly dared move, for Uncle Dan might be watching and go to carry out his threat even sooner.

Or he might tell Little Mother, and next time the punishment would be even worse.

"I got this idea," Rex said in a low voice, his eyes on the house. "This here Little Mother, she gives all the orders. Dan, he just carries them out. She can't get out of her room much, or she don't want to get out of her room or something. So if she likes us, we'll be okay. Whata you think?"

No one answered him.

Somewhere in the house was a definite sound, a door closing, a voice speaking, another, lighter voice answering, and steps on a weakened board.

A harsh warning issued from Rex's mouth: "He's coming. Don't move. Pretend you don't know yet. Don't look up until he says something."

The back screen door of the house opened and closed softly, and then came the clapping sound, palm against hard palm, and Uncle Dan's silky, deceptive voice calling cheerfully, "Come children, don't be shy. Little Mother has sandwiches for you."

Timmy felt himself incapable of moving, so consumed was he with a sudden terror that weakened his muscles and caused his tongue to turn to leather in his mouth. Rex tugged at him though, stretching his sleeve upward, demanding wordlessly that he rise.

Timmy's legs obeyed, and Rex whispered from the corner of his mouth, "Don't make him mad again."

They moved woodenly to the wash table, and Rex pumped water, a cold, clear, steady stream that fell from the rusted metal mouth like a miniature waterfall. Joey cupped his hands under it and drank.

"I'd kinda like to go to the creek again," he said. "It's so hot today. Whew. I wonder if Uncle D- if Papa would take us to the creek."

"Yeah, he might," Rex said, "if he don't get mad again. We can ask him after we eat."

"Not me," Timmy said. "I'm not going to ask him." Uncle Dan would have to go with them, he'd not let them go alone. "I don't want to go anywhere with him, not ever, anymore."

"Then," Joey said, sympathetically, "why don't we pour water on each other from the pump? Why don't we dig us a bigger hole right here under the pump and make us a real honest to goodness swimming pool?"

"Yeah, that's a good idea," Rex said, again agreeably, "Maybe we could. Okay now, we gotta eat. You gotta eat, Tim. Remember."

Timmy knew he was right. The less attention he drew to himself the better it would be. Even if he were sick in the toilet later, where no one would see.

He looked around for Susie and found her not far away. She didn't cringe when he looked at her, and he made his silent gaze tell her he was still her friend, and he knew she was his. She was just a little girl, and she needed a mom like his own. He thought of them together, his mom and this little girl, and it made him feel warm and safe during the firefly lighting of the thought.

They ate in the backyard, sitting on the ground. Uncle Dan brought out sandwiches and lemonade and placed them on a cloth he had spread down on the grass.

The sandwiches wadded in Timmy's mouth, threatening at times to choke him, but he washed it down with lemonade, which was cool and refreshing though made without ice.

Uncle Dan was talking again about monsters and snakes and other even more horrible, unnamed creatures that lived in the woods, that dwelt in the trees, that even came up out of the ground, but Timmy heard only a word now and then and the false timbre of friendship in his voice.

From the house at times he thought he heard the sounds of singing, and he wondered, is she singing to Dale? Are they having their own picnic in her room?

After the sandwich platter was empty and the pitcher of lemonade drained into the last glass, Uncle Dan gathered it all up and went back into the house. Timmy followed him in his thoughts and wondered if he had gone into the bedroom to talk to Little Mother, of if she had come into the kitchen and was standing back in the shadows where she would be unseen, but where she could look through the window and see them. He felt chilled knowing that she might be watching him and could see how hard it was to eat the sandwich her hands had prepared. Would she be angered again?

Joey said, "I wonder if Dale is eating with Little Mother?"

"Sure, he is," said Rex.

"How do you know?" Joey asked, not challenging, just wanting confirmation.

"I just know."

Joey seemed satisfied. He smiled to himself, pleased with the thought of Dale's lunching with his new mother.

They finished the last of their sandwiches in silence. As the sun climbed in the sky, the shade moved away from Timmy and the sun shined down upon his back. It felt stiff now and sore, no longer alive with pain.

After a long while Uncle Dan came out again. The face he wore was pleasant and smiling, as though all was well with Little Mother.

"What would you children like to do this afternoon?"

After a long pause, during which no one else ventured a response, Joey said timidly, "Could we play in the water at the pump?"

"At the pump! Don't you feel that's a bit cold?"

"It ain't bad," Rex said, and punched Timmy. "Is it, Tim?"

"Uh—no. No."

Uncle Dan turned a slow grin upon Timmy. "Well, the cat didn't get your tongue after all, eh, Timmy boy?"

Timmy kept his eyes down. He might be forced into politeness, but nothing could make him look into those slitted eyes again. "No sir," he said briskly, daring not to call him by any title, not Papa, not even Uncle.

Joey said eagerly, "We—we—could we make us a swimming hole under the pump, Uncle Dan? I mean—I mean, Papa? It's already got a little bitty hole started, and we could dig it out and make it real deep and pump it full of water and have us a place to swim."

"Oh my goodness, what ambition my youngest son has. I used to be like that. I was always thinking up interesting things to do, even though I wasn't the youngest, like you, Joey. I was the oldest. My, but we had a good time, just like you're going to have from now on!''

Uncle Dan stood up and slapped his hands against his heavy, bulging trunks of thighs. "I know, children, we have the big old galvanized bathtub. I'll bring it out and you can use it for a swimming pool. Of course it will only hold one child at a time, except in a tight squeeze, but at least it holds water and you can cool down. And do remember to bathe yourselves with soap while you're playing, so Little Mother will be pleased with your cleanliness.''

He went to the rear of the house and lifted down the bathtub that hung on cedar posts. He dragged an old bench and the tub near the pump and stood back, smiling.

"All right, children, go at it. You can lay your clothes on the bench. I'll be back out to check on you later, and I'll be looking behind every ear here, so take care in washing. And, I might add, keep your voices down. I don't want you to disturb Little Mother during her afternoon rest.''

Timmy pumped water, draining fear, anger, and time in the physical labor of swinging with all his weight on the iron pump handle to bring it down squealing and groaning to the depth required to send a rush of well water squirting from the protruding lower lip of its iron snout. He found a mind-occupying interest in the gushes of water, and if he swung hard enough and fast enough on the rusted old handle, the water kept up a fairly steady expulsion.

His arms began to tremble with weakness, but he hung doggedly to the handle, keeping it jumping like the pump car he had seen once on a railroad track at the antique city of Olden Days. The tub filled and overran, and a small stream issued onto the ground, cutting a narrow path among the pine needles.

Joey waded delightedly in the miniature stream and began to laugh with the joy of mud squishing between splayed toes.

Susie stood aside and watched, and finally ventured in, barefoot, and the mud delighted her, and for the first time Timmy saw her smile.

Rex sat down in the tub of water, legs and elbows hanging out like a skinny spider, and leaned his head back, face toward the sun's heat, his eyes closed.

"More, Tim, more," he cried in pretended ecstasy, and Timmy rode the handle in even greater fervor, his feet leaving the ground each time the handle soared toward the sky, his weight bringing it down again.

It was like seesawing, in a way, only without a partner on the other end, just the weight of the water. This way he didn't have to worry about someone's jumping off and leaving him to crash his tail on the ground.

When he was finally exhausted, he dropped into a limp pile beside the spider boy in the tub. And after awhile Uncle Dan came out again and started his campfire for the evening cookout, and the sun turned into a red ball behind the trees, and shadows lengthened, and the silent woods darkened even more. A bullfrog far down the mountainside near the creek began a low-voiced bellow that touched the ridge air as faintly as a wisp of mist rising.

They remembered suddenly to wash their ears, but they forgot their muddied feet until Uncle Dan came over and herded them back to the tub of water. But he didn't make them take off their clothes and wash all over. He was glum and yawning, not seeming to be interested in talking or teasing or even noticing that they were there, and it made it easier for Timmy to sit near the bench and eat the hamburger he gave him. Although, covered by creeping darkness, Timmy threw bits of it into the weeds for the ants to find and carry off to their ant hills. Little bits of treasures, so big in an ant's eye it took two to carry.

Timmy became aware he had a stomach. A strange, rebelling section in the middle of him that had griped and ached before the hamburger now pulsated like a red dwarf in the heavens and sent waves of nausea to his throat. He threw away the rest of his hamburger. He refused potato chips and cookies when Rex silently held them out to him. Everybody sat yawning, it seemed. Except Uncle Dan who had gone into the house again, and except Timmy, who pressed his hand to his mouth to keep the glowing star of his stomach from erupting and spewing and turning into a black hole.

Uncle Dan came back bearing a tray with four glasses of liquid. He gave one first to Susie, then Joey, Rex, and finally Timmy. "Drink it up," he said. "Every drop. Good for you. Make you sleep good."

The dying campfire created in Dan's face hollows, caves, and dark pits and made his nose long, pointed, and lighted on the end like a witch's nose with a wart. His black hole eyes paid particular attention to Timmy. "Drink it. I want to see that glass emptied."

Timmy raised it to his mouth. The ants would not like this orangy drink, could not carry it away and

199

save him. He set the empty glass on the bench, and his revolting stomach expanded and came closer to his throat. He got up and tried to look casual and strolling as he went down the path to the toilet in the evening mists. Alone, he closed the door, and in the created lightless and smelly dungeon he fumbled for the long seat at the back with the three holes. He thought fleetingly of the spider in the corner. His hands found the edge of a hole and he put his face in and was achingly sick. But his emptied stomach settled back, leaving him weak and dizzy but relieved. He leaned against the seat as the trembling stopped and he began to feel more like Timmy Malcolm.

When he returned to the others even Rex was yawning. And his own eyes began to feel as though their lids were being dragged downward by little invisible weights. The sun was still a glow in the west, and the moon a great glowing ball coming westward through the eastern trees like a mirrored reflection of the sinking sun. On the hillside sloping toward the hollow a screech owl began its eerie night cry, but Uncle Dan said nothing about ghost children tonight.

"Early to bed, early to rise, makes children happy, wealthy and wise," he sang instead as he stood up and stretched and his belt slipped and settled beneath his belly. "Come on, children."

They were left in the hall to find their way to bed, and they settled into their bunks too tired to stir.

The pillow cradling Timmy's head was a soft cloud that comforted and carried him away where he was safe for another night.

Sixteen

Dan stood on the porch and stared out into the darkness, his face puckered into a frown of concentration. The faint light from the kerosene lamp in the living room, beyond the uncurtained window, cast a yellow glow on the hood of his van. Darkness came early here among the tall trees. Far beyond the mountaintops there was still a trace of pink in the western sky.

He had just remembered something that stirred a faint uneasiness in the middle of his belly, like indigestion beginning. He had promised old Steve he would call. If he didn't make that telephone call Steve and Connie would have the police out looking for him, thinking he might have driven into a canyon or something. He could see now that bringing Timmy along might make complications along the way, but he would never admit it to Little Mother. She hadn't ever wanted him to bring a child of living parents. It was so hard to wean them away; but Timmy was such a beautiful little boy he couldn't resist. He was a perfect addition to their growing family.

He'd better get to a telephone now and make that call, and make it sound good. Set old Steve's mind at ease. He could tell him they would be going camping deep into the mountains, perhaps the Rockies, and wouldn't be close to another phone for several days, and that would give him plenty of time to figure out how to handle Steve and Connie, the only people he knew who might try to interfere with his plans to build a happy family life. He didn't want to have to destroy them in order to shut them up, but if he had to, he would.

But meantime, while he was doing a lot of thinking about it, he had a phone call to make.

He stuck his head in the door long enough to call to Little Mother, "Want anything from the store down the valley way? I'm going down for some cigarettes."

A little lie wouldn't hurt. It was better than letting her know that he still hadn't solved the problem of Timmy's parents.

He looked to see if she might be sitting in the only comfortable chair in the living room, beside the lamp, reading a magazine. She had always liked magazines.

Dan withdrew before questions could be asked. She was not sure that Timmy even belonged in their family, and if she knew about Steve and Connie and that they were both still alive, she would be very disapproving. She might even get angry.

The road down the hill was long, steep, and treacherous, part of it with layers of rock like tiered

tables, one above another, as though at one time long
ago a stream had flowed there. Dan drove it as fast as
he was capable of handling the van, dropping off at
last into a road that was less rocky but filled with ruts
that were, much of the time, mud holes. The road
wound on down a narrow, tree-filled valley alongside the widening creek. Here he gained more speed,
and the van bounced from mud hole to mud hole
along the bottom of the hollow.

The easiest way out, he decided as he drove, would
be to leave a message for Steve. Not talk to him at all.
That way, he wouldn't have to answer any questions.
Steve would have to take the message and like it.

He saw with relief that a light was still on in the
little country store. One bulb burned brightly at one
side of the sagging screen door, calling to it every bug
in the neighborhood. The owners of the store, an
elderly man and his wife, sat alone in rocking chairs
farther along the narrow front porch that ran the
length of the building, watching him, watching
everything that occurred within their sight. Here the
graded, gravel county road came, made a wide spot
and a turn in front of the store and the single gas
pump, and then went on past to cross the old iron
bridge above the swelling creek. Most of the cars and
trucks that came this way and stopped at this store
belonged somewhere in the neighborhood farther
along the widening valley and back in surrounding
hills. The owners of the store stared at Dan harder
than they would have a customer they were used to
seeing, but neither of them moved.

Dan got out of his car, leaving the door open. His
friendly salesman smile was on his face. "Good

evening, folks. Do you mind if I use your telephone?"

"Help yourself," the old man said. He was wearing the old timer's native dress of overalls and blue shirt, and looked as though he hadn't a worry in the world. "It's inside the door hanging on the wall."

After the screen door had closed behind the man, Evelyn Gunning cast a sharp sideways glance at her husband and then stealthily eased her chair nearer the door and leaned far over the side, her ear sharply in search of any stray word. Her husband gave her a silent and critical glare, but she paid him no attention. She had been watching the world go by this particular corner for fifty years, and when something as unusual as the man at the telephone came along, she intended to hear what he had to say. She repeated from the corner of her mouth, in a low voice, the conversation as she could hear it, and even though her husband had shown disapproval at her eavesdropping, he allowed her to pass the word along.

"He's calling a hospital somewhere," Evelyn hissed, leaning farther toward the door. "It's long distance, taking a lot of change."

Irvan Gunning smoked his pipe and watched the lightning bugs in the trees across the road and the light and shadows cast by the rising moon. Somewhere down the valley a truck was climbing a hill. Its low whine was almost musical it was so far away, so intermingled with the calls of the whippoorwills and the katydids and the frogs.

"Shhh," Evelyn said, even though Irvan hadn't spoken, and then, "there, he got someone. Leaving a message, I reckon. Everything's all right, Timmy having great time, he says. Hmmm. Listen. Short phone call." She straightened up and adjusted her chair.

The door squeaked open. The heavyset blond man came back out onto the narrow porch, gave them his wide smile, thanked them, and drove back the way he had come.

Evelyn stared after him, watching the tail lights disappear into the trees.

"I hadn't noticed that truck going up that road lately, had you, Irvan? Where could he be going but to the old Clanton place? And that place was abandoned years ago, except—"

"No, it sold a couple of years ago. That's probably the owner."

"But I thought those people were gone. I don't remember seeing that woman down here since, let me think. Was it last summer or a year ago last summer? And is that the same man that was with her?"

"I think it is."

"Remember her, Irvan? A tall woman, with black hair that hung nearly to her waist. She had it pulled back into one of them ponylike tails."

"Naw, she just had it tied at the nape of her neck."

"Well anyway, I wondered what she wanted with so much hair. She didn't say much as I remember. But I hadn't seen that van around here. That wasn't the car they were driving then, was it?"

"I think so."

"No, it wasn't. They were driving a blue pickup with a camper on the back. They came down three times for groceries, and I hadn't seen them again for a couple of months, and then they came for groceries

205

again. Then last summer—oh yes, I remember now. Last summer I don't think she came down at all. Just sent him for groceries. They don't show up very often. I hadn't even seen that van go by. I didn't know they were back."

"Went by at night probably."

"Had to."

"I figure they just stay up there for their vacations."

"Well, maybe. I asked her once if they were going to make their home there, but she didn't answer me. Not very friendly people, or something."

"Didn't figure it was any of your business, maybe."

"Well that's not a friendly attitude. Why wouldn't I be interested in whether they were fixing up the old Clanton place to live in or if they were building a new house somewhere?"

"I guess that people who get that far back want to be left alone." Irvan puffed on his pipe and tried to listen to the gentle night sounds of nature. His wife had a love of the unusual that struck him as a borrowing of trouble, and he wanted none of it.

"It seems to me," she said after a thoughtful pause, "that something odd is going on here, Irvan, something odd."

"Ahhh—it ain't, Evelyn."

"Where's that woman? And didn't they have a child once, Irvan?"

"Once, I think."

"There's no other way in to that place except past here, and that man had to have made a point in coming by after midnight or I wouldn't have missed seeing him. Why does he only go by after dark?"

"Just happens that way, I expect."

"Something strikes me as odd. Why don't we call the sheriff and tell him to drive up there and meet those folks?"

"What for? It ain't none of our business, Evie, none of our business at all."

"It's the sheriff's business to see that the county don't harbor no fugitives. I think you'd better call him. It wouldn't do any harm that I can see."

"Well, I *ain't* calling him. And neither are you. Leave the folks alone, Evie. Mind your own business for once."

She let out a sniff of indignation and then was quiet, except for the angry little creak of her chair as she rocked.

A nurse looked in to the private room where Connie lay in the raised bed and motioned for Steve. He left the chair at Connie's bedside and went out into the hall.

"There was a phone call and a message left at the nurses' station, Mr. Malcolm, if you'll go there they can give it to you."

She went on into the next room with a tray of medicine, and Steve hurried to the nurses' station, an island in the center of a network of hallways and waiting rooms. A nurse with a blue stripe on her cap looked up, smiled, waited.

"I'm Steve Malcolm. There was a telephone call for me?"

"Oh yes, a message just came in from a . . ." She picked up a note pad and looked at the scribbles on it.

"From Dan Walker. He said to tell you all was well and Timmy was having the time of his life. He said also to tell you they would be going camping back into the mountains and wouldn't be near a phone for several days, but not to worry, everything okay."

She looked up smiling, a pretty, middle-aged face beneath neat hair and sharply clean cap.

The first quick pang of relief Steve felt was instantly wiped away. "Why wasn't the call given to me?"

"He said not to bother you, that he just wished to leave a message."

"Did he say where he was calling from?"

"No, he didn't."

"Thank you."

Steve wandered slowly back along the hallway toward Connie's room. What did the phone call really mean? Why hadn't Dan asked to speak to him, or why wasn't the call relayed directly to Connie's room? Dan had to have deliberately chosen to leave a message only at the nurses' station, had to have chosen not to talk to him.

Instead of being relieved by the phone call, he felt a sudden and more urgent need to find Dan, to find Timmy before . . . *what*? He only knew he had to hurry. There was no time to be lost. The police had finally told him they would issue an alert for Dan Walker and the purple van, but the day had dragged by with no further word.

He paused outside Connie's room to compose himself. To force his own features into the expressionless mask that the professional people so often wore.

She was watching for him, the light on the head of her bed turning her fair hair golden, shadowing the depressions in her face.

"Was it Dan?" she asked. Her voice was faint, and a bit weak, softened and slowed by painkillers. The nurse with the medicine was beside her bed, preparing another hypodermic. This one, Steve guessed, would put her to sleep for the night.

"Yeah, it was Dan."

"And Timmy—did you talk to him?"

He had to think fast. Somehow, he had to go after Timmy and Dan without alerting Connie to any of his feelings of danger. A shock now, he was afraid, would kill her. The doctors said she was doing great and would be home on time, running races with him and Timmy in three months. But instinct told him that now was a crucial period of convalescence, and she needed no worries. But how was he going to go after Timmy without alarming her? He needed more than one night.

He held her hand and leaned over to kiss her. "Timmy's fine, but Dan fell and broke his ankle," he said, surprised at the smoothness of his lie, "and they're at a place miles from a bus line, so we'll be bringing Tim with us after all. I think he'll get along fine here, and the doctors say you're doing great, so he can hang around with me until you get home, even go to work with me, I guess. Will you be all right if I go on and get him? It'll take me a couple or three days probably—"

"Yes, I'll be fine. I'm glad you're going. I wish we'd made other arrangements for him anyway."

"It'll take me two or three days." Or more. How

many more? And perhaps it would never end, this search for his son. But he couldn't think of that, not while Connie was watching him so closely.

"That's all right," she said, "just keep in contact by phone, okay?"

"You know I will."

He kissed her, and then he left her, hurrying down the stairs rather than waiting for an elevator, running to the car lot, making plans as he unlocked the car, as he began to drive.

First, a map of all states north, west, and east. The Boston Mountains were in Arkansas, he was sure, and if Dan hadn't gone there, he was lost.

He stopped at a service station only long enough to fill his gas tank and check an Arkansas map. The Boston Mountains covered a large area in the central west, a large gray area into which only a few roads trailed their thin little dotted lines. From the south there were four major highways, widely spaced. Dan had to have entered on the most convenient one of those, and Steve would do the same, driving all night, stopping at the sheriff's office in each county seat, and somewhere along the way maybe God would be on his side.

Seventeen

Timmy's sleep was black and heavy, without the wanderings of the creative dream mind, so that he hardly knew when the dim light went out in the room and the door closed firmly, closing in the dark.

When he awoke, grasping the edge of a cry in the night, it seemed that only a moment in time had passed. But the night was deep and silent around him, as though the hour were much later than it seemed. The jarflies and katydids had stopped making their summer noises and were asleep now in the dead of night, the last hours before the dawn. But echoing in Timmy's mind was the sound that had awakened him, returning hauntingly to make him wonder. The cry had been a part of a dream? Or the owl that might not be an owl?

He listened, intently, searching for a repeat of the sound that had brought him so suddenly awake. Someone in a bunk across the room breathed in slow, heavy rhythm, but there was nothing else, not even the cry of the screech owl.

The silence began to throb in his ears, sounding like the waterfall far down the hill, and a closer, more definite sound emanated from the wood of the house, of movement somewhere. He lay very still, ears pounding with the beat of his quickening heart, and a definable sound broke free and became footsteps in the night.

The door opened so softly, so stealthily, and the footsteps padded on bare feet into the room. Timmy held his breath, feeling its pressure swelling in his lungs. From across the room the deep, rhythmic breathing went on, and on, undisturbed by this alien presence that stood among them.

The soft, plodding steps crossed the room, past Timmy's bed to the other bunk beds, and paused.

Bedding rustled softly, a bedspring squeaked like a tiny mouse in fear or pain. There was a soft sigh, and a long moment of utter silence except for the undisturbed sleeper.

Timmy mentally traced the intruder and came to Susie's bed. The lower bunk beneath where Rex slept.

The footsteps moved again, less slowly, came past Timmy's bed and went out into the hall, and the door closed. Timmy lay unmoving until the footsteps blended into the whispering movements of the house.

Someone had come and taken Susie from her bed, and had carried her away? She had not cried out. She had not awakened. Had he taken her to see Little Mother? Did he take her while she slept so that she wouldn't cry? Or was it Little Mother herself who had crossed the room in darkness?

He threw off the blanket and slipped out of bed and made his way through the total dark to the bunk where Susie should be sleeping. His hands groped at the mattress edge, found the pillow, and touched the baby fine curls tangled there. His fingers felt the velvet softness of a round cheek. She did not stir. Her breathing was slow and nearly inaudible.

He moved back, only partly satisfied. They had not taken her away. Then why had they come? Whoever they were, human or nonhuman. What had they wanted with the sleeping girl? Since they had not taken her away, then they must have brought her back from somewhere. Or had Little Mother just come in to look at her?

Could she see in the dark?

He climbed onto the middle of his own bed, his disturbed thoughts circling like doves in a clouding sky, finding no branch of freedom upon which to light.

There were movements in the house, undefinable now, indistinct, the merest whisper of a voice, of Little Mother's voice? And then there was silence again, and the silence seemed more ominous than the other. He did not lie down again but sat hunched, listening, waiting for he knew not what—but something, something that screamed its happenings in silence.

The room gradually took on a gray shadow-and-light quality. The sharp corners and posts of the bunk beds grew visible. The pulled blind at the window became a lighter rectangle. A bird chirped the coming of day, and from somewhere in the early, misty dawn came the faint, ringing echo of hammering, as of a metal stake being driven into the ground by a maul. The sound seemed both eons distant, and yet somewhere near and frighteningly personal.

Timmy sucked in his breath and listened, and every sharp drive of the stake trembled in his flesh. He left his bed and moved soundlessly to the door. The hall was silent, dark, empty, doors along its length closed. The driving of the stake, or the hammering, became inaudible now, and Timmy wondered if whoever was there had finished.

He went on through the kitchen, his bare feet soundless on the floor. He found the back door unlocked and stepped out into the damp fog rising from the mountaintop, forming a cloud in the treetops. He pulled the door shut behind him, and again now he heard the echoing ring of metal against metal, or metal against stone, from somewhere down the fog-shrouded ridge behind the house.

He followed the sound, bare feet tender against unyielding rocks. Thick undergrowth foliage dripped morning dew, and night's darkness lingered in the clutches of heavily leafed bushes and drooping tree limbs. Weeds and briers scraped his bare legs and caught his undershorts and knit undershirt with thin, grasping hooks and burrs. A morning whip-poorwill called from a deep hollow, and the hammering paused for a few moments, then began anew.

The sound became loud and clear as he moved cautiously nearer through the woods, going beyond the blackberry thicket, and on farther than he had gone when he had searched for Dale.

Timmy saw the man suddenly and unexpectedly,

and dropped to his belly behind the twisted roots of a large tree. He was in the edge of a tiny clearing, shaded by tall pines whose tops were lost in the fog, and it wasn't a stake being driven but a hole being dug by a pickax that rang again with each powerful drive into the rocky ground. Uncle Dan's large wedge-shaped back rippled when he raised the pickax and drove it a few inches deeper into the stony ground. Timmy had not been seen, not yet, but his breath choked his heart with the realization that if Uncle Dan turned toward him there would be no way to make himself invisible. He lay on the damp leaves of the ground, his fingers digging into velvet moss at the base of the tree, and watched spellbound the rise and fall of the pick. The red clay hole at which Uncle Dan dug was about the size of his dad's old army trunk, three feet long and two feet wide.

And then Timmy saw the other thing.

It lay upon the ground just beyond the hole and looked like a bundle of blankets wrapped in a short, round oblong shape like the cocoon of an unborn butterfly. Parts of the blanket were stained almost black, and Timmy recognized the pink and blue plaid with a stinging coldness growing and spreading over his skin. It was a blanket from one of the bunk beds. It was a blanket like the one on his own bed. And on Susie's and Joey's and the others. But there was a difference in this blanket. There was a large, red flower among the pinks and blues, the edges curved and curling and turning black.

Blood on the blanket.

Not a red flower, but red, fresh blood with the edges dried to blackness.

Time hung suspended in Timmy's moment of mesmerized horror.

Uncle Dan put down the pickax and picked up a shovel. He bent at the waist, scraping clay from the bottom of the hole. He threw aside the shovel, and it clanged metallically against a rock. He stooped again and picked up the bloody blanket and tossed it into the hole, and it dropped heavily with the burden it covered. The man stepped upon it then, trodding it down with his feet, forcing it to fit into the tiny, shallow grave. He took the shovel again and scraped the pile of soil back into the grave, tamping, prodding, packing.

Timmy began pulling away, backing like a crawfish searching blindly for safety. The scrape of the shovel covered his movements, the sounds of rocks turning beneath his body, of disturbed leaves and crashing twigs that were like gunshots in Timmy's ears. When he had reached the shelter of heavy undergrowth he pushed himself to his feet and hands like a woods creature who had never learned to stand upright and ran in that four-footed crouched figure tearing through the underbrush like a frightened wolf-child.

Timmy took refuge in the toilet, his labored breathing burning his chest and his throat, while behind the toilet, coming through the brush was something following. It made no effort at stealth but clamored through and went on past, now distinguishable as the steps of a man who was in no particular hurry. Timmy saw him through the crack in the door, shovel and pickax in hand. He did not leave them outside the back door but carried them with him into the house. The door closed. Timmy waited, fear of meeting Uncle Dan in the kitchen or the hallway draining his mind of rationality. Would he know, on looking into Timmy's face, what he had seen?

And what had he seen? He didn't know. He couldn't think. His imagination, even his logic, had turned to red clay in his brain.

Eighteen

There was no movement around the house, no sound coming from within. An ugly gray structure, it hovered upon its secrets in stolid silence. But within that house were his friends, Susie, Rex, Joey. He needed the comfort of their presence. He needed to share his secret. Rex would know what to do. Together the four of them could discover what had been buried in that grave.

There was no alternative that came to his mind but to walk boldly to the kitchen door just as though nature had called him early to the toilet. If Uncle Dan saw him, perhaps he would ask no questions.

The kitchen, though, was as silent as when he last saw it, and the doors along the hall were still closed. He slipped into the bedroom unseen and rushed to the ladder to Rex's bed. He climbed and clutched the arm that was flung loosely over the side of the bunk.

"Rex! Rex, wake up." He had to keep his voice down, he reminded himself as he desperately shook Rex's arm. "Come on, Rex, wake up, please wake up."

The boy continued sleeping, mouth open, red hair tousled and mussed. Timmy edged closer and began patting the slack jaws.

"Rex. Rex."

His gaze passed beyond Rex and fell upon the bunk bed where Joey slept. The upper bunk, the one Dale had used, was nothing now but a bare mattress. And the lower bunk, Joey's bed, was hidden in the shadows. But the blanket that should have been there was gone.

Timmy stared at the shadowed edge of that bed, at the white sheet tucked under the mattress. He sought to visualize that blue and pink plaid blanket and the boy who slept beneath it, but he saw nothing but the white sheet. Slowly he backed down the ladder and went to look into the dark corners of the other bunk bed.

Joey was gone.

He knew where Joey was. In the blue and pink plaid blanket with the spreading red flowers and black, dried edges. They had killed and buried him. They had killed . . .

He felt her looking at him, and he turned in slow motion toward her, and saw that her blanket was still clean, still did not have red spreading and seeping out from her.

"Susie . . ."

She did not move. He went closer, seeing her stare from narrow half-moon eyes in strange half light. Was she really alive? He bent down to her and found her stare fixed beyond him and not moving from that point near the bed where he had stood. Her mouth drooped, moisture beaded at the corners, and for a stifled instant Timmy thought she too was dead.

She breathed, though, softly, slowly.

She was alive, but she wasn't really awake. She was sleeping with her eyes half open like a doll whose eyes had stuck halfway down.

In the upper bunk Rex made a smacking sound and turned, and his deep sleep breath quieted as he settled into a new position. A soft snore escaped.

Timmy couldn't lose him again to the deep sleep from which he could not shake him awake, and he scrambled rapidly up the ladder and fell on Rex and shook him savagely. Rex stirred and blinked open his eyes.

"What the hell you doin'?" he demanded in sleepy crossness.

"Rex, wake up. Come on, I've got to talk to you. I *saw* something Rex and I think Uncle Dan—or *she*—killed Joey."

"*What?*"

"He's gone! Joey's gone, just like Dale. They killed him, Rex, and buried him out there. And maybe they did Dale, too. And there's something wrong with Susie, Rex."

Rex sat up and forced Timmy to back down the ladder. He came down after Timmy, long growing legs sticking out from short outgrown pajamas.

"You're crazy," Rex said. "You're crazy as a loony bird. What's wrong with Susie?" He bent and looked in upon her.

"Look at her eyes. They're not shut. They look funny."

Rex gazed upon her. He put a finger on her eyelids and pushed gently downward, and they remained closed. He straightened, grinning at Timmy. "Didn't you ever see nobody sleep with their eyes partway

221

open before? Lots of people do that. I've seen it before. It's nothing to get so scared about. There ain't nothin' wrong with her. How come you woke me up, anyway? It's not even daylight yet."

"Yes, it is." Timmy dug his finger into Rex's arm. The larger boy tried to pull away, but Timmy hung on all the harder. "Joey's gone, Rex. They buried him. I mean, Uncle Dan did."

Frowning, blinking, Rex pried loose Timmy's fingers. He looked in upon the empty bunk that held only a sheet that was still wrinkled from the tossing body of the boy who should have been there. "Where is he?" he asked, as though he hadn't heard Timmy's soft cry, "Out in the woods, behind the house. I saw Uncle Dan bury something there. I think it was Joey."

Rex looked cautiously over his shoulder. His face had grown white in the dimness of the room.

"Shhh. They'll hear you. Let me get my jeans on, then we'll go outside."

Timmy waited, and then he remembered that he wore only his underclothes, and he joined Rex in dressing, in jerking on jeans and shoes and running his fingers through his hair in shaky urgency in place of comb and brush.

When they reached the backyard, Timmy tried again to explain, to get through to Rex. "I followed Uncle Dan, Rex. I mean I followed the sound he was making, and I saw him dig the grave, and he put—he put—" His voice failed him, for there was no way to stop them now from burying Joey.

Rex gazed down at him in hostile aloofness. Only the bloodless, freckle-shot ears betrayed his growing fear that Timmy was right. "They wouldn't do that.

222

Uncle Dan may be a little crazy sometimes, but he wants to adopt us and he wouldn't kill Joey. Why would he kill him? Joey went to bed when we did last night. He didn't do anything to make anybody mad or anything."

"Where is he then? Just like Dale, he's gone."

Rex looked about, from house to wash table to toilet and beyond. "Dale went to—Little Mother. Maybe Joey did, too."

"I saw Uncle Dan dig a grave," Timmy persisted, close to tears, yet too afraid now to cry. "And he put something in it that was wrapped in a blanket like ours. It had blood all over it. It was Joey, I know it was."

"You're crazy. They wouldn't do that. Why would they do that?"

"I don't know. Rex, let's go—" *to the grave. Let's dig it out again and see what is wrapped in the plaid blanket with the black-rimmed red stains.* But could he find the courage to go there again? Yet he had to. It was the only way to really know. "Before they see us, Rex, let's go find it. I'll show it to you."

Rex squeezed his head between both open palms. The pressure twisted his features out of shape. "I feel funny," he muttered. "My head feels funny. It kinda hurts."

"I'll pump you some water." Timmy ran to the rusted brown pump handle without thinking, and it squealed metallically as it moved. "Maybe it'll feel better if you pour water on it."

Rex grabbed Timmy's sleeve, his eyes cut toward the house. "No. Stop. You wanta wake Uncle Dan? He got real mad yesterday when he found out you'd gone back in the woods to look for Dale. And *she* got mad, too, I think. Little Mother."

"Then that's why, Rex, don't you see? Maybe Dale's buried there, too. Maybe he's not with Little Mother after all. Maybe she didn't like him after all!"

Rex shook his head, but his answer was not so negative. "All right, you show me where the grave is. We'll dig it up and see what's there. What did he use to dig it with?"

"A shovel and a pick."

"We'll need the shovel then. Where did he put it?"

"In the house. He took it in with him."

They stood side by side and looked at the house, then turned in unison toward the back woods.

"It was just a little grave," Timmy said. "We can dig it up with our hands."

"Yeah. I never saw no shovel in that house. He must keep it in his own room, under the bed."

They reached the blackberry thicket and went around it, and were in the silent woodland of tall trees and thick undergrowth. English ivy pulled at their feet like green shallow quicksand.

"Maybe it's in that room they keep locked," Timmy said intuitively. "The one where Little Mother stays most of the time."

Rex stopped, looking down at the ivy as though he were trapped in it and could go no further. "Hey! This here is poison ivy. I had that once, and I don't want it no more. It's worse than chicken pox, and I had that too, once."

"No, this ivy has five leaves. Poison ivy's got three. Like that, see?" Timmy pointed to a thick woody vine that coiled around a nearby tree like a long snake climbing. Here and there along its fingered length

224

were twigs of three-leafed ivy with red, poisonous veins. *"That's* poison ivy. Don't touch it."

"This is the same stuff!"

"No. This has got five leaves," Timmy said in exasperation, feeling a sob rise like a bubble into his throat. "Rex, don't you want to find Joey?"

"He's not out here! He's not! Uncle Dan wouldn't hurt him that much. Little Mother wouldn't let him hurt Joey or Dale that much!"

Timmy started on, pushing aside the yielding limbs of a young oak sapling. "Then you stay here. I'm going on."

"All right. But it was something else you saw, I know it was." And he followed behind Timmy reluctantly, unwilling to accept the truth of Timmy's words.

The forest became more impenetrable, the ground boulder-strewn and sloping downward, it seemed. The damp beneath the trees sent gnats fogging into their faces at times, blinding them, getting into their eyes. Timmy tried to orient himself, admitting at last this was not the way.

"We're too far downhill," he said, turning his path sharply right. "It was up high on the ridge. Let's go this way."

"I don't like it out here," Rex whined, batting with both hands the gnats that fogged in humming aggravation about his face. "I can't see a goddamn thing but these little bugs."

"It's this way," Timmy said, battling his way uphill to more level ground, leaving behind the murky dark of junglelike growth and the hordes of insects. "It was beneath some pine trees."

They pushed on, and the nightmare quality began to seem endless, to blend night into day, reality into non-reality as the red on the blanket had blended so gradually to deep and ominous black. He was living in a terror-filled dream that had started days ago, and there was nothing real about it. The burying of the killed creature in the blanket was like the screech owl that was really the crying of lost ghost-children, like the monsters that hid invisible behind each tree and the writhing, waiting snakes in the thick and clinging ground ivy. Reality lay beyond the treetops where the morning sun turned the rising fog to gold and pink and warmth, and where the birds sailed free through the sky. Reality was home, and Mom and Dad and a friendly puppy named Kazan. This was only a nightmare. Rex was part of the nightmare, and Joey, and Dale, and even Susie.

And the mysterious person who lived beyond the door of the locked room. She, perhaps, most of all.

Rex's voice broke through with a stab. "Let's go back. There ain't no grave. You had a bad dream, that's all. I don't like it out here."

Timmy turned right again, choosing the least obstructing way through the brush, hoping he hadn't lost their way permanently in this shadowy world of nightmare dreams. *There is no grave*, he thought. Rex was right. But no, Rex was wrong. There was a grave. But where?

"We'll go back," he said. "And I'll go find it myself, today, or tomorrow. I'll find it myself. I'll keep looking till I find it, and then you'll believe me."

Like a miracle they glimpsed the gray shingle roof

226

of the house through the holes in the canopy of understory trees. They came upon the blackberries and the narrow backyard where the weeds were trampled, where the tall pine trees reached toward the sun.

Rex sat on the bench morosely and nursed the cuts and scratches on his arms with a finger dampened with spit. Timmy looked with puzzled and confused thoughts back the way they had come. Where was the grave? Straight down the ridge, a block away, maybe two blocks. Where were the pine trees that stood sentry over that tiny, new graveyard?

A sudden and terrible urgency gripped him again. "Rex, we can't stay here. We have to leave."

"Why?" Rex asked, dabbing at his scratches. "Uncle Dan wants to keep us, and if Little Mother don't get mad and likes us they're going to adopt us."

Timmy saw that Rex clung stubbornly to his own non-reality, as lost in his dream world as Timmy was still shocked and dazed by his nightmare. The wall between them was as impenetrable as the forest, and Timmy felt lost in his efforts to reach Rex.

"I'm leaving," Timmy said, standing still in front of Rex, his muscles frozen by helplessness. "I'm not going to stay here."

If you disobey, or if you try to run away, I'll kill your mom and dad, Uncle Dan had said. And he had not dreamed that. Any more than he had dreamed this other.

Rex stood up. "Let's go back to our room," he said, 'and wait for Joey to come back."

Timmy went with him, following along because here was nothing else he could do. His mind searched for a solution, and his mind discarded each one that came up. If he could get to a policeman—but no. The hands of the police were tied these days, Timmy's dad said in anger every time he read a newspaper. These days, he said, the courts turned killers loose to kill again. The world of the police went for nothing so much of the time, and criminals went free. Timmy knew the police would not be able to stop Uncle Dan from killing his mom and dad. A threat was not illegal.

If he could reach his dad and tell *him*, maybe then he could stop Uncle Dan. Yes, somehow he could.

Timmy went to Susie's bed and looked in upon her. Blue eyes looked back at him from a hole in the blanket that was pulled into a shawl around her head. He leaned closer, staring into those eyes to be sure they were awake, and he knew they were when she shrank further into her blanket.

"Susie's awake," he said.

Rex made no answer. He paced the room, encircling the small space between beds. And each time he stopped and looked in upon Joey's empty bed, as though somewhere back in the shadowed recesses the little boy had been overlooked. Then he went on to pace a circle around the floor again.

Timmy waited by Susie's bed a moment for a response from her, but she stayed hidden in her blanket with only her eyes exposed. And today they were as wild as the eyes of a trapped animal, and unfriendly, as though she had forgotten who he was.

Timmy moved away, took his pen knife from his pocket and played with the small blade. But there wasn't much a boy could do with one blade, so he pu it away and climbed onto his own bed and sat watching Rex wander the room.

Timmy wished he had not fallen on his Christmas watch that day playing touch football and broken it. If he had it now he could see what time it was. It seemed hours and hours ago that he had watched Uncle Dan bury that thing in the woods.

"Children!" the voice called just before the door opened.

. Uncle Dan peeped in with a face smiling like an evil Santa Claus, an imposter who really didn't love children at all but who offered candy and gifts to trap them forever.

"Come on, children, rise and shine."

Rex pressed his back against the double bunks that had been Dale's and Joey's beds. Uncle Dan came on into the room, pushing the door back against the wall. The smiling lips, the slitted eyes, the bouncing jowls, came toward them. The moist, fat palms clapped for attention.

"Well, look at the boys, all up and dressed? My, but you're early birds, aren't you? My mother always said early birds are good birds, and only the good birds don't have to be punished. How nice that Timmy and Rex don't have to be punished this morning."

Rex stepped forward. "Joey's gone too," he said.

The smile didn't stop. "Joey was a good boy. He went out for a drink last night, and he stopped by to see Little Mother. But then—ah—we just keep losing our boys, don't we, because boys are so bad, so bad. But we still have our Susie girl, don't we? We can't get along without our Susie girl. My no. She's sometimes bad, and sometimes she has to be punished, but one of these days she's going to be as good as Joey and Dale and get to go be with Little Mother. Come on dear, hop out of bed and get a clean dressy on." He held out his arms to her.

Timmy watched amazed as the little girl slowly pushed aside her blanket and crept across the bed on her knees toward the waiting arms. Her mouth had drawn in to a puckered little hole, held tightly, and her eyes continued wild and filled with trepidation. But her body obeyed the command, and she let him pick her up and hold her, and pull over her head a short garment from a suitcase under the bed.

He talked all the while, crooningly, a kind of baby talk that sounded to Timmy more fake than his smile.

"There, that's a nice girl. Susie won't be bad like Timmy and try to run away where the old mountain witch can get her. My mother always said bad things get bad children. The boys are bad. We can afford to lose our boys, but we can't lose our girl. Not yet. No, not yet. Little Mother is so eager for Susie to be a really good girl so she can come in and be with her."

He carried her as though she were two years old instead of a small five.

"Come on, boys, let's go wash up and have our breakfast."

They followed him to the wash table and the bench where he used his hands to wash Susie's face. By the time he set her upon her own feet she reminded Timmy of a real-life robot. She moved, she walked, but she neither spoke, nor smiled, nor seemed alive as she had just yesterday. And Timmy sensed it had something to do with Joey's death.

230

Nineteen

The day moved on into heavy, still heat. Jarflies buzzed in the trees, crickets chirped in the grass. Susie sat in one place hour after hour and played with a small pile of pebbles and sticks she had gathered. Timmy stood for awhile and watched her, and saw she had built a house with pebble walls, and filled it with furniture made of small groups of pebbles, and the sticks were her people. There was a tall stick, and a shorter, fatter stick, and several small sticks. They moved about woodenly in her pebble house, pushed into motion by her fingers, and sometimes the tall stick beat savagely upon the smaller ones, and sometimes the smallest one broke the largest one in two, and it became divided, and instead of being one large adult, it was two children, and they in turn were beaten by a larger stick, and killed.

Timmy moved away, frightened of her game.

Rex was still walking, hands in pockets, around the pine tree, around the bench, and the table, just around. Timmy thought about trying to talk to him, but gave it up as hopeless. Rex hadn't believed him this morning, so why would he believe this afternoon?

If he had a car, and if he could drive—

Suddenly he remembered the van parked under the trees at the front of the house. He had watched his dad drive, and he tried to remember how it was done. First, the key inserted and turned. Then the brake released. But from then on it was a combination of shifting, and guiding, and pedals. He wasn't afraid to try. He could drive, he knew he could. He hoped he could. It was the only way he could keep Uncle Dan from catching him.

He looked around for Uncle Dan, but he had gone into the house.

Like Rex, he put his hands into his pockets. Unlike Rex, he looked at the sky and hummed a tune. He made his stroll seem casual and wandering. He went around the north side of the house and over toward the van.

Footsteps rustled the leaves behind him, and his heart leaped and choked on the tune in his throat. But then he saw it was only Rex.

"Where are you going?" Rex whispered.

Timmy saw the nervous shifting of Rex's eyes and the pale skin behind the darkened freckles.

"Just walking around."

"I been thinking," Rex said, leaning close, his hands in his pockets. "You may be right about some things. Dale and Joey gone, and not a sound out of them. If they're in the room with Little Mother, why ain't we heard their voices?"

"I saw Uncle Dan bury someone. He was wrapped

in a blanket like the ones on our beds, and Joey's blanket is gone. And besides, it was about his size. Little and short." Timmy was shivering again, the scene vivid in his mind. "I know they killed him. I just know they did."

"The thing is," Rex said, "why would they? I believe you," he added hastily, "but I can't figure out why. But if they killed Joey, they must have killed Dale, too. But why?"

"I don't know why. Maybe they made them mad."

"Well," Rex said, "when you leave, I want to go with you."

"Can you drive a car?"

"I did once."

They looked at each other, and the message passed wordlessly between them. Rex eased up to the door of the van and looked inside. Timmy, too short to see, watched the blank and reflecting windows at the front of the house for signs of Uncle Dan or the shadowy Little Mother who might even now be watching them from a window, or a crack in the log walls.

Rex withdrew from the van.

"No keys," he said, low voiced.

They strolled on, behind the van, under the oak trees, around a clump of flowering shrubbery someone had once planted, and to the other side of the van.

"The doors weren't locked though," Rex said. "We could get in."

"What good would that do?"

"We could hot wire it."

Timmy looked down the road. It dropped out of

sight within yards, disappearing over the brink of the hill, canopied by shading trees all along the way. At any other time, with his mom and dad and his dog, it would have been a wonderful road to walk along. But now, it only looked dark and scary. Still, it was the only way to safety, to distance from Uncle Dan and Little Mother.

"How do you hot wire a car?" Timmy asked.

"I don't know," Rex admitted. "I only heard about it from guys."

"Then what will we do?" Timmy cried. "I don't know how to hot wire a car, either!"

"Burgle," Rex said, his eyes shifting from car to house to all hiding places in the overgrown yard.

"What?"

"Burgle," Rex repeated. "Tonight, when everybody's asleep."

"You mean *steal*?"

Rex's eyes settled like wood gnats upon Timmy's face. "Sure. You got scruples or something? You wanna leave here, and you got to have a car, or you won't get nowhere. It's twenty goddamned miles to the closest town, did you know that? I came through it, and I know. There's not anybody living on that road out of here for twenty miles, except at that store down at the crossroads by the river, and that must be ten miles. It don't even deserve to be called a road. It's just a track. If I owned a van like this one, I sure wouldn't have driven it up that rocky road."

"But where would we look?" Timmy asked, hope rising. "Where do you think he keeps his keys?"

"Probably in his pockets. But he takes off his pants to go to bed, don't he? Well, then I'll slip in and ge the keys. You just be ready to go."

"I will," Timmy said. "But what if they don't sleep? Sometimes in the night I hear footsteps and voices. And this morning, when it was still dark, somebody came to Susie's bed and looked at her. But—I don't know why. They didn't take her away. I guess they just looked at her, in the dark. I think Little Mother can see in the dark."

Rex moved away from the car. "We better go. They might see us here."

They gave the van a wide berth, going past with assumed disinterest.

Susie was still sitting by her pebble house, her hands moving slowly and with little enthusiasm. Rex jerked one shoulder toward her.

"What about her?"

"Can't she go, too?"

"She acts kinda dopey. So maybe she won't yell. She either don't say anything, or she screams like double hell."

"Is she sick?"

"I don't know. Maybe." He turned his back toward her and his nervous, darting eyes toward the back door of the house. "Another thing. Don't drink any more of that stuff than you have to. I think he put something in it last night."

"What?" Timmy remembered being sick and losing not only the liquid, but the food. "Why?"

"Who knows? Drugs. Something."

"How do you know?"

"The way your head feels, you know. Didn't your head feel funny?"

"I vomited my food up last night. I didn't feel

anything but sick," Timmy said.

"Lucky you. Get sick again if he makes you drink anything, but don't let anyone see."

"How can I just get sick because I want to?"

"Stick your fingers down your throat, that's how."

"Rex?"

"Yeah?"

"I'm glad you changed your mind about going away. This morning you didn't want to. I was afraid you wouldn't go."

Rex shrugged both shoulders and walked away. Over his shoulder, as an afterthought, he said, "I just been thinking today." He retraced his steps suddenly to stand over Timmy. "Stay awake tonight. Pretend you're going to bed, then put your clothes back on. I'll stay awake, too. When everybody else is asleep I'll go burgle the keys, and then I'll come back and get you. Be ready to go, okay?"

"Okay."

Rex's eyes fell upon Susie again. He snapped his fingers at Timmy, with some of his old confidence, and motioned toward the little girl. "I got an idea," he said. "Come on. I wanna ask her something."

They moved upon her, but she didn't seem to notice. Rex went down on his knees in front of her, scattering one wall of her pebble house. She gazed at it, then raised her eyes.

"Where'd Dale and Joey go, Susie? Did both of them go to see Little Mother? Did Joey go, too?"

She stared at him, unmoving, unyielding.

"You can tell me," he said. "I won't hurt you, or tell that you told."

Timmy asked, "How would she know, Rex?"

236

Rex ignored Timmy. His eyes held Susie's as an adult demanding truth from a child. "You know, don't you, Susie? You know where they are."

Slowly her head began to move, back and forth, in a wordless denial. Her mouth drooped from the white strain of the pucker it had held all day. Her chin trembled.

"Leave her alone," Timmy said. "How would she know?"

"She knows," Rex said. "She knows something, can't you see? What, Susie? Tell me where they are."

Her denial became more vehement. Her breath pulled in, heaving her chest with a long, audible gasp. "I don't know," she whispered, "I don't, I don't."

Rex leaned closer. "If you don't tell we'll leave you here and the same thing'll happen to you that happened to them. You gotta tell."

"No! No! No!" Soft, terrified gasps were now tearing out of her, and she started to roll away from him, going down on one elbow, her bare legs scraping through the ruins of her pebble house. But Rex lashed forward, trapping her with his hold, pulling her back, forcing her head up.

"You know where they are!"

And suddenly she was screaming again, her fists pounding against her own ears.

"I don't! I don't! I don't! I don't!" And on and on, denial after denial, thrown from her with all the terror of her endless hell. "Little Mother—she got them—she did—"

Footsteps clamored through the house, like background drums beating to her screams of fear. The door slammed. Palms clapped together sharply.

"Here! Here! What's going on?" Uncle Dan shoved between Timmy and Rex and rushed to Susie. "Shut up! Shut it up I say!" His voice came almost as loud as hers, and his chin quivered with anger as hers quivered with fear.

She caught her breath the moment she saw him, and the silence was as sudden and unexpected as the screams. Timmy's ears buzzed and throbbed with the dying echoes, and his heart beat rapidly in his chest.

He saw the mirrorlike exterior of the window reflecting trees and sky, shadows of light and dark, and he couldn't be sure whether he saw Little Mother move beyond the glass or if he only saw the reflecting shadows change, but the sight chilled him so that he began to shiver in the hot summer air, a terror growing as great as Susie's. Susie knew—Susie had seen—what had she seen?

"What did you say to Susie?" Uncle Dan demanded. "To make her scream like that?"

"Nothing," Rex said. "Did we, Tim?"

Timmy pulled his eyes from the changing window. "Uh—no—uh, not much. We asked her if she wanted to play, that's all."

"Oh come now. All that fuss over a simple request like that? Don't underestimate my common sense, Timmy boy. What did they want, Susie? And don't give me any more of that silent treatment. If you can scream you can talk. What did they want?"

Timmy heard the soft intake of Rex's breath and felt his own body tense with waiting for her answer, if any, and whatever repercussions it would bring.

She whispered clearly, "They asked me if I wanted

238

to play, and I didn't."

"I'll be goddamned," Uncle Dan said to himself and got up. He dusted his knees and then his hands. He motioned carelessly toward her. "Well, play with her anyway, boys. Do what you want with her. But you'd better keep her quiet. I don't like my sleep interrupted by some dizzy female screeching like an alley cat in heat."

He went back into the house, trailing laughter faintly, and Timmy and Rex looked down upon Susie in consternation.

"See," Rex said. "I told you she knows."

"No, she doesn't," Timmy denied, although in his heart he agreed. But Susie must not scream again. The punishment might come the next time.

"She knows something. But she won't tell." He gave Timmy a sudden, impish grin. "Did you hear what he said? About playing with her?"

Timmy withdrew a bit. Cautious and suspicious. He didn't like the look on Rex's face.

"Do you know what he meant?" Rex persisted.

Timmy turned away abruptly. "Come on, let's go get a drink of water. I'll pump and you hold the bucket under the spout."

Rex's grin faded, his attention wandering. "There's water in the bucket already."

"It's warm. I want some cold water."

Timmy swung on the pump handle, up, down, up, down, until the water gushed forth cold and clear and fresh, deep from some cavern beneath them, and created a small stream in the bed it had run through the day before. And that reminded him of Joey and the mud squishing between his toes, and his delight

239

and his laughter. And Timmy stopped pumping and let the water settle back with a deep gurgle into its underground home.

Everywhere he looked then he saw Joey laughing, his round face vague in the trees, the weeds, even the windows and walls of the house, like a picture puzzle where you find and count all the hidden faces. And beside the faces was the grave, with its bloodied blanket.

He wished for night to hurry, and for the world to sleep.

"What if they catch you?" Timmy asked Rex.

"They won't."

"But what if they did?"

"I said they won't. Okay?"

"But what if they don't sleep? I mean, at all?"

"Whata you mean, don't sleep. Look at 'em, they sleep half the time. Or something quietlike. You know Uncle Dan sleeps, you saw him once."

"But maybe they don't sleep at night." Timmy frowned away into the distance. It was in the early dawn, late in the night, that Dan had dug that grave. That he buried the thing in the stained blanket coffin.

Twenty

The day stretched long ahead. The heavy still heat suggested a trip to the creek might be nice, but Uncle Dan didn't offer to take them, and Timmy's heart wasn't in play of any kind, even in the creek.

He went to stand behind Susie again for awhile, watching her robotlike play. She sat moving her stick and pebble dolls about almost mindlessly, as though to keep her hands busy was the important thing.

Timmy put his hands in his pockets and wandered over toward the pump. The small depression in the ground beneath the spout was slightly muddy, and a mud dauber wasp was busily gathering up a tiny round ball of mud.

Because he had nothing better to do, Timmy followed her when she flew. She went to the eave of the house and disappeared beside a rafter. In a moment Timmy heard the buzz-buzz of her busy homemaking.

A small rock hit the roof near Timmy's head and rolled off to drop at his feet. Timmy turned and saw

Rex, with a mischievous grin on his freckled face, aim another small rock at the roof above Timmy's head.

Timmy's heart lurched, and his body felt as though it shrank several inches as he waited to hear the rock hit the roof and roll. What was the matter with Rex? What if he woke Little Mother from her midday nap?

Timmy ran out into the yard. Maybe if Rex's target were changed, the rock throwing wouldn't be heard.

"Stop it!" he hissed. "Do you want her to hear you?"

Rex only grinned, his hands filled with more rocks; and Timmy felt himself relax. Just having Rex look and act more like his old unafraid self was a help.

"Uncle Dan will be out here after you," Timmy warned, not yet as unafraid as Rex. "What if he—"

As though in answer to Timmy's fears, the screen door opened and Uncle Dan came onto the step. Both boys stared at him. He was wearing the apron again, and the expression on his face was benevolent and effeminate. He had the smile in place, that half smile that now terrified Timmy more than the mean, teasing Dan. His hair was neatly combed straight back from his forehead, fine ridges showing damply the recent separation of blond strand from strand by the teeth of the comb. It was as though it had been raked, Timmy thought, and remembered that Uncle Dan always combed his hair this way when he wore the apron. It was something he just hadn't noticed before.

Timmy thought he might be after Rex because of

the rocks, but Uncle Dan was looking instead at him. He put one hand palm up, fingers curled into palm, and motioned him with one finger.

Timmy moved stiffly forward, afraid to go, afraid not to. When he reached the step he could hear Uncle Dan humming that high-pitched little song.

Dan turned back toward the door and led the way into the house. He went to the rocking chair at the end of the room and sat down. From the small round table nearby, the one on which a kerosene lamp sat, he took a small white jar like a cold cream jar. Timmy found he was having trouble taking his eyes off the jar. He had seen several just like it in his mother's part of the bathroom dressing table. But when Uncle Dan screwed the lid off, Timmy saw that this was different from his mother's. Instead of the white cream, this one held a green ointment.

Uncle Dan sat with his knees pressed together, and he motioned for Timmy to sit down at his feet. Timmy obeyed, slowly, going first down to his heels, then twisting around, and when Uncle Dan's hand pressed downward on his shoulder, he at last sat down with his back to the strong, apron-covered knees.

Dan lifted Timmy's shirt, and humming on and on, pulled it up until it was pressed to the back of Timmy's neck. Then, to Timmy's amazement, he heard the man make a sympathetic moan, and his hand began rubbing the cool ointment over the still tender marks caused by the whipping.

Rex came into the kitchen and stood staring openmouthed. Timmy dropped his head in embarrassment and didn't look at him again after the first glance.

He was vastly relieved when Uncle Dan dropped the shirt over his ointment-smeared back and gave him a gentle push. Timmy stumbled up to his feet. He glanced at Rex again and saw that a wicked one-sided smile had edged onto Rex's face, but instead of being the target this time, Timmy saw that Rex was watching Uncle Dan.

"Hey," Rex said in a low voice and jabbed at Timmy with his elbow. "Watch this. As soon as he gets up and starts cooking, watch this."

Humming, Uncle Dan seemed now to be unaware the boys were still in the kitchen. He put the lid back on the jar, carefully wiped his hands on his apron, and pushed himself up out of the rocking chair with a small grunt.

He went to the cabinet and reached into the canned food section, and now that his back was turned toward Rex, the boy stooped into an exaggerated position of slipping up on someone with bent knees, crooked arms, fingers in claws, and tiptoed slowly toward Uncle Dan.

Timmy pressed both hands to his mouth to hold back the giggles. Rex looked like a cartoon character sneaking along, with the caricatured facial expression of the devil himself, and Timmy couldn't hold back the laughter. It spewed out, between his fingers, and encouraged Rex to act all the more ridiculous, which brought on such hearty laughter from Timmy that he was sure Uncle Dan would forget he was wearing the apron and turn upon them in a fury.

But Uncle Dan seemed unaware. He brought out a can of green beans, and a can of salmon, humming high in his throat, smiling his enigmatic little smile.

Timmy stopped laughing when he saw that Rex was actually going to do something to Uncle Dan, and the thought of it mixed terror with the humor, leaving only a nervous smile that wavered behind his fingers.

Rex carefully reached out and caught the end of the apron tie between two fingers, then with a wink at Timmy, he gave it a hard yank. The apron came untied and sagged forward around Dan's belly.

A frown came and went so quickly on Dan's face that it was little more than a grimace. The humming continued, with only a slight catch. He bowed his head and looked at the billowing front of the apron, then he reached around behind and tied it again into its little bow.

Rex danced backward away from him, and as soon as the bow was tied, he began tiptoeing in again, reaching out to untie the apron.

It was no longer funny to Timmy. He had a queer, uneasy feeling in the pit of his stomach as though he might be sick at any time.

"Hey, Rex—"

Rex grabbed the end of the tie and ripped it undone again, then unable to contain himself he burst into giggles, and with his hands over his mouth, went running out the back door.

Timmy backed away, watching Uncle Dan reach once more to tie the bow. He saw the little smile was gone, and for a moment the humming was silent, but by the time he reached the door Dan was humming again. The smile, though, did not come back.

Timmy escaped into the backyard where Rex sat

doubled over on the grass laughing.

"Hey Rex," he said, squatting nearby. "I don't think you should have done that."

"Why not? Two to one the old bird won't remember a thing. He's crazy when he gets that apron on." Rex stopped laughing and stared at the back door. "I'll be glad when we're outa here."

"Why don't we go now and just walk away? Now while he's got the apron on and won't notice we've gone?"

"For one thing, I don't think he's that crazy. He'd probably see us. And for another it's like I already told you. We'd never get anywhere."

"I gotta go call my mom and dad and warn them against him. He said he'd kill them."

"He did?"

"Yes. He told me not to tell anyone that he whipped me or anything, or he'd kill them. So I have to get to a phone."

"We'll never get there walking, I know. But we can get to one in an hour as soon as I get them keys. Don't you worry, we'll get away."

Timmy glanced over his shoulder at Susie. She was still sitting under the lengthening shadows of the tree but was no longer playing. She appeared instead to be staring at the remnants of her play. And Timmy saw that she had dashed it all to scattered bits. The little walls of the house were gone, and the stick and stone people were thrown into the weeds.

"I better tell her," Timmy said, "so she'll know and won't scream."

He got up and went over to bend down by Susie.

246

"Tonight," he whispered, "we're going to run away, me and Rex, and we're going to take you along. So when I wake you up, don't scream."

She looked up. Her lower lip drooped open, her eyes rounded. She whispered, "No."

"Don't you want to go?" Timmy cried.

She nodded. "But Little Mother won't let you."

Timmy frowned. "She won't know. And neither will he. We're going to slip out."

"Little Mother knows everything. She won't let you go. She'll keep you with her forever, just like she's keeping Dale and Joey, and the little boys and the baby that came with me, Charlie and Teddy, and Terry."

Timmy sat down on his heels, staring into Susie's face. She was talking, at last, but the things she was telling chilled him to the bone. In his heart he was terrified that she was right. He could feel the eyes of the strange Little Mother boring into the back of his head, reading his thoughts, listening to the whispers from the little girl.

Timmy wanted to ask questions of Susie, but his throat closed in his fear. He swallowed, and croaked, "No—Joey isn't with Little Mother, Joey's dead. Maybe Dale's dead, too."

She shook her head. "No, they're with *her*, with Little Mother."

Timmy tried to think of an argument and couldn't. Someone was dead, or something was dead. He had seen the burial. But Dale had gone in to see Little Mother, and maybe Susie was right, and he was still there, with her. But he was so quiet. Why

247

couldn't they hear him talking, laughing, playing? Or crying. Timmy had heard him crying, once, at the beginning.

To be taken to Little Mother was too terrible to contemplate.

Timmy withdrew from Susie, backing away still in a squatting position. Just as he started to rise the screen door opened and Dan, without his apron, stepped out.

"Come on, children, suppertime. Move it!" He was scowling darkly, and his hair had been tousled, as though he had run his fingers through it many times. It fell sideways on his face in a kind of long bang. "If you haven't washed up, you should have. Now I don't want to mess around with you. Rex! Little Mother told me you untied her apron strings this afternoon, not once but several times."

Rex made a noise in his throat, and Timmy thought he was going to say something, to object, probably, denying that he had untied the apron more than twice, but instead of speaking at all, he went passively into the house.

When Timmy followed him in he saw that Rex was already seated at the table, his face long and morose. He didn't meet Timmy's eyes.

"Now then," Uncle Dan said, as he shut the door behind Susie, "I'm going to light only one lamp. You're going to have to go to bed as soon as you eat, before it gets dark, because there's not going to be a light in your room tonight. There'll be no niceties tonight, not after the way you treated Little Mother. I'm not going to eat with you, either, and I want you to know I will tolerate no noise out of you while I'm out of the room."

Without a word, Rex helped himself to green beans and cold salmon. Timmy was afraid to look up at Uncle Dan, but he saw from the corner of his eyes that Dan carried a food-laden tray as he went into the hall and out of sight toward the front of the house. Or perhaps to the door that was kept locked. He didn't know exactly where he stopped, for the footsteps seemed to go on and on, as though someone walked slowly and softly in a circle, never stopping, never resting.

After a long while there came the low mumble of Uncle Dan's voice, and answering, a finer voice, only a word spoken, or a murmur, floating through the air as thinly as a spider's web.

Shadows fell as the children ate. The glow from the lamp on the small table by the rocking chair grew in long, yellow streaks across the bare wood floor. When they had finished, Susie slowly adding to her mouth the last green bean on her plate, Rex got up and gathered the three plates and set them carefully on the cabinet. When he started down the dark hallway toward their room Timmy and Susie followed. Light edged the locked door and fell in a tiny figure eight through the old key hole. Susie pressed to the wall away from it, and, Timmy noticed, Rex gave it a berth as wide as possible in the narrow hall.

The footsteps were quiet now, as though someone had stopped to listen, and perhaps to watch, as the children slipped into the darkening bedroom.

Timmy found his bed and slipped into it without undressing. Now, in the comparative safety of his bed, he felt suddenly and overpoweringly sleepy. Tonight none of them had been taken to see Little Mother. Tonight—they would escape. Susie was wrong, wrong. They could—they would get away. All of them.

Twenty-one

Timmy sat in the dark in the corner of his bunk trying to stay awake. He could hear Rex moving on the other side of the room. There was no sound from Susie's bed. The house crackled now with silence, and Rex's subtle movements were like those of a small, soft creature in the walls. The footsteps were mere whispers crossing the room to his bed.

"Are you dressed?" Rex's voice hissed in the dark at the side of his bed.

"Yeah," Timmy whispered back at him.

"Then lay down and pretend to be asleep in case they check on us. I'll lay down, too. I'll come and get you when I've got the keys."

"Okay."

The footsteps whispered back across the room and became a soft rustle of bedding and yielding bedsprings. Timmy stretched out on his bed and pulled the blanket to his chin. His heart disturbed the silence and sent blood rushing through his strained hearing and gradually became calm and settled. He breathed softly, aware of each breath, and the night settled with its quivering screech owl serenades and the unafraid mating calls of the whippoorwill.

From somewhere then in the throbbing house came the faint vibration of music. He heard the even beat of country blues, felt it in his flesh; and after a long while it had the effect of a lullaby, and his mind drifted and wandered in and out of sleep like mists in the forest trees that finally claimed him against his will and swept him softly into total darkness.

The voice rose in his consciousness, ripping sleep to shreds with all the power of a terrifying nightmare. Someone, somewhere, was screaming, a horrible belly-deep cry that could be human or animal.

Timmy jerked upright in bed clutching his blanket against his heaving chest.

The scream gasped to an end, then rang out again, and this time within its framework a voice cried, "My God! *God, get her away from me!*"

Rex!

Timmy saw in the light that emanated from somewhere in another part of the house that the bedroom door stood open, and as he stared at that faint rectangle of light, he saw a small figure run on bare feet across the room and pass through the doorway. Susie! Susie was going . . . to Rex?

Moving automatically, without plan, his body acting without benefit of conscious thought, Timmy was out of bed and following in Susie's footsteps.

The hall was softly flooded with light at the center, where the locked door now stood open. Rex's screams vibrated in the walls and the ceilings. Susie stood for a moment outlined in the doorway, and then she disappeared into the lighted room that belonged, Timmy was sure, to Little Mother.

Uncle Dan's bellow rang out, competing with Rex's cries, "Get down on your knees, you ungrateful boy, and ask Little Mother's forgiveness! Ask her! *Ask her*!"

The sounds of gagging and revolt came from Rex's throat amid indecipherable cursing from Uncle Dan. There, too, was a sound from a child, or a woman. Susie or Little Mother. It was almost lost beneath the other, and noted in Timmy's awareness only as part of the confusing sounds.

Suddenly Rex cried out tearfully, "You're crazy! You're insane—"

The very walls of the house seemed to be splintering as something crashed into wood; and beneath it Rex's sobs went on and on.

Timmy stumbled half blind in the shadows of the hall, caught in the added guilt of knowing this was his fault. He had wanted to steal the car keys, too, had been willing for Rex to steal them. And now Rex had been caught, and they were hurting him. They were—oh God, what were they doing to Rex?

The screams rose again, both Rex's and someone else's, but there were no distinct words this time, only a horrible gurgle in a throat that could not articulate. Rex needed help. Oh God. *Why couldn't he move faster*? He had to stop them.

Timmy blundered into the wall and felt for a door frame that seemed to be moving erratically in this pale, golden light; and the crashing of the house went on around him. The strange gurgling screams had only the edges of words, the suggestion of communicable phrases, like a tortured animal making a last effort at human speech.

He grasped the door frame for balance and jerked himself to the threshold. The room, lighted by a brighter lamp than the kerosene lamps, blazed out a yellow-white swathing that included a bed with a patchwork quilt and a braided rug on the floor. At the edge of the rug, back in the corner, was the rocking chair whose wooden arm Timmy had seen in what he at first thought was a dream, and sitting in the chair . . . tied in the chair with rope that had turned dark with old blood, sat a human skeleton with long black hair still adhering to the half-decayed scalp, grinning a horribly permanent grin that showed two rows of perfect, white teeth in a lipless, gumless mouth, in a face that had only part of a nose, part of one cheek, and eyes sunken back and eaten by insects that still crawled over the remains.

Susie stood halfway between door and corpse, staring, unmoving, no longer making a sound.

Timmy stumbled past her and to the light-flooded area beyond the bed. Rex had crumpled between bed and wall and was holding his arms up against a pickax that Uncle Dan was swinging high into the air before the final, thrustful drop. The pickax came down as Timmy reached out, and Rex was able only to lift feeble hands against it before it split into his brain.

Timmy fell backwards. He rose facing Susie, and he stumbled to his feet and ran past Susie, grasping her dress and jerking her with him. The material tore, coming loose in Timmy's hands. He turned back to see that Uncle Dan had spotted them. With the pickax raised over his head, and with a roar of determination and madness, he swung at Susie. The ax whistled close to Timmy's arm as he reached back for her, caught her by the wrist and pulled, oblivious to her cry of pain. The pickax missed its target and cut into the floor. Uncle Dan wrenched the sharp blood-stained point from the wood like it had been wrenched from the red, sticky soil of the grave in the woods and from the wound in Rex's skull.

Timmy's body hesitated only a second as he stared at Dan and the ax, as he took in the entire room in his consciousness, Rex now dead on the floor, and in the chair the bound skeleton of a woman who once had lived in this house. He hesitated only a second, and then his body jerked to life and he lunged backward and pulled with him the soft and yielding form of Susie. He reached down instinctively and clawed her arm more safely and securely into his grasp and jerked her after him, through the fading light of the hallway. Behind him Dan screamed, "Come back here, you bad children! Don't you dare turn your backs on Little Mother!"

Timmy found the back door and turned the lock with a nearly nerveless hand, pulling Susie out into the blessed cover of the black night. Behind them in the house came thudding footsteps.

Uncle Dan's voice screamed out, "I'll find you, Timmy! I'll find you! And you'll have to account to Little Mother for this—your disobedience—Papa Dan always wins."

Timmy heard Susie gasp sharply, but he pulled her on and felt the weeds and brush growth surround them. His fingers dug hard into the soft flesh of her arm, dragging her behind him. They were silent players in a horror show, protected now by the darkness they had feared, guided toward the creek in the deep hollow by the faint bellow of a bullfrog. And the sounds of nature became their only friends: the screech owls overhead; the quick rustle of fleeting movements of things they could not see.

The hillside became a slide, dropping downward in the dark, with only the boulders and the tree trunks and vining roots stopping their fall. All flesh felt torn from Timmy's hand as he reached out to steady their way. He became aware of a whimper coming from Susie, and he looked over his shoulder and saw her close against him, a pale, short little ghost. It would be daylight soon, then, if he could see her now. And the daylight would make them easier for Uncle Dan to find. But it also would make it easier for them to get away, if he could only see where to go, if he could only cross the creek and climb the hill beyond and go and go and keep going.

Mist rose from the murmuring creek below and turned grey in the withdrawing dark. Timmy pulled Susie inexorably on, deaf to the small sounds of pain and protest, downward, sliding, falling, coming up against boulders of varying sizes and with varying sharpness. Every few feet of progress he threw a look over his shoulder back up the hill where now the mists were lifting and uncovering the arrival of daylight. And he saw, once again, that Susie was naked, except for a pair of panties. In trying to take her with him, away from the horrors of Uncle Dan and Little Mother, he had inadvertently ripped her dress away.

He had known that she was naked, but that had not penetrated his awareness before. All that had mattered was getting away, escaping. He stopped now, resting against the cold stone of a moss-coated boulder, and pulled his tee shirt over his head. The cool morning air struck his bare chest with its own chilling wrap.

"Here," he said, and jerked the neck of the shirt over Susie's head and over her scratched shoulders. She looked as though she had been dragged through the blackberry thicket, her body, face, arms, and legs crossed and crisscrossed by a network of red and angry marks.

He jerked at her now to hurry her on, but there was no arm to hold. They both were encased within the tee shirt. He looked at her helplessly a moment, then reached through a sleeve and pulled her arm through while she struggled with the other to find the sleeve. He saw she was barefoot, too, but there was no time now to try to solve that problem.

"Come on, Susie. Hurry and keep up with me. He's coming after us. We're going to cross the creek."

She whimpered again in protest, but he went on, steeply down, sliding past one boulder and on to the next. When he paused and looked back he saw her struggling downhill behind him, bare feet bleeding from rock-torn flesh.

He sat down and took off his shoes, and when she reached him he helped her get them on and lace them. She fumbled at trying to tie the laces like a baby who had never tied a shoelace, and he took over the job in impatience and faint disdain. On his own feet yet were his heavy white cotton socks with the blue

257

and red figures at the top. They were scant protection against the small, sharp rocks that littered the dropping hillside.

The creek sound grew louder, water running, swift and dangerous and pulling into its rapids all loose objects it touched. Where was the still, shallow water in which they had played that first day? On the bank overlooking the creek, Timmy watched the swirling water suck at the soil between the roots of the tree by which he stood. Across the creek the bank rose steeply, washed out for a depth several times his own height. Susie hung back, several feet farther up the hillside, arms holding desperately to a slender, bending sapling, her eyes pulling away from the menace of the water.

"We can't cross here," he said with the creek roar, looking upstream and down for a suggestion of gentling breadth and depth in the stream.

He climbed the hill again to stand beside her, to cast a slow, measuring gaze upward for the figure of a man standing among the tree trunks or crouching within the hillside brush and boulders. He had no doubt Uncle Dan knew which way they had gone and would follow and kill them when he wished.

Upstream was the waterfall. He was sure of that, for the path they had climbed that first day had brought them out on the ridge east of the house. And just below, the waterfall and creek spread in glassy smoothness, reaching from willow-drooped bank on the far side to rocky cliff on this. They might be able to swim it at that point and pull themselves free with the help of the willows. And then, they might escape.

"Come on," he said. "Follow me. Be careful and

don't slip.''

It was a steep drop into the water, and he crept along on hands and knees, clinging to whatever he could find. He glanced back occasionally at Susie and saw she was following in his path, grasping what he grasped. Bit by bit they made their way over the cliff above the water and down the other side. The roar of the waterfall filled the narrow hollow that was, at this point, a canyon. But here now was the path, and the going became easier.

A choking thought came to Timmy's mind: Uncle Dan, with the bloody pickax, waiting somewhere on the path ahead. He pushed forward anyway, for there seemed no other way out, around boulders, under bushes; and the path ahead held no one.

They slid down the drop in the path and were on the narrow beach suddenly where the water lay smooth and deep. He gripped a tree root that was washed clean by the water and eased down, down, searching for bottom with his feet. But there was nothing but still, cold depth beneath him. He looked up at Susie standing in the nearly invisible, mud-slick path at the base of the leaning tree and said, ''We got to swim across. Just catch hold of this root and slide in. I'll go first, and when we get to the other side I'll pull you up on the bank.''

But she was shaking her head, her eyes looking past him at the water and widened in a continuation of her night of horror.

''Come on, Susie!'' he commanded, ''he'll catch us if we don't.''

She whispered loudly, ''I can't swim! I can't swim!''

He hadn't thought of that. A portion of his life passed rapidly through his mind as though a part of himself were giving up to die. Red Cross swimming lessons, beginning when he was three years old. His dad had said, "You never know when your life may depend on your ability to swim, and I want my boy to be able to survive this world." Why hadn't somebody taught Susie to swim?

Timmy's teeth began to chatter from the cold of the mountain stream. He looked at the far bank, measuring distance. He had never tried swimming with the weight of another person, but there was no other way—unless they could cross beneath the waterfall? But no, the cliff rose straight toward the sky on the other side. At no point in the creek had he seen a place that could be waded.

"Come on," he commanded through chattering teeth. "Get hold of this root and slide in. Don't hold your breath unless your head goes under water. Breathe slow and easy, like this, with your mouth open." He ignored her shaking head and gave her a brief example of deep breathing. "Then, put your arms around my neck and hang on, don't let go, but don't choke me, and I'll swim us to the other side."

She hung back, sitting down and pushing against the tree, her fingers digging into crevices in the bank. "No! No! No, I can't!"

"Susie! *Come on.*"

"No! No!"

"I'm gonna leave you here and let him get you then!"

She began to cry, her lower lip trembling and we by the tears that squeezed past her closed eyes.

Far up the hillside above her a rock began to roll, to bounce, to gain momentum as it plunged downward toward them. Timmy watched it in petrified fascination. It bounded high, passed over Susie's head and splashed into the still water behind Timmy. But his eyes were held up there, at its source, for something, *someone* had jolted it loose and started it rolling.

Uncle Dan was coming down the hill.

Timmy waited no longer. He reached up, grasped her ankle and pulled. She slid downward on her back, her arms flailing and grasping futilely for support. Her mouth grimaced and opened in a scream that was choked off by water as she plunged under. Timmy dragged her up, his arm around her neck. She coughed water and her fingers dug into his naked back.

He hissed furiously and in desperation into her ear, "Someone is coming down the hill! You want him to kill you like he did Rex? And all the others? Now don't fight and you won't go under again. Hold on. I'm going to turn around and start swimming."

He turned slowly, easing his back toward her, and she clasped her arms around his neck and lay her chin hard on his shoulder. He held to the root a minute longer, measuring again the wide, deep pool between them and safety, and then he turned loose and began to swim.

Her weight dragged him under and he fought water to surface. Her grasp began to slip in her panic, and he had to use one hand to pull her back again. There was no breath to waste, to tell her again to not let go, please Lord.

As though she heard his silent prayer she stopped

struggling suddenly and locked her fingers together against his throat. He gulped air and began swimming slowly and carefully, an under-water stroke that carried them inch by inch toward the leaning willows on the far side. At one point he felt the swift, cold pull of an undercurrent, and a new kind of panic took hold of him so that once again he had to fight to stay afloat. For the first time in his life he was afraid of deep water. Something under water touched his foot and he jerked it free, and Susie's hands slipped and slid away from his neck. He turned to reach for her and felt her hands grip the belt of his jeans. Her head was barely above surface, her eyes bulging in her silent fear. But she was holding on, and he stretched out high in the water and began an overstroke that carried them more quickly to the bank and the drooping limbs of the willow tree.

He reached up, grasped leaves that tore loose in his hand. He reached again and caught the limb.

They climbed out on their bellies and lay panting and gasping. When Timmy raised his head and looked at the hillside where they had been, where the rock had fallen, he saw movement, and a brief flash of blue. His fingers closed over Susie's wrist, and he pushed and dragged her deeper into the shimmering cover of willow foliage. Then, lying on his stomach, he watched the far hillside.

Uncle Dan came in view, moving as surely as a mountain goat to stand on the path where they had stood. He took a cigarette from the blue pocket of his shirt and lighted it, and stood smoking and looking, and at last he flipped the smoking butt into the water and moved away, following the path upstream toward the waterfall.

"I don't think he saw us," Timmy whispered to Susie. "But we can't stay here. We got to climb this hill and the next, and as far as we can go." He stumbled up, jeans water-soaked and dragging, his upper body cold in the morning air. They began climbing the hill, pulling themselves up, and up, with the help of anything they could hold.

Susie stopped climbing and lay huddled against a boulder, and Timmy urged her up again and on. Far above, over the thick canopy of treetops, sprinkles of sunlight came through like golden raindrops.

"See Susie," he said, his tired voice encouraging, "up there the sun is shining. If we keep going we'll reach it soon, and then we can rest."

She raised herself to hands and knees and climbed slowly past the boulder. And then on, toward the promised sun.

He was too tired to look back, to see if Uncle Dan was behind them. He was too tired to notice how empty and flat his stomach was. He remembered Rex, and the sound the pickax had made in his head, like the splitting and bursting of something ripe; and he remembered the last look in his eyes. But he remembered with a distant part of his mind, as though it was blocked off from his emotions.

The top of the hill leveled off, and Susie crawled into a spot of sunlight and collapsed, already asleep. Timmy curled against her, then pulled over them the end of a fallen branch that still clung to crisp, brown winter leaves. Thus partly covered, they slept.

Twenty-two

An owl heralded the coming of night, and in her exhausted sleep Susie heard, and cried softly, and pressed closer to the warmth of Timmy's body. Her movement woke him, and he stared upward where moon drops replaced the sun. He listened. Soft movements in the leaves, but not footsteps, not these, but the slithering of something small, something without feet or legs. He lay still, hoping it would go away. And it did, movements growing softer and farther off to the right. The lost owl moaned again on a nearby tree limb. But that was all right, too. All the snakes, and the monsters, and the ghost-beings of the forests were not as frightening as the man who hunted them. As the man who would find them, eventually, and kill them.

He sat up, feeling the eyes of the darkness all around, afraid to make a sound, to move, to rustle the leaves as the snake had. Little sparkles of light, of fireflies turning on and off, were like cigarettes in the dark held in the patiently waiting fingers of Uncle

Dan. And perhaps *she* stood there too, ghostly, patient, one on one side of them, and one on the other, waiting for them to move, to reveal exactly where they hid.

But no, it was only fireflies. Uncle Dan hadn't found them yet.

Timmy slipped his palm over Susie's mouth so she wouldn't scream and whispered in her ear, "Wake up, Susie."

He felt her stiffen against him. He heard her breath suck in and hold.

"We're going on," he said, "down the ridge. When day comes again we'll cross the next hollow. Are you ready?"

She nodded, a jerking movement of her head as she rose to her feet. He took his hand away from her mouth. Her lips felt dry and rough beneath his fingers as he slipped his hand away, and he was aware suddenly of a desert dryness in his own mouth and a thirst for water that far exceeded his hunger.

"We have to find water," he said.

She dug her fingers into his hand. "Not the creek," she whispered. "I don't want to go back there."

"No, not there. Somewhere else. A spring, maybe."

They walked slowly, hands clasped for comfort and guidance, his sneakers slipping on her small feet, the cotton socks on his feet torn and cut. He tried not to limp, but the tenderness and the pain increased with each step forward.

The moon moved on ahead of them, westward down the ridge, and paled and dispersed beyond the trees. Its light had not touched them anyway, and they did not mind its abandonment. They trudged on, silent in the dark, scratched and tortured by weeds and vines in some places and by sharp rocks and boulders in others.

She began dragging behind again, and he could hear her free hand scratching at her skin. He tightened his hand on hers when he felt the fingers turn soft and lax and try to slip away.

"No, no," she whispered in tired remoteness. "I want to stop. I'm tired." Her scratching made a soft sound in the night.

"We can't stop. You want Uncle Dan to catch up with us? You want him to kill you?"

"I'm tired," she repeated, without hope.

He stood helplessly waiting, knowing he could not leave her there, yet he could not stop again tonight. He said, "You want *her* to come and take you back?"

"No," she whispered after a long and thought-filled moment.

She began moving again, a turtle's pace beside him, and the soft scratching of chewed fingernails against tender skin moved with them.

He didn't notice when the night became less dark, but suddenly it seemed he had developed an animal's vision, for there ahead were distinct outlines of tall trees and boulders, and dips and rises in the mountain ridge. Then, faintly through the air, like a call from a world he had almost forgotten, came the awakening crow of a rooster. He stopped abruptly.

Susie pressed against him, and her cry was low and timorous, "What was that?"

"That was a rooster!" Timmy answered, forgetting to keep his voice down. "That means there's a farm there, because roosters are boy chickens and they live on farms. Maybe there'll be a telephone and I can call my dad and mom. Hurry, Susie, let's run. Listen, it's crowing again. Didn't you ever hear a rooster before?"

"I don't know. No."

"Come on."

But he couldn't run. His feet felt like stubs of raw flesh, and every leaf, every small stick he stepped upon was like a hundred piercing knives. "Wait," he said, and sat down and picked off his socks. The bottoms had worn out. He folded them and wrapped them around his feet, and from the precious hoarded collection in his jeans' pockets he pulled forth a wad of string that was still wet from the creek and tied the wrapped socks firmly, creating a cushion sole of thick cotton. Beside him Susie scratched, on and on.

He looked at her through the gray mist of receding night and saw her red and blotched, from her bare legs beneath his tee shirt to her neck and face. She scratched tiredly. Beyond the soft noises of Susie came the welcoming crow of the rooster, and the beginnings of bird calls high in the treetops above.

"What's wrong with you?" he asked. "Have you got measles?"

She looked down at her legs and nodded. "The other time I had measles I got real sick. I want to lay down now."

"You had measles before?"

She nodded again.

"But you can only have measles once," he said. "I think."

She sagged toward the ground, but he held her, pulling on her swelling and spotted arm. "We got to go, Susie. When we get to the farm, you can sleep. I promise.''

In the growing light of day he could pick an easier path to follow, around clumps of weeds and thick growths, around boulders and ravines that dipped sharply toward the faraway bottom of the hill and the creek that flowed there. He pulled Susie along, relentlessly, and the continual crowing of the rooster grew closer and more comforting.

They broke through a dense plum thicket into sunlight and a small cleared area no larger than a tennis court. Within steps of them was a tiny log barn, and perched upon its low roof was the rooster. Timmy stared at this miniature hill farm in dismay, and at the rooster on the roof, and the rooster stared at him. Then, cackling in alarm, the rooster flew down among the few hens scratching the grassless yard, and they all flapped away in raucous escape from this unexpected danger.

Timmy blinked against the dust their leaving fogged into his face. Beyond the dust he saw a slightly larger log house with a tacked on front porch, and beyond that a small patch of growing corn. A plump-bellied, scrawny-faced mule grazed in a pen made of boards behind the house, and tethered in the front yard of the house was a nanny goat.

As they stood looking upon this scene, a man came out onto the porch and stood gazing about. He was a scrawny little man, with a flowing, stained white beard. He looked like a distant relative of both the mule and the goat. He turned to go back into his house, and his eyes fell upon them. As the goat raised her head to stare, so did he.

Susie whimpered low in her throat and pulled back toward the plum thicket so suddenly that Timmy almost lost his grasp on her. He dug his fingers into her wrist.

"Come on, Susie, maybe he's got a wife, and she'll take care of you."

She came with him reluctantly, and they approached the old man on the porch. Old eyes, still as black and as sharp as a raven's eyes, looked down upon them.

"Howdy," he said, his eyes darting to the plum thicket and back again. "You've more or less come the long way around, didn't ye? You shorely ain't out here in these woods alone, are ye? Got your folks waitin' somewheres?"

"No sir. Yes sir," Timmy answered, confused by the disconnected questions. "Have you got a telephone I could use, sir?"

The black eyes fell upon Susie and raked over her. "My God a mighty," he exclaimed. "What's wrong with you, little girl?"

She pushed in against Timmy's back, trying to hide. Timmy said, "I think she's got measles or something."

The old man stepped down off the porch, tugged at the white beard that was stained dark around the hole of his mouth, and peered around Timmy at Susie's legs.

"That there looks like a bad case of poison ivy to me. A real bad case. Come on in here and let me doctor that."

He reached out his hand and let it drop when Susie did not respond.

270

"She's afraid," Timmy said. "She won't talk. If you've got a telephone sir—"

The old man's eyes darted toward the plum thicket again. He shook his head. "No telephone, little boy. It's more 'n seven miles down to the closest telephone, at the Gunning store, in that direction. Back the way you came in it's probably twenty or thirty miles, as the crow flies, and no habitation and no roads that I know of except a logging trail here and there, and the forest ranger trails. So, pray tell, where'd you'ns come from?"

Timmy almost told him, but just as he opened his mouth the old man said, "Only house I know of in these parts is the other side of the river. Belongs to a man and his wife that come up now and then by the name of Reilly. A short, heavyset man. Wears his hair down to here. It's the style, I guess. Seems like a pretty good fellow."

"You know him?" Timmy asked in dismay. "Does he come to see you?"

"Me? Mercy no. Just seen him once or twice down on the road." He turned and pointed down the hill. "I don't have much of a road, I don't need much. It goes down and fords the creek there where it spreads out, and goes on down and runs into this road to the old Clanton place. That's the one Reilly bought, ye know. I run into him on that road one day when I rode my mule to town for supplies. He said he'd bought the old Clanton place and planned to fix it up for a home for him and his wife some day. He's from some big town somewheres, I forget what one. I seen him once more after that, when he passed me and my mule on the road."

"He doesn't come to visit you?" Timmy asked.

"Lawsy no. Why would he want to visit an old man like me? You'd better come on in the house, little girl, and let me doctor your poison ivy. You don't got no call to be afraid of me. I don't even hurt the flies." He stumped back up onto his porch and through the door into his house. He called back, "How long's it been since you two et? I got a pan of bread in here."

It was the magic word. They moved side by side up the step onto the porch and into the one big room of the house.

There was a square, rough board table with a bench, a board nailed to the log wall for kitchen supplies, a squat, black stove with a pipe going out the ceiling. And back in the corner was a bed built in and made up neatly with a tacked quilt pieced awkwardly from squares of old denim. There was one rocking chair with a broken arm.

"Set there," he said, motioning toward the bench. "Help yourself to the bread in that pan. I'll pour you both a big cup of goat's milk. Ever drink any goat's milk before?"

"No sir."

"Well you've got a treat coming."

He took a stone jug down off the shelf and poured creamy liquid into two granite cups and placed them with two spoons in easy reach on the table.

"Just crumble your bread in the milk. After awhile I have to take this here milk down to the spring house or it'll sour on me."

They ate voraciously. It was a strange, too-rich taste, but it was filling and thirst quenching at the same time. Susie paused occasionally to scratch. The old man filled their cups again, and in a metal bowl mixed something into a paste. Timmy grew sleepy and put his head down upon his arm.

"Here now," the old man said, pushing the bowl of paste toward him. "Rub this on your little sister's poison ivy so she can get some relief from her itching. Then you can both stretch out on the bed yonder and sleep." And he added to himself, "You musta come a long way, but it beats me from where."

Timmy looked at him in satiated, sleepy dullness, thinking he should say something, some kind of lie about where they had come from, because if the old man knew, might he not tell Uncle Dan where they were? He gathered the dish of paste into his hands and approached Susie. She stood still and allowed him to smear her arms, legs, face, and neck. She was almost sleeping on her feet when he finished.

The old man grunted approval. "Now you two young'ns take your naps and I'll trot this here milk jug down to the spring."

Was he going to a spring, or was he going for Uncle Dan? The spring, he was only going to the spring, Timmy felt, needing desperately to rest unafraid. He sank to the floor under the shadows of the table and pillowed his head on his arms, facedown, the cool, rough boards pressed against his cheek.

Twenty-three

When he woke he lay still and listening, tense without knowing why, his memory blurred and garbled like a movie camera moved too swiftly over a passing scene: He was begging his mom and dad to let him go to the farm with Russ; he was watching a horse, small with distance, cross a field with a rider on its back that might have been him or might have been Russ; he was in a moving vehicle, tossed about on a bed that had no inner spring, just a foam mattress that did not cushion the rough ride, and his sides and back and bottom hurt, and he felt he had to go to the bathroom; he was watching a little girl with long, tangled curls bouncing down her back run screaming through the shallow edge of a creek of water with her panties stretched high under her arms; he was being carried into a room filled with a golden shadowy light, and he saw on the wall a framed needlework that read Home Sweet Home; then he was lowered into the arms of a hideously grinning skeleton; and he watched the pickax sweep downward and burrow into the splitting skull of a boy with red hair and freckled skin, because he wouldn't call the skeleton "Little Mother."

He sat up too quickly, still disoriented, and cracked his forehead against the edge of the board bench beside the crude, handmade table. The blow made him feel dizzy and nauseated. He put his hand on his forehead and felt an almost instant rise of a bump there. He eased out from under the table and the bench and looked around.

The small house was silent and stifling hot. There was one door and one small square window beside it. He remembered now where he was, and he looked around for Susie and saw that she was lying asleep on the bed in the corner. Her skin was angry red under the splotched white mess of medicine he had smeared on her. It had dried to a tissue thinness that let the red rashes show through. Sweat glued her hair to her forehead and neck, and below his tee shirt that she still wore, that had slipped up across her belly, her thin panties were black with dried mud. Flies buzzed above her, droning, and sometimes they sat on her, but briefly, as though the white medicine, or the poison ivy rash, repelled them.

He twisted around, moving in utter silence, and his eyes fell upon a short, stocky, double-barreled shotgun standing in the corner. Its twin barrels were as shining and black as the skin of a freshly washed black snake sunning himself after a rain. He eased closer across the floor, on his hands and knees. His dad had taken him skeet shooting because he said everyone should know how to handle a gun the right way. "But don't ever shoot a living thing, son," he said. "Unless you're needing food. Our wild animals aren't here for your sport. I wouldn't want to know that you ever needed to kill for pleasure." And his answer, given so sincerely, "Oh I won't, Dad." What reason would he ever have to kill a living creature?

A soft cough issued from somewhere beyond the thick, log wall, and then the lazy creak of a rocking chair.

Timmy stood up and found his feet hurting in their tight sock bandages. He limped through the open door and sat down again, and the cool south breeze wafting up from dark, deep hollows dried the sweat on his head.

"Well, you woke up," the old man with the white beard said as he rocked slowly. "You musta been plumb tuckered out. I picked up your little sister and put her on the bed, but you had crawled so far under the table I was afeered I'd wake you up trying to drag you out."

"I was okay," Timmy said. He bent over his feet and tried to untie the knotted nylon string that held his socks to his feet. He finally resorted to his pen knife and cut them off. The old man watched him with interest.

The cloth had stuck in places and came away reluctantly. Timmy twisted the bottoms of his feet so that he could look at them. They seemed to have toughened in some areas and gone raw and bleeding in others.

The rocking chair groaned like old, tired bones as the old man bent down. "Looks like you walked many a mile barefooted. That's the trouble of wearing shoes at all. It makes you a cripple when you

277

don't. You may not think it now, but you keep walking barefooted and they'll toughen up all over just like a mule's hoof." The chair sighed as he sat back again. "Just let them dry in the air. Don't cover them up again, and they'll be all right until you can get you a new pair of shoes. Though I don't know any reason a boy needs shoes except when the snow flies. There was many a time I went barefooted even then."

"Yes sir," Timmy said politely. Then, "I saw your gun. What kind is it?"

"My gun! Now, don't you be touching my gun, boy. I keep both them barrels loaded. You never know when you might need a loaded gun. It's not a toy. It's an old twelve gauge short barrel. Good, straight shooter. I try it out once a month just to keep it in practice."

"Is it the only gun you have?"

"Yeah. One's enough."

They sat quietly together, the chair moving, the goat in the yard munching grass closer and closer to the porch with fast little rabbit chomps, its little beard bouncing. Timmy watched it and the dark shadowed woods beyond the yard. He turned the soles of his feet toward the sun and breeze to harden, as the old man had said, into something tough enough to walk on, for he figured he had a long way to go on foot.

"You don't have a car, I guess," he said.

"No car. How would I get one down or up that hill yonder? A path's all I need, me and my mule, down to the creek."

"How far is it to the creek?"

"About a mile, I reckon, though I never measured it."

"Where do you buy your groceries?"

"At the store, Gunnings Corner, about seven, eight mile down the road on the other side of the creek. It's a good slow day's ride, there and back, and I don't need many groceries. Fourteen, fifteen miles on a mule is too much mule."

"Is there any way to get there besides on the road?" Timmy asked cautiously.

"Well, I'd hate to try any other way. It's easy to get lost in these woods if you don't know them very well. Is your little sister still sleeping?"

Timmy almost said, *she's not my sister*, but bit the words back. How could he know if the old man were to be trusted? He had been good to them, but Timmy's trust was weakened and almost nonexistent now. He didn't know what they were going to do, he and Susie, but he had to talk to his dad, some way, and as soon as he could reach a telephone. The woods lay still and dark and waiting, endless miles of them, and he could not go back into them. Not yet. And perhaps there was another way down to that store seven or eight miles away.

"Are you planning to go to the store for groceries very soon?" Timmy asked, picking intently at a piece of loose skin on his foot.

"Why do you ask? Is there something you want?"

"I just thought me and Susie could ride along with you. Is there a telephone there at the store?" But what if Uncle Dan were waiting there, knowing they would come because there was no place else for them to go and stay alive. And even then how could they stay alive? The people at the store would not believe, ever, because who would believe that a nice-acting man like Uncle Dan would kill boys and bury them on the mountain ridge? Who would believe that he had tied his wife in a chair and killed her and left her body to rot, while all the time he acted as if she were alive?

No, no one would believe.

Timmy became aware that the old man had answered him, and he, deep in his troubled thoughts, had not heard. "I beg pardon, sir, what did you say?"

"I said, yes, they got a telephone all right, but I wouldn't know how to use one because I never had call to use one. I recollect now, that was the first thing you asked for. Who is it you're wanting to telephone to?"

"My mom and dad."

"Well, Lord, where are they?"

"At home, down in Louisiana." It was all right to tell him these things. *These* things, he would believe. He would never believe the other, about the nice man who had bought the old Clanton place on yon ridge.

"Louisiana?"

"Yes, sir."

"Then what, pray tell, are ye two doing up here in the mountains at old John's place like two abandoned kittens?"

Timmy picked intently at his other foot for awhile and thought about how much to tell. "We kinda got lost," he said, "from a summer camp."

"A summer camp. Hmm."

Timmy could feel the dark and penetrating eyes crawling all over him like beetles on a carcass, probing, examining.

"I didn't know there was any summer camps back this far in the hills."

Timmy said nothing. The goat had come close enough to nibble with curiosity at his toes. It tickled, and he laughed a little. It felt strange to laugh again, but it was only a surface thing, while behind it the fear swelled and ebbed and swelled again with each beat of his heart.

"Your folks send you to this here camp?"

"Yes sir, they kind of did. But they didn't know we would get lost."

"Well I reckon not. Are you lost or just kinda lost."

"I don't know where we are," Timmy said in honesty.

"But you know where you been?"

"Yes sir. Kind of."

"Then maybe you ought to go back and wait for them to come and get you. Don't you reckon the folks at the camp there will be getting worried?"

Timmy licked suddenly dry lips and withdrew his feet from the goat. He was glad now he had not said where the camp, the house, was. Very glad. He knew for sure the old man would take them back, for he would never believe . . .

The rocking chair groaned as its occupant leaned forward. His beard jutted out and the black hole of his mouth said, "What's that?"

Timmy saw he was looking beyond him, beyond the goat, and, it seemed, beyond even the edge of the woods. Timmy looked and saw nothing but the weeds and the brush and the dark green solid forest wall. Above it, sailing effortlessly in the cloudless blue of the sky, was a buzzard. He saw nothing; still, the skin on his arms turned cold and the hairs wiry stiff with warning. He got to his feet and backed cautiously to the door frame, and stood there with his hands behind him gripping the sharp edge of the door.

Then the goat jerked her head up and twisted the supple neck, and looked over her back. The old man sat back in his chair.

"I thought so," he said. "Heard a crow squawk, and that means something is moving around. And now old Sally knows someone's coming up the path."

Timmy stepped back farther into the doorway. "Who is it?"

"Don't know yet. He'll be in sight in a minute."

Timmy backed on into the house and stepped out of sight against the wall near the one window. The glass was coated with several years of dust and grime, so that it was like looking through colored glasses. Even so, he saw the figure emerge from the forest. A man dressed in gray slacks and a floral gray and green shirt, buttoned high on his chest. A short, wide man with wide, powerful shoulders, and long blond hair falling across one side of his face. The window grime blurred and distorted his features, wavered his frame, but the sunlight caught and glistened in his hair, and his soft face widened in a friendly smile.

Timmy gasped for air and flattened against the wall beside the window. His eyes sought a method of escape at the back of the house, but there was no way out other than the front door onto the porch. And

Uncle Dan, with his charming smile, was almost there.

Timmy crouched beneath the window, pressing as tightly to the wall as a poster glued. He was afraid to move. Afraid to breathe. His senses picked up the approaching steps as if electrified, and the voice burst soft and cultured upon his ears, beguilingly friendly.

"Hello there, Mr. Alcorn, how are you today?" A boot touched the board step but came no farther.

"Howdy."

"Nice weather we're having."

"Yelp, usually do this time of year. I ain't sure I know you, sir."

"I'm Dan Reilly. My wife and I bought the old Clanton place. We met you a couple of times."

"Sorry, didn't recognize you there for a minute. How's Mrs. Reilly?"

"Oh she's fine. Enjoying the pleasant weather."

"I see. Give her my best." Mr. Alcorn did not invite the man onto the porch.

"We seem to be having a lot of sunny weather this July," Dan said, as though he had come for nothing but to talk about the weather. "However, there's a cloud in the west, so the dry weather might break. I guess the farmers need rain."

"Farmers almost always need rain. I noticed that there bank in the west. The day's sultry here at my house, which always means a change in the weather. You had quite a walk up the hill, Mr. Reilly."

"Yes, sir, I did. It must be a mile down to the creek."

There was silence from Mr. Alcorn. Timmy heard

the beating of his own heart and was terrified that Uncle Dan would hear it, too; he was even more terrified that the old man would any moment, with his next breath, tell Uncle Dan that he wasn't the only visitor.

"Mr. Alcorn," Dan said, "I suppose you're wondering why I'm here. The truth is I'm looking for my two children. They seem to have wandered away and become lost in the woods."

Timmy's heart roared in his ears, taking all the strength of his body to keep it supplied with its sudden demand for blood. This was it, and what could he do? He alone might get away, if he ran and ran fast enough. But that would leave Susie for Uncle Dan again. And he couldn't let Uncle Dan take her. She was still sleeping on the bed, with no warning that he had come. And Timmy could not reach her without passing the open door.

Mr. Alcorn said, "Yours? Your young'ns?"

"That's right, sir. Have you seen them by any chance? Or any signs of them?"

"What are they, a couple of boys?"

"No. A boy and a girl."

"What do they look like?"

Timmy's heart slowed in surprised hope. He could tell by Mr. Alcorn's voice he did not like the man Dan Reilly. He was not going to tell him, not yet, anyway. Timmy looked again for a way to escape, as though a wall might have opened up for him and Susie in their need. But there was nothing, no miracle, no way out. He began instinctively to back farther into the corner, and his hand touched the cold, smooth double barrel of the shotgun.

"Two little tow heads," Dan said. "The boy's about ten, the girl five."

"And what was these two young'ns wearing?"

Uncle Dan's smoothness failed him. There was a long pause.

Mr. Alcorn said testily, "Don't you know what your own young'ns was wearing, Mister?"

"Well—just the regular things that kids wear. Jeans, shirts." His voice changed suddenly and became less smooth and more urgent. "I really must find my kids, Mr. Alcorn. Their mother is worried sick. And there are other dangers to them as well. These woods are filled with dangers, and they may be dead or dying right now. I don't know why they did this to me. Yes, yes, I do. They're a couple of little tale tellers, and I gave them both a spanking, so they got mad at me and ran away. But if you see them, I'd appreciate very much if you'd bring them back to me. I'll pay you well, of course."

Mr. Alcorn said, "If I see them, I'll keep it in mind."

Timmy squeezed his eyes shut and hoped with all his being that Uncle Dan would go away now. Go away and never come back.

"I'd appreciate that deeply, Mr. Alcorn," Uncle Dan said in false sadness that sounded like the voice he used when he talked to Timmy's mom and dad.

And then Mr. Alcorn said, "Are ye running some kind of summer camp for young'ns over there on the old Clanton place?"

In the significant silence that followed all the sounds of nature intensified. The buzz of the jarflies in the trees shrieked in warning. The flies darting above the unwashed cups on the table vibrated the hot, still air. And Timmy's body sagged with hopelessness. Mr. Alcorn had just told Dan Reilly, without realizing what he had done, that not only had he seen them, he had talked with them.

"I think, mister," Dan said in icy, chopped tones, "you got my kids in your house."

There were boot steps on the porch now, hard and purposeful, leading straight toward the door.

"Just a minute!" Mr. Alcorn cried out. "You can't go in there."

"Don't stand in my way, old man."

Instinct took over Timmy's muscles, and he moved like a jack-in-the-box sprung loose from its moorings, and the shotgun came up gripped hard in his small hands. He met Uncle Dan in the doorway and there was a briefly flashing expression on Dan's face of satisfaction.

Then the blast of the shotgun filled the small room, and its repercussions shot Timmy back against the table as though he had been picked up and thrown, and in front of him Dan's face showed shock as it turned pale and trembling, and he staggered and crumpled into the doorway and hung there a moment, his fingers gripping the door frame, then settled slowly backward onto the porch.

Blood stained the shoulder of his shirt, slowly edging outward, soaking into the material.

Timmy used the table to pull himself off the floor. The room echoed the gun shot, on and on, and the air was filled with that strange, sweet smell of gun powder. In the long slow-motion moment that followed, stung so permanently and sharply upon

Timmy's awareness, he saw Susie stand looking down at the prone figure of Uncle Dan, and the blood on his shoulder, and her lips curved gently in a smile of angelic innocence and wonder, and full, personal satisfaction.

On the other side of the door, just beyond Uncle Dan, Mr. Alcorn stood, his feet splattered with tiny drops of blood. The black hole of his mouth gaped in stunned silence.

Sobs rose screaming into Timmy's throat and died there, unable to find expression. In terror he ran. Past the partly blocked doorway, the body lying on the porch, the frightened goat tethered in the yard. He ran until the dense gloom of the forest covered him, and behind him he heard the voice come alive and follow.

"Boy!" It shouted. "Boy! Wait!"

He stumbled and fell, and stayed where he was, his face pressed into the vines that had tripped him.

He heard the footsteps pounding through the leaves behind him, and he waited. The sobs kept filling his chest and throat, yet still found no outward expression, and he trembled all over, his body cold in the still humid heat that wafted down from the sun-scorched clearing above.

The runner caught up with him and fell gasping for breath at his side. It was Susie, not the man, after all.

From back on top the hill came the call, "Boy!"

Mr. Alcorn was coming after him, because now he was a murderer. Mr. Alcorn would take him to the police, and no one would ever believe him, that he shot Uncle Dan because there was nothing else he could do to save himself and Susie. Even then it was wrong, wrong, something hard and knotted in his body cried out, *wrong*. ". . . never shoot to kill . . ." And he had, he had shot to kill.

He wanted to scream, but he couldn't.

Susie was on her feet, bending over him and tugging at his arm. "Come on. Come on, Timmy. The man is coming after us. And Uncle Dan, too. He got up off the porch and he's coming, too."

Timmy noted with part of his mind, the part that was not numb with horror, that Susie had not whispered, she had spoken aloud. But it was a mute and accepting edge of consciousness that asked no questions and gave no answers. Still, the hard knot in the middle of his body began to dissolve.

He had not killed Uncle Dan after all?

Not dead . . . not dead. . . .

Twenty-four

Timmy gave in to Susie's tugging and with her at his side began running again, into the ravine that dipped downward between tall trees and obstructing boulders. Mosquitoes and gnats rose in angry fogs from the small springs that trickled out from beneath wet leaves and moved with them into the deepening ravine. Fallen logs and boulders made the passing increasingly difficult, and in silence they turned their steps upward away from the depths, and on the rise of the hill they came upon the path.

It wound upward between the trees toward the small ridge farm that was far behind them now, and downward in the other direction, disappearing in the sunless tunnel made of trees and brush and creeping vines.

"Where are we going?" she asked, her voice low, but not whispering.

"We'll go this way," he said, leading the way downhill.

He began running again, slowing occasionally to

find Susie was keeping up, the sneakers flopping on her feet. He thought in the numb part of his mind, the separate part that looked and saw and heard but did not feel, that Mr. Alcorn had been right. His feet had toughened in the air of the afternoon and no longer hurt. Or was it that they, too, had gone numb?

The hill settled into a narrow valley of trees, oddly level in this area of long, high hills and deep hollows. The path went straight to the edge of the wide, shallow creek bed and stopped. The water ran clear and murmuring over a gravel bed, and they waded through, and at no point was it over waist deep. On the far edge the path resumed, climbing a low, sloping bank and going again into a nearly impenetrable growth of low bushes and vines.

They came suddenly upon the van, driven as far in along the path as it could go. It looked strange and unfamiliar, a car that belonged to no one. Its sleek nose was pushed into a stand of undergrowth, of wild grapevines and poison ivy. They stared at it in startled and suspicious silence. But it sat alone like a ghost car that really did not exist at all.

Timmy remembered suddenly. He had stood beside it with Rex; he had ridden in it from his home; he had seen it parked before that in his driveway. How could he have forgotten what it looked like, even for a minute?

"I know whose car that is. It's Uncle Dan's."

"Yes."

Timmy crept upon it, and without touching the dusty, pollen-covered metal, peered in.

"But he took the keys," he said.

He stood looking at the car, and recognized finally

the danger of being near it. Uncle Dan would be coming here, now, any minute. He backed away from it, into the vines, and around toward its rear.

"The road is close, though," he said. "Or else he couldn't have gotten the car in here. When we get to the road we can go toward the store. And the telephone. I got to call my dad."

She followed in the path he made around the van, moving slowly against clutching limbs and tangling vines. He tried to make the path better for her, pushing aside and holding back growth that scratched his hands and arms and bare chest. Her short stature was dwarfed by the lush, damp foliage.

Timmy heard the sound, the odd, dry rattle that seemed so alien to these creek-damp vines and the muggy ground. The direction of its warning emanated up from all around him, confused and angry, as though he had stepped into the center of its deadly coil. Susie heard, too, and returned in silence his gaping stare. And then, with a swift piercing pain, like the sting of an angry wasp, it struck the top of his foot. He reached instinctively for Susie's hand, holding away from her face a threatening limb, and jerked her with him away from the dry rattle and the invisible coil. They stumbled on, around the van, and into the faint foliage-free road track.

Timmy sank down upon the ground and gripped his ankle in both hands. The pain was hot and racing now, no longer as innocent as the sting of a wasp. He rocked back and forth, holding the ankle and venom-pierced foot aloft.

"It bit me," he sobbed, "it bit me. A rattlesnake. It hurts. Oh, it *hurts*."

She bent above him, her hands on dimpled, rash-covered knees, her worried face close to his. "Timmy, don't die. Please don't die."

Cub Scout training flashed back to him suddenly, laying out orders in the calm and unfeeling part of his mind. "Get my knife, Susie, out of my pocket. Hurry. There. There." He nodded toward his left pocket, his fingers tightening on his ankle to delay the blood from mingling with the snake venom and from working its way toward his heart and his brain. She dug one hand into the pocket and came out with the small knife, and as he gave the orders, her clumsy obeying fingers opened the blade.

"You've got to cut it," he said. "Push the blade in as hard as you can. Right there, where it bit. One on each red spot there."

The opened knife shook in her hand, poised inches above his foot. "I can't. I can't."

"You got to, Susie, or I'll die." He fought to keep hysteria from his voice. "Put the point against the bite, and *cut. Cut, Susie, cut a cross on each bite.*"

It trembled in her hand a second longer, and then she plunged the blade in, the cry of her own pain swelling and blending with his. Twice, three times, four, he felt the cut of the knife, but it was a pain that gave relief to the dark threat of death that was moving with invisible surety toward his heart.

He raised the foot to his lips, bending over his twisted leg, to suck the blood that beaded along the tiny cuts. He drew on it until his mouth ached from the strain, and the taste of blood was indelibly etched into his memory. Susie sat on her heels beside him watching in worried silence, the knife still gripped in her hands.

He stood up, finally, testing the foot upon the ground. Already the top of his foot bulged swollen and discolored.

"Can you walk?" she was whispering again.

"Yeah, I think so. I got to. We can't stay here by his car. Uncle Dan will come to get it, and then he'll be looking for us. He can't let us go, Susie. And he can't let Mr. Alcorn go. Before he quits he'll find us. We have to hurry."

"It's bleeding," she whispered. "Why does it keep bleeding?"

"It's supposed to. It'll quit after awhile. Come on, let's go find the road. When we hear the van we'll hide in the bushes at the side of the road."

He limped on ahead of her down the path, using his injured foot as little as possible, his teeth clenched against the pain that radiated upward through his leg.

Behind them something splashed into the creek and came splashing on across. It climbed the bank with a plodding clip clop, and then its hooves became whispers of movement, deadened by the vines. It paused at one point a few yards back, just beyond the van.

Timmy and Susie sank to their hands and knees into the vines and brush and huddled together in silence.

The heavy steps moved again, came on around the van and into the path. Through the thick of the foliage covering them, Timmy glimpsed the long ears of the mule and the white beard of the rider. They went on, hoof thudding against the packed mud path in slow, determined progress. Ahead of the mule a small flock of birds rose chattering toward the sun-touched tree canopy.

When the silence had returned again, she asked, "Is he looking for us?"

Timmy's mind swirled, trying to follow the logic of the white-bearded rider. "He might be going after the police," he said in hushed tightness, his clenched jaws aching.

"To take you to jail? Because you shot Uncle Dan?"

"Yes. Because—maybe now he's helping Uncle Dan."

The call drifted back to them through the growing distance, "Boy! Yeh, boy?"

"It's me he wants," Timmy said, in returning hopelessness. "He's still looking for me."

"Why? Because you shot Uncle Dan?"

"I don't know. I don't know." But yes, he knew, and the memory was a blood-washed pain that made him writhe internally. He had disobeyed the old man and touched his gun, had picked it up and used it to kill, and even though he had only wounded, it did not excuse him. So now again he was hunted by two men, one of them to kill him, and the other because he had tried to kill.

"Timmy," Susie pleaded, "maybe he'll help us. Let's tell him where we are."

"No! Uncle Dan is here, too, somewhere. You said he wasn't killed."

She shook her head. "No, he got up. He wasn't killed. You only shot his shoulder."

"Then they may be working together now. We

have to stay out of the road. We have to watch where we walk. We have to listen and hide when they're coming."

They chose the path anyway, following along in the distant wake of the mule, listening for the van behind them. Timmy paused and used his knife to slit the lower part of the pants' leg that was growing snug on his swelling ankle, and paused again to adopt for a crutch a dead, sturdy stick he found beside the path.

They reached the road at last, a rocky, weedy double track over which tree limbs hung and underbrush crowded. It disappeared into wilderness in both directions, corners turned and lost in the waning day. They listened and heard throbbing silence. Beating pulse and rushing blood deafened Timmy, fighting the poison that had escaped into his system. He couldn't be sure that the heartbeat was not the pounding hooves of the mule or the throbbing engine of the van.

"Do you hear them?" he asked.

"No."

"We go this way then, to the right. The cabin is back up there, on the hill."

They moved along, in procession, at the edge of the narrow, turning road, ever ready to hide from the rider and the driver. Shadows deepened and lengthened. And ahead of them, dipping low, the sun became a red witch's pumpkin beyond the trees.

Her fingers dug into his arm. "A car!" she whispered in harsh anxiety. "A car's coming."

They stumbled backwards into the roadside brush, not so much aware of the serpent dangers behind them as of the danger coming creepingly slow, crunching through the twin path of the canyon road. Purple mingled with the solid, varying greens as the van moved along, bit by slow bit. Uncle Dan, his superficial wound no more than a dried bloodstain on his shoulder now, his face set and determined behind the wheel, looked right and looked left, slitted eyes ferreting into the soul of hell itself. Timmy shivered in his hiding place and felt his fear and trembling move into Susie as she pressed against him as though he could protect her from her memories.

The van moved on, out of sight, and finally out of hearing, going toward the store, the town, away. The swollen leg throbbed with each beat of Timmy's heart, and weakness crept into his muscles, so that it seemed a rest in bed was now the most important thing in life.

"He's gone," he said to the cooling air, running it through his mind verbally. "There's no one at the cabin. I'm thirsty, Susie, and my foot hurts. Let's go to the cabin before it gets too dark to see. Tomorrow, we can go away, too. Tomorrow we'll find a telephone and call my dad."

"No, Timmy," she cried, "she's there! Little Mother is there!"

"But she's dead, Susie. She's been dead a long time."

"No! I heard her walking at night. I heard her. I saw her come and look down at me. I saw her take the baby away."

Timmy remembered the times he had thought he heard voices that weren't Uncle Dan's, and footsteps too soft to be his—but it couldn't be so. Little Mother was not the one to fear.

"Susie, she's dead. We have to go back. It's getting dark. There's lightning in the sky. See, Susie?"

She whimpered softly, but objected no more.

He hobbled back against the coming dark, going east now into its face, meeting it headlong in the steep climb up the long hill that at times seemed endless. He stumbled on a jutting bluff invisible in the pocket of darkness and fell with a grunt of pain upon his foot. Susie's limited and weakening strength helped him up and on.

To the west the silent swells of lightning in the sky gradually became more distinct and cutting, and soft rumbles of thunder reached their ears. Timmy tried to hurry, the approaching storm in the western sky a reflection of the burning, jabbing pain in his leg, slowing him, yet pushing him on with its intensity and its threats of worse to come.

They came out on top the hill with the moon rising low in the still cloudless east, shaped into a bright pie with one wedge bitten away by the peak in the house roof that rose against it. Blank windows stared at them, dark and glittering with the faint white light of the moon, and streaking too with darts of lightning. All horrors past issued from the walls, as though the ghosts of all the children who had died there breathed on in their helplessness, and the skeleton of Little Mother walked threateningly back and forth in the hallway.

They hung back, the house no longer the sanctuary it had seemed.

Chill night air washed over Timmy's naked chest in icy ripples, and he shook with the beginning of a fever that made his head feel strange and floating.

"There's no one there," he said, teeth clenching together in his chill. "It only seems like someone's there, but no one is. She's dead. And besides, she was tied in her chair. It only sounds like someone's walking."

Susie whispered, edging behind him, "Rex is there, too."

They were silent together for a long while, their hearts pounding with their fear, their visions trapped for a moment by the room where Rex lay on the edge of the rug, the room where the skeleton was sitting forever in her chair.

Timmy said, "We won't go in there. Not in that room."

"No."

"We'd be safer in the house," he said, trying to convince himself as well as all who listened. "We could go to the kids' bedroom."

"Y-yes."

"Uncle Dan's gone. He won't be back."

She didn't answer.

He tried not to look at the blinded windows of the house as he limped past it, tried not to see Uncle Dan burying the blanket-wrapped body of life-loving little Joey, nor the pickax splitting deep into Rex's brain. They needed a night's shelter, and the house was here, and empty now, and alone except for the dead and for the lingering echoes of voices gone.

The kitchen door stood open, and Timmy hesitated only a moment before he braved the darkness, the waiting walls, the strange and unpleasant smell that oozed into his fever-chilled pores. He leaned upon his makeshift crutch and dug into the comforting odds and ends collection in his pocket. And then he remembered the swim through the creek. What matches he might have garnered would be worthless now anyway.

"I don't have a match," he said, and found the sound of his voice small and defenseless in the haunted house.

Outside a screech owl quivered a call into the forest depths. Susie slipped past Timmy in her over-big shoes and went straight to a corner of the kitchen. He heard the fumbling rattles of matches in a box. She struck one on the stove and turned with it aloft, like a miniature candle, its limited light making an odd shadowy caricature of her face, and looked about for the oil lamp. She found it neatly put away on its small shelf. She reached for it, but it remained on its nearly inaccessible perch far above. The match burned low, and she shook the light out, and in the darkness Timmy heard her drag a chair from the kitchen table and strike another match. She did not ask for help. She went about her self-appointed duties as though she had never known what it was to ask for, and receive, help.

She stood on the chair, stretched on her tiptoes, removed the globe from the lamp and touched the match flame to the wick. Carefully she replaced the globe, and soft yellow light dispersed the strange black holes of the room. Still stretching tall, she eased the lamp down.

Timmy watched her, his breath held. If she fell, she would be in flames. He began limping toward her, but she successfully balanced the lamp and climbed down from the chair with it still upright in her hands.

A pail of water sat on the cabinet and Timmy drank, and then like a tired, sick pup he crept down the hallway past the door that was once again closed, perhaps locked, and on down the hall to bed in the bunk where he had slept, under which his suitcase still lay. He pulled on a heavy, long-sleeved knit shirt for warmth against the chills that claimed his body, and rolled into the blanket.

Twenty-five

Evelyn Gunning had just finished waiting on a local customer and returned to the porch, talking, discussing weather and how the fish were biting. She took her usual place on the chair next to her husband and watched the pickup truck move away into the growing darkness. Ahead of it, reaching in fingers from a black sky, lightning signaled the slow approach of the storm. There was a moment of silence during the settling of the dust left by the truck. Irvan took his pipe from his mouth and tamped a bit more tobacco into the bowl.

"Moon is coming up full tonight," he said. "But it won't last long. It looks like we may get some badly needed rain. Quite a bit of electricity in the air. Might get more'n we bargained for once that storm hits."

Evelyn leaned forward abruptly and hissed, "Shhh."

"What is it?"

"Something coming down the old road yonder, sounds like a horse in a hard run."

301

"A horse?" Irvan started to dispute her word. There were no horses in that direction that he knew of. "What would a horse be—"

The apparition appeared suddenly in the darkening overhang of trees, peeling free from the shadows of the narrow little road to the old Clanton place. With white beard streaming, his legs sticking awkwardly out on each side of the mule's round, fat belly, old man Alcorn rode as if he had young Indian blood still pounding in his veins. He was kicking and yelling and urging his mule to the fastest trot it had ever run. One of his arms raised in a greeting the moment he came in sight of the store, and his voice floated thinly above the steady thud, thud of the mule's hooves.

"Call the sheriff! Call the sheriff! There's been a shooting up yonder at my place! Call the sheriff! A little boy used my shotgun on a man! And now he's after them. Two little kids. Somewhere between here and God knows where! Need help!"

Evelyn gave her husband a piercing look as she got out of her chair, a gleam in her eye that he was destined never to live down.

"I told you so!" she said. "It's got to do with that man in the van, just you wait and see."

Steve drove wearily in to park under the trees surrounding the square in the little county seat. Street lights sifted down upon the emptiness, upon grass and flowers and benches unoccupied. A friendly dog crossed the little park in the center of the square, paused briefly and wagged his tail for Steve before he went on. Only a few lighted signs above closed stores suggested this was not a ghost town, that people were somewhere beyond the walls, that they moved along the sidewalks during the day and shopped and talked and lived.

In this small town the sheriff's office and the jail both, judging from the bars on a couple of windows, were all in the courthouse. That made it handy. Not only for them but for Steve, too. This was his fourth night on the road, bringing an end to his third long day. He had stopped and talked to the sheriff's department in three counties, with no luck. He was exhausted. He had followed roads that weren't on any map, and asked questions of almost everyone he saw. No one knew anything about the van he described. In the past three days he had seen some of the most beautiful scenery in America, and at times he had felt smothered in its lushness, its everlasting greenness.

Yesterday when he called Connie, he was gratified to hear her voice was strengthening. She had been up walking, she said, and was eager for him to bring Timmy to the waiting room downstairs so she could see him. When he called her tonight, what was he going to tell her? He'd been putting it off, all day, until soon the switchboard in the hospital would no longer put through any calls to the rooms. But what could he say? Connie, our son is gone, disappeared. I won't be bringing him to see you after all, I won't be bringing him home.

He was torn between going on with this fruitless search and turning back to be with Connie. He had progressed into the heart of the Boston Mountains, where even here he found beautiful valleys and farms and quiet civilization amidst the uncharted mountain ranges, the steep hills, the deep hollows, all covered with the endless trees. But no one had seen a purple van exactly like the one Dan Walker drove. There were a lot of vans, but none of them was the right one.

He got out of his station wagon and slapped some of the dust off his clothes. The color of his car was almost blotted out beneath the road dust. Not many of the roads in this area were paved. He came close to staggering as he mounted the steps of the courthouse and headed toward the lighted doorway that opened beneath a sign that read Sheriff. At least they hadn't locked up yet and turned out the lights.

It was a small room, with one desk, and one deputy in charge here. Through another door he could see another desk and another man dressed in a neat, sharply pressed uniform, wearing the badge of the sheriff. He was stacking some folders into a neat pile, tidying up his desk as though getting ready to leave, and probably to lock up.

The deputy looked at Steve with faint surprise, nodded, spoke, smiled. But his eyes revealed his curiosity, for Steve was most obviously a stranger in town.

Steve dropped into the closest chair. Before he could state his purpose for being here, the phone rang. In the next room the sheriff picked it up, but it silenced any conversation in the front office as the deputy turned his head to listen.

"Sheriff speaking."

The expression on the sheriff's round face underwent a rapid and revealing change. His eyes bulged, his chin dropped slightly and for a moment he said nothing, then he dropped the phone into its cradle and began to run, through the office door, across the front office.

"A shotgun shooting up at old man Alcorn's, on the other side of Gunning's Corner. A little boy involved. And a man named Dan Reilly. Call the state police and run a check on Dan Reilly. Call the ambulance. I don't know how bad he was hurt. Find out what you can about him. Then follow me on up!"

Steve leaped to his feet, caught in the sudden whirlwind of activity in the small office. The deputy was on his feet now, even though he was pausing to make the phone calls. The sheriff was already on his way down the steps. Steve followed behind him.

The sheriff seemed not to notice the dusty station wagon at all as he cut a U turn in the wide, quiet street and headed east on another of the graded county roads, this one leading to and following the bank of a full-running stream of water. Dust fogged heavily in the wake of the sheriff's car, and Steve drove in the midst of it, his headlights dispersed within it, nothing at all visible most of the time other than the huge cloud of dust.

Mr. Alcorn stood on the porch of the Gunnings' store and told the story again, and again, his white beard bobbing, his hands motioning.

"And before I knowed what was going on, *bang*, and that man fell, and them little kids was running like you never seen, then that man got up and I could see on his face he didn't know he'd been shot he was that mad, and he was going to get 'em if he could. So I took out to find them and couldn't, so I run back after my mule and let me tell you we hurried right along.''

"I'll say!" Evelyn broke in with her comments regularly and automatically. "My Lord a'mercy!"

"Them little kids just come out of nowhere and was scared to death, and tard and hungry, and I put them down to rest after giving them a bite to eat, and then this here man showed up with them grins as nice as you please hanging all over him, and I knowed there was something putrid somewhere—"

"I knew it! I knew it!"

"And the next thing I knowed, *bam*, and I thought for a minute the man's head was gone. But it only scraped his shoulder. Slowed him down some. He was going right into my house without a here-you-by, and ran smack into something he wasn't expectin' at all!"

"Oh my!"

Irvan puffed furiously on his pipe, unaware that it had gone out, and stood with Mr. Alcorn and Evelyn near the corner of the porch, listening intently. The chairs were forgotten. The overweight mule stood just off the porch with her sides heaving.

Mr. Alcorn suddenly jumped to action again. "Them little kids are out there somewhere in the woods, all alone. I'd better go see if I can find them before they get hurt worse. I'll go home and get my lantern, and my gun, and you can tell the sheriff to come on up toward my place. I don't know where he'll find Dan Reilly. But me, I'm going to look for them little young'ns.''

"Wait!" Irvan said. "I'll go with you. Let me get a lantern."

Evelyn snapped her tongue against the roof of her mouth. "I knew it! We shoulda called the sheriff when I wanted to."

Her husband ducked his head and ran for his lantern.

No one saw the purple van ease quietly down the narrow road with only its park lights on, stop, back up, turn and disappear again into the dark tunnel of trees toward the old Clanton place.

Twenty-six

For Timmy, small awarenesses came and went. Susie brought the lamp in and placed it on a chest of drawers against the wall. She changed her clothes, taking off his tee shirt and replacing it with jeans and shirt of her own, and then she sat on her bed and ate crackers. Once she tried to feed him one, but he could only stare at her from his burning eyes. When she perceived that he was freezing she brought the blanket from her bed and prodded it into all the crevices around him. After that she sat on her bed and watched him, and gradually her eyes drooped and she leaned her head back into a corner between the bunk and wall.

Timmy's foot hurt, with a throbbing, stabbing pain that shot up his leg like the darting, fiery tongues of a thousand snakes. Time dragged in a night unending, and he was frighteningly alone, for Susie slept now, slumped upright in her corner, oblivious to the growing sounds of thunder and the bright flashes of lightning. Oblivious also to sounds that moved through the house in ghostly gatherings, woman and children, on footsteps that made the floor boards creak, and through walls and doors that whispered and coughed with the disturbance of their passing.

Ghostly voices laughed and sang, and wept. And sometimes he heard the screams again, so loud and so clear, of Rex at the last moments. He heard, too, the whimpers of Dale the night he was taken to see Little Mother, and he heard him yet, whimpering there in the room where he was locked in with her forever.

Yet Susie slept, unaware of the sounds that Timmy heard.

He closed his eyes and prayed for day, and for the pain to stop and the fever to go away.

He slept, and he woke. The lamp still burned on the chest of drawers, and now Susie had slipped down in a crumpled heap. The blankets upon him were thin and cold, and fever-driven chills rippled over his skin like the creek water over layered stones.

The rain was beginning, driven by thunder and lightning, and struck the window with large drops. Wind came screaming between the logs of the outside wall, finding small holes from which the plaster had dropped long ago, causing the lamp to flicker.

The voices came and left again. He thought he heard his mother's voice saying softly, "It's all right, darling, Mama's here." And he heard his dad's voice too, only it was far, far away, and calling to him in a darkness like the deep interior of a cave, on and on, "Timmy . . . Timmy . . ."

He wanted to cry, for he knew he would never be able to find his way through the black labyrinth of the cave in which he was trapped. He put out his arms, searching for his dad, but suddenly looming up in front of him was the poor skeleton of Little Mother, and she could see him, though she had no eyes, and behind her was Uncle Dan shouting, "Papa . . . call me Papa . . ."

He touched reality again, briefly, knew the voices for what they were, only tricks of memory and imagination, and hoped they would not return to haunt him.

He heard a footstep in the hall and trembled with instinctive fear though he knew it was only the waking nightmares in his fever-tossed mind.

And then Susie sat up suddenly, her eyes as wide and as round as the full moon that was now hidden beyond the clouds. She stared at him a moment, unseeing, and then her full-moon stare leaped toward the bedroom door, and she shrank back in the bed, her hands going to her mouth in pure, silent terror.

Timmy jerked up, clumsy in his blankets, and faced the door.

Uncle Dan stood there. The evil slit of his eyes no longer carried their masks of kindness.

"Well," he said softly, closing the door behind him and leaning against it. "So my children came home. You've made Little Mother very angry running off like that. Now I have to punish both of you, you know, and soon, because you've wasted too much of our time. We'll have to get other children, for you have disobeyed. But how shall we punish you? You must suffer for all this trouble you've caused me and Little Mother."

He eased away from the door and pulled from his hip pocket a thin, white nylon rope.

"Shall I tie you together and leave you to starve? Or throw you into the creek, perhaps. Since you chose to run away together, then it's only right that you shall die together."

Susie leaped off her bed suddenly and ran toward Timmy, dodging the arm Uncle Dan thrust out to grab her. She tumbled up beside Timmy, and Uncle Dan laughed.

"Oh, Susie, my girl. You're just making it easier for me. Go on, cuddle close."

He stretched a section of the rope between his hands and watched them, and slowly circled the room. Susie pressed against Timmy.

"Leave him alone," she cried aloud.

"Oh, another little mother." His smile was gone and he stared at Susie with cold, planning, hate-filled eyes. "Come here, Susie."

She pushed harder against Timmy. "No."

"*Don't you say no to me, you little bitch!*"

He lunged at her in unexpected swiftness, and Timmy shoved against her, pushing her into the corner, crouching with her in helplessness away from the hands that clawed the bed. There was no way to escape Uncle Dan now. He could only delay that final moment. He shoved his blankets into the fury-contorted face. The room rang with curses and screams and shouts, and somewhere in it all there stood a small bent man with a white beard, and the door banged against the wall, and the lamplight glinted on the black double barrels of the shotgun.

"*I said hold it!*" The old man shouted again.

One loud blast split the air in the room, and the scene stopped, still and unmoving, and in the ceiling was a strange black hole through which small bits of debris fell to the floor.

Uncle Dan gaped openmouthed at the specter of the little white-bearded man and short double-barreled shotgun.

"The next one," the old man said, "goes where your fat belly is right now." He jabbed the gun toward him.

Uncle Dan backed away, his eyes flickering through a dozen expressions as his thoughts changed and raged through worlds both outward and within.

"That's good, Mr. Alcorn," a deep, calm, male voice said. "We'll take care of him now."

Timmy saw two men in uniforms of tan and brown, with guns strapped around their waists and handcuffs shining as black as the shotgun in Mr. Alcorn's hand, and then he saw the apparition of his dad, coming out of his dreams, only he was as real as all the other men in the room, and his arms were reaching for him and holding him. When he felt his dad solid in his own arms, warm against him, he knew at last that he was real. He knew the nightmare was ending.

There was a bellow of rage, and Dan flung out his arms against the sheriff and deputy, knocking them backwards. Then he had turned and was gone, into the hall, and to the locked door. He wrenched the door open and passed through it into the room with the skeleton.

A deafening crack filled the air and shattered the walls of the house, and with a roar the roof was

313

burning; old wood, dried, exploded like kindling, the beginning rain no competition for the fire.

A voice shouted, "Lightning struck! Get out!"

Timmy felt himself lifted and carried. He felt the jolt of running steps, and heard them all around him in darkness that was pierced only by the full force of an electric storm, and the fire that was eating through the ceiling and into the inner walls.

Steve ran into the full force of the rain and hunched his body over Timmy's to protect him.

"Take the kids into my car," the sheriff shouted. "I'll go around the house and see if I can get through a window to Dan Reilly."

From the car Timmy and Susie watched the house burn. The mule stood with its head alert under the dripping limbs of the oak tree not far from the car, its eyes reflecting in fear the light of the fire. Tethered to a limb, at times it moved restlessly as though it would like to break free.

Timmy hunched into the corner of the car, with Susie pressed against him. The man who had carried her withdrew with his lantern, a feeble, reddish light against the flames of the burning house. Timmy was beginning to feel warm and damp, and he knew his fever had broken. The worst of the snake bite was over.

Figures moved about in the light of the fire. Flames were shooting heavenward, as though no rain was falling, and the fire ate the house like a monster, its sounds persistent under the crashes of thunder and lightning.

The men fought through the brush around the end of the house. The trees that grew close to the south

314

side of the house were tossing in the heat of the fire like creatures desperate to escape the flames. The roof of the house had turned orange red, and bits of fire-crisped shingles were dropping into the wet leaves.

With one arm up to protect his face, the sheriff moved in closer to the nearest window that was, as closely as he could tell, approximately opposite to the door that Dan Reilly had locked behind himself.

"T'aint no use," the old man shouted. "Better not get too close to the side of that house, Sheriff, it might explode!"

The old man was right, the sheriff thought, yet sometimes there was a chance that a room was not burning yet, and rescue could happen.

The room beyond the window though was brightly lighted, the fire working at the ceiling and into the walls. Dan Reilly had gone into the room by choice, knowing he was trapping himself. The window was closed. He had not tried to escape by that avenue. The sheriff could not help the sense of horror that rushed through him when he saw the figure of the man through the window. He was kneeling by a rocking chair, and someone was sitting in the chair. He could see the pattern of her dress material.

Good God, why wasn't she trying to escape?

He moved nearer the window, shielding his face the best he could. He heard the shouts of the men behind him, and he saw from the corner of his eye that the father of the kidnapped boy was coming in closer.

The sheriff stepped to the right, and for a moment before the ceiling of the burning room fell, he saw what was sitting in the chair. Even in the terrible heat of the fire he felt a sudden, unforgettable coldness in his soul.

Steve grasped his arm with a firm hand and pulled him back into the damp safety of the forest.

The burning roof of the house caved in slowly with a great sigh, and the window was forced outward, the tinkle of bursting glass barely audible.

The sheriff turned his back to the house and the sight that would stay with him the rest of his life. He saw that his deputy had caught up with him. The faces of the men now standing in a close group reflected the red of the fire.

"Did you find out anything about this man, this Dan Reilly?" the sheriff asked.

"Yes, he's got no record, but his mother did. She, Amy Reilly, died in a hospital for the criminally insane. She burned down the family home, killing four of her five children. Dan was the lone survivor. He was twelve years old at the time, and spent several years in a mental hospital. His mother had been abusive, so his problems didn't all stem from the fire. He got out of the hospital about six years ago and married one of the nurses. After that he dropped out of sight, and disappeared from police files."

"Poor devil," Mr. Alcorn said. "Looks like the fire aimed to get him sooner or later."

They stood together in silence until the fire had settled and quieted somewhat, the house becoming a huge, shapeless, smoldering mass in the wet forest."

Steve was the first to move. "I've got to get to my boy."

Mr. Alcorn said, "Yeah, and I gotta get my mule home outa this here rain, though a good washing down don't hurt him as much as he thinks it does. Nor me either, I reckon."

They went around the smoldering remains of the house. The automobiles now were not so brightly lighted, and the mule stood in deep shadows, its head twisted about and its reflecting eyes watching for its master. It made a sound deep in its throat at the sight of him.

Mr. Alcorn leaned into the car and clasped Timmy's hand in an adult shake. "Son, I'm mighty proud to see you going home, safe and sound, you and your little sister both."

Timmy smiled his gratitude and glanced at Susie, to see that she too was smiling. He was not going to say, no, she's not my little sister, for he was beginning to feel that she really was. He was going to ask his dad if Susie could go home with them, since she had no home of her own. His parents could be her parents too. And he would even let her name the puppy, and it would be part hers. She would never again be afraid to speak.

THRILLING FICTION
from Zebra Books

THE LEADER AND THE DAMNED   (1718, $3.95)
by Colin Forbes
Only Martin Bormann knew the truth of Hitler's death until Ian Linsey stumbled onto the incredible deception. Now the gestapo is out to capture him and torture him to death because he holds the knowledge that Hitler is a fake.

FIREFIGHT   (1876, $3.95)
by Richard Parque
For Marine Captain Montana Jones, the war was over . . . until the cablegram arrived from 'Nam that said, "Please help me!" Montana knew he had to go back to find the raven-haired wife he thought was dead . . . to rescue her from the Cong in one final blood-drenched FIREFIGHT.

DEADLY ERNEST   (1909, $3.95)
by Daniel Lynch
Lt. Murphy had never seen a woman as brutally beaten as the murder victim just a few blocks from his home. It looked like a random killing which meant it would happen again—and again—until Murphy caught the killer, or the killer caught him.

HIGH COMMAND   (1910, $3.95)
by Anton Emmerton
As Great Britain falls to the Communist tanks, Ex-British Intelligence agent, John Sulley, must mount a daring commando raid on the isolated hideout of the Supreme Commander of the Soviet forces.

BLOODLAND   (1926, $3.95)
by William W. Johnstone
America's farmbelt had changed, and Key Lessard knew he would have to go to war again—only this time against a secret army of his own countrymen, against a neo-Nazi army of vengeance and hate.

Available wherever paperbacks are sold, or order direct from the Publisher. Send cover price plus 50¢ per copy for mailing and handling to Zebra Books, Dept. 1571, 475 Park Avenue South, New York, N.Y. 10016. Residents of New York, New Jersey and Pennsylvania must include sales tax. DO NOT SEND CASH.